The Devil's Advocate

Artemis Greenleaf

Marti Keller Mysteries

Book Three

PUBLISHED BY:
Black Mare Books
Houston, Texas
www.blackmarebooks.com

ISBN: 978-1-941502-88-4
The Devil's Advocate
Copyright © 2016 by Artemis Greenleaf

Acknowledgements

Acknowledgements

As always, thank you to my wonderful family. This endeavor would not be possible without your love and support. I also appreciate the invaluable editorial and structural help of my critique groups and beta readers. You know who you are, and I couldn't do this without you. Finally, a big shout-out to the law enforcement officers I've had the opportunity and privilege to interact with. Thank you!

Table of Contents

The Devil is an optimist if he thinks he can make people worse than they are. — Karl Kraus

Chapter 1
Space City Sizzlin' Summer Literary Conference

Wednesday, August 3
Houston, Texas

When my husband, Ryan, died and left me alone and six weeks pregnant, I thought I'd never be happy again.

But here I was, not quite two years later, relaxing on the couch, drowsing against Quinn's perfectly muscled chest, watching TV. Maybe it was too soon to call him my boyfriend, but in a few short weeks we'd already taken turns saving each other's lives, and it just felt right to be with him.

No matter how dangerous he was.

"Arf!"

"I think Cú needs to go out," I said.

"Probably," Quinn replied.

The black puppy got up from gnawing on his rawhide bone and trotted towards the back wall. As he approached it, he began to fade out into transparency. By the time he reached the wall, he had vanished. A few moments later, he faded back in as he trotted to his favorite spot on the rug, barked twice at his toy, and began chewing it again.

"I'm still trying to get used to that," I said.

"One of the benefits of owning a Faery dog."

"Hmmm."

He squeezed me a little tighter and kissed my temple. "I should probably go, while it's still a respectable hour," Quinn said in his sexy Scottish accent.

"Probably," I replied, though I made no move to get up.

"As you wish," he mock-chided, "but it's your mother that lives next door."

I sighed and sat up, and he pulled me back down, laughing.

But that all stopped when a piercing wail punctured the moment. "Mamamama! Mamamama!" shouted Cassie between sobs.

"Poor baby – she's teething. I'd better get her some ibuprofen. It may be a long night."

As I entered her bedroom, I saw Cassie standing in her crib, little tears running down her cheeks as she gnawed on her fingers. She stamped one foot, wailing and reaching out to me with her other hand. I scooped her up into my arms and turned to go out to the kitchen. I accidentally knocked a gaudy paper hat off the dresser. It was left over from her first birthday party last week. Mom insisted that I bring it home for the baby scrapbook that I hadn't actually kept up with. Hopefully, I'd remember to pick it up before the puppy found it.

I carried her into the living room, and she was getting more worked up by the minute.

"I'll take her," Quinn said.

"Thanks." I handed her off so I could get her medicine.

By the time I got back, Cassie was asleep in his arms, and he gently rocked her back and forth. Guess I didn't need the eyedropper full of ibuprofen after all.

And that ability to bend humans to his will, like pipe cleaners around a pencil, was the least of the weapons in his arsenal. But I wasn't going to wake Cassie up for the sake of a principle.

I was a little surprised to see a U-Haul truck in front of the Tenth Sphere when I got to work. Belinda Tate, one of the metaphysical shop's co-owners, stood on the ramp, hands on her hips.

"Hauling something in or out?" I asked.

"Loading up books and stuff for the conference tomorrow."

A youngish man with glasses poked his head out of the cargo area.

"Hey, Ben," I said.

"Hey." He waved, then blotted the sweat off his forehead with the bottom of his tanktop. "Okay, Belinda, I think I've got everything but your cardboard cutouts loaded up."

Lulu's nephew had recently been arrested for murder. He was exonerated and released, but he'd still lost his job, and was at loose ends. Belinda was paying him to be her roadie for the *Space City Sizzlin' Summer Literary Conference* at the George R. Brown Convention Center. He and I would take turns manning her booth on Saturday while she was speaking on the romance writers' panel and in breakout sessions. I wasn't looking forward to the crowds, but I could use the money.

The shop traffic was about average for a Thursday afternoon – customers came in waves. But we were currently in a lull. I cleaned fingerprints off of the glass countertop that housed the Belinda's Blessed Beads section. I'm not sure how she found time to do it, between the shop and writing, but Belinda made gorgeous beaded bookmarks, notecard stakes for plants or flower arrangements, and jewelry.

Lulu propped her elbows on the glass display case. "Have you been practicing with your cards, honey?"

"Been kind of busy," I replied scrubbing a little harder.

She raised one eyebrow.

I looked at the front door, hoping a customer was on the way in. No such luck. "Sorry."

Lulu came around the display and pulled a carved wooden box from a shelf underneath the cash register. Inside the box was a red silk bag containing a deck of Tarot cards.

"Shuffle," she said. "And think of a question. You don't have to say it out loud. Usually better if you don't."

I set down my duster and shuffled the over-sized cards. The only question on my mind right now was, *What does the future hold for Quinn and me?*

"When it feels like they've been moved around enough, pick one."

"From the top?"

Lulu stretched her hands out, palms up. "Doesn't matter. Top, middle, bottom. Wherever you like. The point of handling them is to get your energy on the cards."

The big cards were stiff and awkward to deal with. I think I stopped shuffling more because I gave up and less because it 'felt right.' I pulled one from the middle and laid it on the counter.

An ugly winged humanoid stood in the middle with a raised sword. Before it stood two naked people with ropes tied loosely around their necks, and connected to a ring in the floor.

Trump 15. The Devil.

I frowned. "That can't be good, right? Isn't this card about base urges and greed?" *Was the Tarot trying to tell me that Quinn was the Devil, and no good would come of being with him?*

"Depends. Think about your question, honey. It could be about lust, fear, hate, and so on. Often has to do with substance abuse. But it could also be about unexpected challenges, or maybe you have to do something very unconventional to solve a problem."

"My whole life has been pretty unconventional lately."

Lulu smiled. "Well, there's that. Depending on where it falls in the reading, The Devil may also represent the shadow side of the querent's personality, the part we don't really want to look at."

The cowbell on the door clattered.

Lulu glanced at the wall clock. "That'll be my 3:15."

She went to work with her client. A few customers drifted in, then drifted back out with their purchases. A few more readings came in. It was a completely unremarkable afternoon.

Until the phone rang just before closing.

"Good afternoon. Tenth Sphere," I said.

"Yes. Is Belinda there, please?"

"I'm sorry, but she's away."

The woman on the other end of the line snuffled and blew her nose. Her voice broke as she asked to speak to Lulu, the shop's other owner.

"I'm sorry," I said. "She's with a client. Would you care to leave a message?"

The caller sighed. "Would you please have Belinda call Anne Tremont? She has the number," the woman said. "Ellen...Ellen has gone into hospice care."

"I'm so sorry. I'll let her know."

Ellen was a long-time client of the Tenth Sphere, and Belinda's most devoted reader. Just when she thought her battle with breast cancer had been won, she was diagnosed with acute myeloid leukemia.

After Lulu's client left, I gave her the bad news. She closed her eyes and shook her head. "I knew it was coming, just didn't think it'd be quite this soon." She smiled wanly, then said, "I'll close up. Why don't you go ahead and take off, honey? I know you have to go pick up that sweet little Miss Cassie."

I started for the back room to get my things.

"And don't forget to hug your mother."

"I won't forget," I replied.

"Girlfriend, you got to try to get Belinda to skip that romance panel."

"Jeeze, Delilah! Don't sneak up on me like that when I'm driving."

I was almost to Cassie's daycare when my spirit guide popped into the passenger seat of my car. She was generally more considerate than that.

I shifted into thought mode – she could hear what I was thinking, and the other parents leaving the daycare wouldn't think I was insane. *I'm not sure a stick of dynamite could pry her off that panel. What's going on?*

"Something bad is coming, girl," Delilah said.

"Aside from Ellen dying?"

Delilah's head bobbled on her shoulders. She still wore the same red-sequined gown that she'd worn at the Roquefort Club the night she died in 1936.

"Much worse," she said. That's a sad thing, for sure, but death comes to all of us. This thing I'm talking about, there ain't nothing natural about it. Nothing at all."

I shook my head as I pulled into a parking space. *"It's going to take more info than that to get her to think about it. Have you seen how pumped she is for this conference?"*

"I know. But *you* know I can't give you details, girlfriend."

"I can tell her, but I don't think it will help." I looked over at Delilah before I opened the door. But she was gone.

Cassie and Cú were both asleep. I took advantage of this and cleaned out Alpha and Betty's cage. The rats were starting to show their age – I'd had them over a year, and no telling how old they were when my police officer brother-in-law, Nick, rescued them and brought them to me. I had just finished cleaning, and had one on each shoulder when my cell rang. Caller ID said it was Lulu.

"Lulu? What's wrong?" It wasn't like her to call at 10:30 at night just to chat.

"I'm sorry to call you so late, honey. But I need a huge favor from you. Can you run the shop tomorrow?"

"All day?"

"Yes. I'll meet you there at 9:30 to help you get started. There's been a terrible accident here. Regina Dupris, one of the writers on the Romance Panel with Belinda, tripped and fell down the escalator. She was a good friend, and B's taking it pretty hard. Especially since she was at the bottom of the escalator when it happened. The ambulance got here super quick, but Regina, she didn't make it. I don't want to leave B on her own. She's kinda fragile just now."

"Oh, I'm really sorry to hear that. Sure, I can open." *Maybe Mom can take Cassie to Briar Ridge Montessori when she takes Kyle and Aiden.* "Let me quickly try and call my mom before she goes to bed, okay? Give Belinda a hug for me, and I'll see you in the morning."

"Okay, see you then," Lulu said.

I remembered Delilah's warning.

"Wait! Lulu?"

"Yes?

"You know, nobody would think badly of Belinda if she dropped out of the panel. It might be easier on her if she did."

"That's exactly what I told her. But you know B. She's like a terrier with a rat – she'll never let it go."

"Yeah, I know. Goodnight, then."

I petted the rats. "It's okay, girls. Belinda would never hurt you."

I called my mother's land line, but she didn't pick up. I called my sister, Emily, since Mom had been helping her with the new baby.

"Benson," my brother-in-law answered.

"Hey, Nick. It's Marti. Is my mother over there?"

"Yeah. She's changing McKenzi right now, though."

"No problem. Is Em okay?" My sister was recovering from a pulmonary embolism, and that made me a little nervous.

"She's fine. I'll tell Adele to call you, alright?"

"Sure. Thanks."

I hung up with Nick and put the rats away. I smiled at Cú – he was lying on the floor, asleep and dreaming, with his nose twitching and feet flapping, as if he were running at top speed after the most delicious scent ever.

It had been a long time since I'd had a dog, and I guess the canine bug was rekindled a few weeks ago when I'd rescued Bruce. Only Bruce wasn't actually a dog. But that's a whole other story. When Quinn brought Cú as a gift for Cassie (and a replacement for Bruce), I wasn't sure what to expect. I smiled at the snoozing pup. "You sure are a cute little thing, with those big floppy ears. Although, if you ever grow into those feet, you'll be the size of a pony."

My cell rang.

"Hey, Mom," I answered.

"Are you okay?" she asked.

"Fine. Sorry to call you so late, but something's come up at work, and I need to be there all day. Is there any way you can take Cassie to Briar Ridge when you take Emily's boys? I may need you to pick her up, too."

"I'm sure I can. We usually leave from Emily's house at 8:30."

"Thanks, Mom. See you in the morning."

After I checked the doors and set the alarm, I looked in on Cassie on my way to bed. Still sleeping like an angel. I was so tired that I almost forgot to brush my teeth.

I awoke with a start and sat up. The clock read 4:37, and it was very dark. I listened hard to see if I could detect what noise might have woken me up, but I heard nothing out of the ordinary. There seemed to be a dream that had quickly submerged itself deep into my subconscious, because I felt there was something I needed to remember, but no memories surfaced. I started to get up to check on Cassie, but stopped dead when I saw the figure standing at the end of my bed. She didn't glow, but I still saw her as clear as day. She was trying to say something, but no words came. I reached out to her, but she faded away. My heart sank.

It was Ellen.

Chapter 2
Cesar Chavez

Thursday, August 4
Houston, Texas

Nick Benson was the third patrol unit to arrive at the scene, and the stink of diesel and blood made him cough when he stepped out of the truck. The primary officer, Chris Canales, had been heading east on an eight-lane segment of Westheimer Road, in the Energy Corridor District, when a late model black Suburban came screaming out of a parking lot, careened off of a cement mixer, and rolled over twice, right in front of him.

Aside from a few cuts and bruises, the driver was unhurt. The same could not be said for his passenger, who had been partially ejected from the car. Cushioning the fall of a three-ton vehicle with one's body tends not to be compatible with life, and the Houston Fire Department EMS team was going to be spending some time locating all the pieces of him. But that would come later. Right now, they were using the Jaws of Life to extract a mom and her two kids from what was left of their car, which had been crushed by the rolling SUV.

The second officer to arrive, Jessica Collins, was trying to get traffic re-routed around the accident, but was not having much luck with a couple of surly rubberneckers. Nick was 6'4", and when he came striding up with a scowl on his face, the lookey-loos opted to go through the strip center parking lot as Collins had told them to do earlier.

"Life Flight's on the way," she said. "They'll need a spot to set down."

Nick nodded. "I'll go back to the intersection and divert traffic from there."

"What's your cell? I'll text you," she said.

Nick gave her the number, then got in his car. He parked his vehicle across as much of the four lane expanse of eastbound Westheimer as he could and turned on all of the strobes. Nick hadn't been rerouting unhappy drivers north and south onto Dairy Ashford for very long when an orange blob appeared on the southeastern horizon. As the blob got bigger, the thumping of the chopper's rotors got louder. Collins came to help him with traffic, using her patrol car to block the rest of the lanes that his didn't cover. Nick knew both Canales and Collins from roll call – occasionally worked some incidents with one or the other of them, but had never run calls with either.

Nick was glad that the department had recently traded his worn out Crown Vic cruiser for a new Tahoe, because he only had to bend his knees a little to use the truck as shelter from the road debris kicked up by the landing helicopter. Collins came and stood next to him. After a while, Life Flight left the scene with two gurneys. A black body bag lay next to the crushed sedan. HFD now started the gruesome job of collecting the remains of the unfortunate SUV passenger. Traffic Division arrived with survey equipment to begin their investigation.

A call dropped on the radio, asking patrol officers to be on the lookout for a stolen SUV. Dispatch gave a description and plates. Canales replied that he was at the scene of a traffic fatality involving that particular vehicle, making it possibly the shortest BOLO in history.

Not unsurprisingly, the driver had no identification, but he said his name was 'Cesar Chavez.' While the guy looked dead average, Nick did notice a poorly executed star with '713' in the center of it tattooed on the side of his neck. Looked like a prison tat, and it also identified him as a Houstone, a gang banger.

Nick walked up and stood where he could keep an eye on Chavez while he was talking to Canales, and offered to transport the prisoner.

Canales, Nick thought, looked like a Hollywood action hero. Aside from a little acne. He recognized a fellow gym rat, and said, "Those are some impressive guns. Whatcha curling?"

Canales grinned. "One twenty-five. But I press four ten."

Nick nodded.

Cesar Chavez's cell phone rang.

"Gimme my phone, man," he said.

"No," Canales replied.

"Come on, man." He tried to roll his shoulders with his hands cuffed behind his back. "Cut me some slack, huh?"

"If it's important, they'll call back." Canales ran his hand through his thinning hair.

"Yeah, it probably ain't no big thing – just your woman begging me to do her again."

Nick took a step to his left as he sensed motion to his right. Before he could parse what was happening, Canales coldcocked Cesar Chavez, and the man crumpled to the ground.

"Stand down!" Nick said, gripping Canales' shoulder. "That mouthy POS isn't worth it."

Canales sucked in a huge breath, and Nick felt his muscles tense, then relax.

Cesar did not move.

"I'll go get EMS," Nick said, shaking his head. *This is going to get a whole lot worse before it gets better.*

By the time he returned with the EMT, Canales and Cesar were gone.

"I guess he got up," Nick said. *Dude, I hope you haven't gone and done something completely stupid.*

"Guess so." The medic returned to his grim task.

"Hey Benson, you see this?" It was Collins, waving Nick over to the battered SUV. On the way over, he noticed several fluid-filled, capped syringes and two metal boxes of mints lying in the street.

At the SUV, Nick looked at one of the open doors that several officers were gathered around. During the vehicle's roll, the interior panel had gotten knocked loose from the metal, and four sixteen-ounce water bottles peeked out. Each one was filled about three quarters full with a fluid that looked like watered-down iced tea.

"Liquid meth," Collins said.

Nick nodded, "Yeah, I've seen it a few times."

"Owner works at the gym," she said, nodding toward the parking lot.

"Not anymore," he said.

Collins laughed.

After Nick turned in his paperwork for the day and clocked out, he was surprised to find Chris Canales waiting for him in the parking lot.

"Hey," he said. "Look, about this afternoon...I know I shouldn't have let that guy get under my skin. It's just..." His fists clenched by his sides. "I was working a security job last night, and I got home early and found my wife in the hot tub with the neighbor from two doors down."

"Shit."

"Exactly," he said. "You, um, you want to grab a beer?"

"Sure."

"How about that place on Highway 6, just north of Westheimer on the right-hand side?"

"Yeah, alright. I'll meet you there."

Nick got in his truck, then retrieved his phone. He texted Emily that he'd be a little late. He adored his family, and wouldn't trade his kids for anything. But sometimes, the new baby was a little much. She needed so much time, so much energy. Nick didn't always have it to spare, but his wife had nearly died from a pulmonary embolism, and was still recovering, so a large portion of the baby care fell on him. He was grateful that Adele, Emily's mother, lived five doors down and could often help out. And at least the boys were old enough to feed and dress themselves. They could even cook a box of mac and cheese, if they had to.

He eased into traffic and headed up Dairy Ashford to Westheimer. If he hadn't known there'd been an awful traffic fatality there earlier in the day, he would never have guessed it. The pavement was a little wet, for no obvious reason, but that was all.

When he turned into the parking lot of the bar, the first thing he noted was the abundance of parking spaces.

Canales pulled up in his Suburban and got out. Nick did the same. As he walked toward Canales, he saw that the 'Open' sign was not lit, and stopped.

Canales smiled. "My bad. I forgot they weren't open tonight."

"Yeah, well maybe another time, then," Nick replied. Canales now wore a hoodie – a peculiar thing for July in Houston – and had his hands in the pockets.

Nick's skin prickled as the little hairs on the back of his neck rose.

He didn't see the blue arc from the end of the Taser until it was too late. His nerves turned to fire as the charge hit him, and his body went rigid. Canales caught him before he fell, and shoved him into the back of his waiting SUV. As he duct-taped Nick's feet together, Nick tried to force his legs apart so he couldn't be constrained, or at least not tightly. But it was no use. The Taser had temporarily short-circuited his nervous system and every fiber of muscle was on fire. Or at least that's how it felt. An unpleasant buzz vibrated up his spine and rattled his brain.

"No," Canales said. "No, you'll talk to them won't you? I know you'll talk."

He pulled Nick's hands behind his back and duct-taped them, too.

"I'm sorry, Benson. Truly I am, but I don't know another way to handle this. You're going to tell them everything, and I can't have that." He slapped a piece of duct tape over Nick's mouth.

As the voltage dissipated, Nick struggled to breathe. His tall frame was already bent uncomfortably in the back, and his lungs were compressed due to his hands being bound behind him. It didn't help that the back of the SUV smelled like fresh mulch – an unpleasant combination of wood, molasses, and manure. Was he about to meet the same fate as Cesar Chavez? What did Canales think he knew? Did he tell the boys he loved them last night when he put them to bed? Nick exhaled as sharply as he dared. He had to focus, if he had any hope of escaping.

He couldn't see out the window, so he listened carefully, trying to make out any audible landmarks. Nick was able to use the ribbed cargo liner to scrape the end of the duct tape off of the side of his mouth. At least he could breathe now. After a short drive, the SUV left the smooth pavement and bumped along slowly. Nick didn't hear the crunch of gravel, and the terrain was so rough that he figured they must be going off-road. The truck stopped. Canales had muttered to himself the whole way, and Nick only caught occasional words, but as near as Nick could tell Canales seemed to think they were being followed.

The engine stopped and Nick heard the driver's door open, but not close. The cab light did little to illuminate the cargo area. He knew he had one chance, and he had to be ready. He eased himself onto his back. His shoulders screamed as his weight shifted to his trapped hands. Then he raised his feet, cocking his legs back as far as he could.

As soon as Canales released the latch, Nick kicked the door with all the strength he could muster. The lift door connected with Canales' face, and Nick had to scramble to stick a foot in the way to keep the door from slamming closed. He grunted as it smashed into his foot. But the latch didn't catch.

Nick struggled out of the SUV and landed on his side. Canales was just getting up. Blood poured down his face, and Nick guessed he must have hit him in the nose when he kicked the door open.

"Why are you doing this?" Nick asked. He tried to get to his feet, but he just couldn't balance on his duct-taped legs.

"Because," Canales replied, holding his nose to slow the bleeding. "You'll rebort be. I cat hab tat habben."

"What is it you think I'd report you for that's worse than this?"

"You dow. Dote play dub wid be."

Nick studied Canales. And then he realized what was going on. The explosive anger. The huge arms. The thinning hair and acne. The paranoia.

"You're juiced, aren't you?" he asked.

Canales leaned away from him and shook his head. "I cat let you tell adybody. Dot about Chavez, dot about dis. Da guy at da gyb, he tode be I could cleed up boving product on da side for hib. He was right. Hill keep his bouth shut, doe. You won't."

"Dude, I didn't even realize you were nuclear. Can we just talk about it?"

"Shut up!" Canales yelled, then shook himself. "Dere's lots of feral hogs aroud here. Dell fide you before adybody eben realizes you're bissing."

He unholstered Nick's weapon. There wasn't much he could do to stop it.

The sound was the worst part, so close, so loud. There was no pain, only intense pressure as the bullet entered his skull just above the left ear.

Chapter 3
Unfinished Business

4:37 AM, Thursday, August 4
Houston, Texas

I pulled the sheet up a little higher. "Delilah!" I whispered in the dark. "Delilah!"

She materialized slowly, fading in with a yawn and a stretch. "Girlfriend, what do you need at this time of day?"

Catching myself, and not wanting to wake Cassie, who was just across the hall, I switched to addressing Delilah through my thoughts. *I need to know what happened to Ellen.*

"I'm sorry, girl. She just passed. She ain't very cooperative, though."

What do you mean?

"She does *not* want to cross over to the other side." Her head bobbled, emphasizing the 'not.'

Is that bad? Doesn't it mean that she's got unfinished business?

"Sometimes," she said. "But I ain't sure that's what's happening with her."

Isn't there a network or something? Don't you just automatically know this stuff?

One eyebrow arched steeply, and Delilah crossed her arms. "Girl, of course I can find out. It's just I don't go meddlin' in other folks' business if I don't have to. I got enough souls to look out for as it is."

And with that, she vanished.

I tried to go back to sleep. But it just wasn't happening. At 5:30, I gave up and got dressed. Cú heard me moving around and walked through the wall of his crate, tail wagging. I'm not sure why

I even bothered with the crate. Force of habit, maybe. Cú wasn't a tiny dog, but he was small enough to be on the menu if a great horned owl happened by. Or, for all I knew, the owl might be on his menu. So, to protect both, I went outside with him. As a puppy, he was mercilessly cute. But he was a puppy. He had accidents and he chewed anything that fit into his mouth, and a few things that didn't. Sometimes, I really missed mature, house-broken Bruce.

I thought I'd lucked out when I found the huge Lab wandering around in the middle of the night. Especially since he'd saved my life. It was the most natural thing in the world to bring him home. Only Bruce wasn't actually Bruce. He was Quinn. And as it turned out, Quinn wasn't exactly Quinn, either. He was a kelpie, a sort of lake monster, who, more often than not, took the form of a human. But he could also shapeshift into a black horse or a large black dog. So that made it a little awkward – I couldn't have Bruce without Quinn, and I just wasn't comfortable having a man I'd only known a few weeks move into my house. Even if he had saved my life more than once.

I brought Cú back inside. He had a little drink from the water dish, then went back to sleep. I sat on the couch, clicking through the channels with the remote.

A book suddenly fell off the shelf, and I jumped. I walked over and picked up *Dragon by Knight* from off the floor. It's the first book in Belinda Tate's paranormal romance series that she wrote under the pen name Coda Sterling. There was no reason for it to have fallen.

"Ellen?"

The lamp flickered.

I thought for a moment. I'd done this before. "If you're still here, either make the lamp flicker or knock twice for a yes answer, and once for a no answer, okay? Knock or flicker, whichever is easier." *Where was Delilah? She could easily translate this for us.*

At first, nothing happened. Then the light flickered twice.

"Are you Ellen?"

Two flickers.

"Ellen, I am so sorry that you died. Don't think I'm trying to get rid of you, but you know it's best for you to go ahead and cross over, right?"

One flicker.

"Why not?" *That's not a yes or no question.* "Is it...that you're too attached to this place?"

One flicker.

"Unfinished business?"

Three flickers.

Three? A yes and a no? Is that a maybe?

Two flickers.

Well, of course. If Delilah could hear my thoughts, it made sense that Ellen could, too. *So, sort of unfinished business, but not exactly?*

Two flickers came, but they were spaced further apart than the previous ones. *Are you getting tired?*

Two flickers, spaced so far apart, I initially thought the answer was 'no.'

Ellen, why don't you rest? When you get your strength back, you can tell me about your unfinished business. Sound like a plan?

There was no reply.

Friday, August 5
Houston, Texas

Lulu and Belinda were waiting for me at the shop at 9:30. Both of them had puffy eyes and tearstained cheeks, but Belinda was drawn and pale. I understood why – she'd lost two good friends only a few hours apart. I hugged her, then Lulu.

"I saw Ellen," I whispered in her ear, afraid that if Belinda heard, she'd just get more upset.

"What? When?" Lulu asked, pulling away from me.

"This morning," I said. "She hasn't crossed over though — there's something she wants to do first."

"Who are you talking about?" Belinda asked. Her voice was raspy with old tears.

"Marti said she saw Ellen early this morning."

Belinda closed her eyes, but liquid grief leaked out from between her lashes.

I gasped. "I am so sorry. I thought you knew that Ellen had passed."

Lulu shook her head, her own eyes moist. "No. You told me yesterday afternoon that she was in hospice. But I haven't spoken with her sister today - we've been on a video call this morning with the conference organizers. They were trying to decide whether to shut down the romance writers' panel after Regina Dupris' accident."

"We decided to keep the panel, and dedicate it to her," Belinda whispered. "I'm going to splash some cold water on my face." She headed toward the restrooms.

Lulu watched her go, shaking her head gently. "All this has been so hard on her."

"Delilah seemed to think it was really important that she quit the panel. But she'll never do it if it's dedicated to her friend. Doesn't Belinda have her own spirit guide to tell her this stuff?"

"Of course she does, honey. You know, I wouldn't be one bit surprised if Sofia and Ellen hadn't worked together to time Ellen's passing to make it as easy as possible for B to step down. But just because people have spirit guides, doesn't mean they listen to them. I have to tell you, I agree with Delilah. There's something not right about this conference."

I shifted my weight and squirmed. I recalled how Delilah had strongly advised against bringing Bruce home the night I found him wandering the neighborhood.

"I'll be back sometime early this afternoon, so you can pick up Miss Cassie on time. Oh, and before I forget," Lulu said as she reached into her over-sized purse. "Here's your exhibitor's badge for tomorrow."

I forced a smile as I took it. *Should be fun, as long as nobody else dies.*

Ocean folded his wings and crouched on the highest tree limb that would support his weight. His grey skin blended well with the trunk of the tree, and he was unlikely to be noticed by passersby. Leathery wings folded against his back, and he'd brought his hand up to use as a visor to shade the glow of his eyes. He waited. With nothing else to do, he watched the windows of the house. He could see into the kitchen as the woman inside gave her baby a meal in a high chair. She had a black puppy that came outside and wuffed at him a couple of times, but ran back inside, tail between its legs. Ocean couldn't identify what the baby had been eating, but whatever it was, it was smeared all over her face and hands. The woman took her away into another room, and he couldn't see them anymore.

He shrugged and shook his head. If he'd been able to find her so easily, it would be even less trouble for Balcones. That demon ran in human circles more often than diabolical ones, and he'd know all of the human protocols. Still it wasn't his concern. There was no shortage of humans, and two fewer wouldn't make any difference in the grand scheme of things.

Dusk was creeping into the trees, and shadows stretched like grasping fingers across the ground before he heard the sound of a familiar tread coming up the sidewalk. It had been a while, but he did not easily forget such things.

"*Mon Dieu!* Looks like all the monsters are out tonight," he said to the approaching figure. Then he hopped out of the tree, his stone-hard haunches easily absorbing the shock.

"Hello, Uncle," Quinn said. "It's been a long time."

Chapter 4
Orange Badges

10:00 AM, Friday August 5
Houston, Texas

Dinah sat in her car with the windows down, pretending to adjust her makeup. She had come downtown to the GRB Convention Center an hour and a half early so she could park at the very front of the cattycorner lot and watch. The badges that hung from people's necks were her focus. White ones were for regular attendees, green ones were for editors and agents, and orange ones belonged to panelists and presenters who were not agents.

A group of white-badged ladies passed. Then a pair of green. Her pulse quickened when she saw a flash of orange. He was a panelist, but not one of The Five. Or rather, The Four, given that smut-merchant Regina Dupris had taken a fatal escalator trip yesterday evening. She wouldn't be spewing her filth across the printed page anymore.

Dinah smiled, and glanced down at the sheet torn from the conference packet she'd taken from the registration table, the one with the photos and biographies of each of the romance writers' panel members. Regina's had a big red X through it.

An orange badge came from around the corner. Short dark hair, wedge cut. Meghan Palmer perhaps? Dinah couldn't be sure – she was just a little too far away. A tall, lanky woman approached from Discovery Green, a flash of orange against her white blouse as she walked. There was no doubt about it. She'd found that awful Coda Sterling woman. With her dragons and shape-shifting creatures. Bestiality, that's what that was. *Sickening.*

"Hey, Miss B!" a man shouted.

Coda Sterling looked up. Dinah snapped her jaw shut so fast she almost bit her tongue when she saw who had called out to the woman. Medium height, mousy hair with blonde highlights. His teal shirt was the same one from his bio photo.

"Stefán!" Coda changed course to meet him.

If Sterling was awful, Stefán Heidlemann was an abomination. Then Dinah realized she'd hit the jackpot. She could get two with one blow.

She wondered if it would hurt twice as much, or the same, just for twice as long. *Nothing is accomplished without sacrifice,* she reminded herself. Still, she swallowed hard before she tugged at the gold chain, pulled a pear-cut ruby out of her blouse, and held it in her right hand.

Sterling and Heidlemann embraced, then headed away from her and toward a traffic light. Dinah didn't want to stare too hard at them, fearing they'd turn around and see her. She closed her eyes for a minute. When she opened them, they were still waiting to cross Avenida de las Americas to the convention center. This would be perfect.

She squeezed the ruby. "I wish," she whispered, "that you'd get hit by a car." Motion caught her eye as the woman she'd thought was Meghan Palmer started running across the street towards Sterling and Heidlemann. Could she get all three?

Dinah waited, almost holding her breath.

A car pulled out of the parking garage underneath Discovery Green. The driver, cell phone cradled against his shoulder, swerved across several lanes so that he could be in the empty leftmost one. He apparently didn't notice the light turning yellow, then red. He didn't even slow down. At least not until it was far too late. By the time the brakes screamed and started to smoke, Meghan Palmer was already airborne. She landed on the windshield with a crunch, the shattered safety glass cradling her like a broken doll. Bright red blood flowed from the back of her head, pooling in and highlighting the spider web of fractures in the glass. For the space of about three heartbeats, not even the birds twittered. Then the scene roared to life, with people running every which way, screaming, and shouting for someone to call 911.

But Dinah had her own problems. It hit her then – the cold, grasping sensation of pulling, then burning, as if someone had torn off a piece of her and cauterized the wound with a blow torch. And then it was gone. She shivered and wondered if the man had lied, and it was really her soul being torn apart.

She pulled down the visor and looked in the vanity mirror. There were crow's feet around her eyes now. The parentheses wrinkles between the corners of her nose and the corners of her mouth were more pronounced. She even noticed a few strands of grey in her hair. Still, five years older didn't look so bad. It was a small price to pay for taking out a smut-writer.

She tucked the ruby back into her blouse and got out of the car, remembering.

Two weeks ago, Dinah had seen an ad in the paper about a meeting for people who wanted to survive during the end times. She'd expected there to be a full house, but fewer than ten showed up. Perhaps if they'd held it a little earlier, people with children would have been able to come, too. At least that's what she told herself. The alternative was that most people thought the idea of end times was nonsense, and she refused to accept that. What with the apocalypse looming on the horizon, she wanted to save every soul she could before it was too late.

Good looking and about her age, Zachariah was one of the handful of attendees at the meeting. Waiting for the speaker to begin, they'd started a conversation on the corrupting influence of popular entertainment.

"Have you read some of these books nowadays?" he'd asked. "It's appalling."

He'd given her a flyer from his organization, Decency In Literature Drives Openness, and mentioned that they might be protesting at the upcoming writers' convention downtown. The paper contained short excerpts from each of the romance panelists, using their own words to show the depravity of their work. She'd hung on Zachariah's every word. *Finally! Someone who understands.*

Dinah's worn canvas shoes slapped on the pavement as she walked towards the accident. That sound would always make her think of Zachariah. That night at the meeting, she'd been nervous about walking to her car alone in the dark, and he offered to go with her. She told him she wished there was more she could do to stop the spread of moral decay, so people wouldn't be doomed for eternity when the world ended. "How is it that you're still single? You are so amazing!" he'd said.

That's when he'd given her the ruby and told her how to use it. It seemed almost too good to be true. There was only one drawback. She got unlimited wishes, but each wish took away five years of her life. But what was five years to her in these end times, when the world was going to explode at any minute? She was certain that her sacrifice in this life would ensure her a place of honor in the afterlife. A glance at the flyer in her hand told her exactly where she should start the cleansing.

She blinked, stopping her reverie, then flipped the visor up and got out of the car. After she locked the door, she jogged over to the scene of the car accident.

"What happened?" she asked the first person who stood still long enough.

"She got hit by a car. The ambulance will be here soon," the man said.

"Oh dear! Will she be okay?" *Why only one? Why couldn't I get the other two as well?*

"I don't know. Doesn't look good," he said, before melting back into the crowd.

The driver sat on the curb near his car. His head was in his hands and his shoulders shook as he sobbed. Dinah felt a flicker of guilt. She hadn't expected that. It didn't really occur to her when she made the wish that if there was a car, there must be a driver, and the driver might be traumatized from having mowed down pedestrians. *Sometimes sacrifices must be made for the greater good.*

There were a few people standing around him, so Dinah didn't approach. She'd wanted to tell him that even though this seemed like a bad thing, he'd really performed a service, contributed to the public good. After all, the filthy pornography that Meghan Palmer wrote only served to doom souls, not save them. A siren wailed in the distance, and Dinah thought it best not to be noticed, so she went on into the conference.

Two down, three to go.

4:30 PM, Friday, August 5
Houston, Texas

It was late on Friday afternoon, and Hadrian Galanti stood up and stretched. The FBI Special Agent had been listening to a recording of a phone conversation between a pair of Russian mobsters about smuggling heroin. But they seemed to be good friends because they spent more time joking around than doing business. At least that's what it sounded like. He had rewound the recording several times, trying to detect a code, or a pattern that could hide a code, and he was starting to get sleepy.

"Galanti?"

"Privyet, Direktor."

"English, please," Special Agent in Charge Jaimeson replied.

"Sorry." He was fluent in seven languages, and sometimes forgot that not everybody else was. But that was why he was brought in from Quantico to join the Multi-Agency Organized Crime Task Force.

"There's some possible movement on Irina Cherngelanov."

"Oh?" Hadrian suspected her husband's death may not have been entirely accidental, but had no evidence to prove it. She hadn't even bothered wearing black to his funeral, and she'd taken over the operation of his criminal organization swiftly and ruthlessly.

"She's a silent partner in the publishing company Bleu Kat Press. They specialize in romance and chick-lit. Anyway, two top selling authors from Bleu Kat's main competitors have had fatal accidents at that big writers' conference going on at the GRB."

"Sounds like Irina's style. People who get in her way tend to get very clumsy and fall in front of buses or off of balconies." Hadrian clenched his teeth to fight back a yawn.

"Exactly." Jaimeson tossed a manila envelope on Hadrian's desk. "That's your attendee packet. How's your suburb surveillance going? Haven't seen anything about it from you this week."

"Doesn't seem to be much going on. I'm starting to think the subject's contact with Irina's gang was coincidental."

The SAIC nodded. "Let it stay on the back burner for now, then."

10:00 AM, Saturday, August 6
Houston, Texas

Hadrian met Sara for brunch on Saturday. He'd been too tired to see her on Friday, even though she'd left a message asking him to go with her to an invitation-only art gallery opening. He probably should have gone, but he'd been up for thirty six hours, and he just didn't have it in him. Sourly, he wondered if she'd taken her intern, Matt, instead. The one she'd had a fling with. He hadn't confronted her about it, but it had led him to contemplate whether there was anything more to his and Sara's relationship than mutual convenience.

"Hey, Blackbird," Sara said between mouthfuls of poached egg. "What are you doing this evening? They gave away tickets at work for the Alley, and a bunch of us are going. We're meeting at Birraporetti's at 5:30."

If it was people from her work, he was definitely going. But he didn't want to seem over-eager. "What's the play?"

"It's an Agatha Christie. I forget which one. Maybe *Black Coffee*."

Sara had her back to the window, and the sun shone through her messy ponytail, making it look like a soft halo. He smiled. "Sure. Maybe I'll pick up some investigation pointers."

After they finished eating, Hadrian walked Sara to her car and kissed her goodbye.

"You want to come over?" she asked.

He glanced at his watch. "Can't. I've got to go to a conference. Work thing. Maybe after the play?"

She kissed him. "Definitely."

A smile lingered on Hadrian's mouth as he drove to George R. Brown. He didn't really think he'd find anything. It was unlikely that Russian mobsters would be hanging out by the front door, waiting to purge any writer who threatened to compete with Irina's stable of authors. Still, it was worth checking out. Parking was scarce, but he finally found a spot. Hadrian hung the conference attendee badge around his neck and read the schedule. He decided he'd walk through the exhibition hall first, to get a feel for the place.

He strolled from table to table, seemingly studying book covers and other literary paraphernalia. But he was really gauging the security and trying to figure out where the cameras were. Maybe he could obtain some video and feed it through his facial recognition software, just in case.

He picked up a beaded bookmark with a carved skull bead at one end, then almost dropped it. In his head, he heard a child screaming and felt panic, someone else's panic, wash over him. Then it was gone. Psychometry, it was called. The ability to touch something and know things about someone else who had touched that item. It came in fits and starts, sometimes helpful, sometimes not. He had no control over it – it was a fickle talent that came and went at some unknowable whim.

"You okay, Mister?" the young lady behind the table asked.

"Yeah. I'm fine. 'Possum just walked over my grave."

She nodded slightly, apparently trying to humor him.

Hadrian put the bookmark back on the table. "You've never had that, where you shudder for no reason at all?"

"No. Not really."

"Oh. Well, have a good one." He moved to the next table.

"Hunter! Hunter Greene!"

Hadrian froze. That was the undercover identity for his suburban surveillance case. He turned around to see the subject of his investigation waving at him.

"Hey, Marti! What are you doing here?" he asked her.

Chapter 5
Green Fire

Nick gradually became aware of something cold and wet rubbing his cheek. Reflexively, he raised his hand to touch it, and it squealed and bolted. The sky was mostly dark, and his vision was a little blurry, but he was pretty sure that the creature was a piglet running away from him. His service weapon was in his right hand. He sat up and shook his head – he had a little bit of a headache, but nothing too severe. Carefully, he probed his skull above his left ear. Nothing felt out of place. He looked at his hand. There didn't appear to be any blood, and his hand wasn't sticky.

There it was. He had his answer.

When he'd returned from an unexpected trip to Russia a couple of weeks ago, he'd discovered that he'd somehow gained an ability to heal almost instantaneously. He suspected that his sister-in-law knew exactly what had caused this phenomenon, but the answer was likely to be more fantastical than he was willing to accept, so he didn't ask. He couldn't. If he cut himself, cold green fire crackled along the edges of the wound and closed it. Bruises, even bad ones, faded in under a minute. He'd wondered if this healing had limits. Now he knew. Of course, now he wondered if he could consistently cheat death, or if this was his only get-out-of-cemetery-free card.

Fortunately, Canales had removed the duct tape, but hadn't taken Nick's keys or cell phone. Canales had staged his body to look like a suicide. The medical examiner would check his hands for residue, and if they ran ballistics to make sure the bullet in his head was fired from his gun, it would, of course match. Some might question why he parked his vehicle on Highway 6 and walked all the way out into the park, but it would probably be chalked up to one suicidal behavior or another. Nick sighed and stood up.

He pulled out his phone and turned on his GPS navigator app. As he suspected, he was in George Bush Park, known for its feral hog problem. He was just north of the equestrian parking area, so he stumbled through the weeds until he found Barker-Clodine Road, and from there he was able to find his way out via the main road through the park. It might have been geographically shorter to cut across the park, but it had rained heavily recently, and he didn't want to have to wade through snake-infested temporary swamps. He jogged in the grass along the road, on the other side of the ditch from traffic, just to be safe, and it took a lot less time than he feared it would to reach his vehicle.

He had no idea what to do about Canales. If he didn't have the magic green fire, what then? Emily and his kids would be all alone. *Just like Marti.* He smacked the side of his car. *How could a fellow officer do this to me? And what am I going to do about it? It's not like I can tell anybody what happened.* Nick had already had to visit the department psychologist after he'd been falsely accused of using his position to help drug runners. He didn't need his IAD file to get any thicker.

When he got home, Emily was on the couch. Crumpled tissues littered the floor. He thought she was asleep, and he didn't want to disturb her. He was just grateful to be home.

"I thought you were only going to be a little late," she said, opening one eye.

Emily had no idea about the healing green fire, and he doubted she would believe him. Not without a demonstration, at least, and he was far too tired to do that tonight.

"I'm sorry. It took longer than I expected." He looked at the tissues. "Are you okay?"

"Me? I'm fine. Kyle, on the other hand, got sent home early from school."

"What? Why?" Nick scowled.

"He got in a fight."

"A fight? About what? Is he okay?"

"One of the girls in his class, Molly," Emily sniffled, and her eyes started to tear up again, "wanted to play Legos with the boys. Kyle told her girls can't play Legos, and he shoved her and knocked her over. Molly, however, has a blue belt in Tai Kwon Do, and got up and kicked him in the face. He's got a bruise on his cheek and a scraped knee, and his pride is deeply wounded, but otherwise he's fine. He sure could have used a talk with you this evening."

Nick winced. "Why didn't you text me?"

"Why didn't you come home when you were supposed to?"

I didn't plan on getting shot in the head and having to run all the way back from the park. "One of the guys I worked an incident with was having some issues and wanted to go for a beer. It took a lot longer than I expected. I'm sorry. If I'd have known about Kyle, I would have said no." *If I'd known he was planning to kill me, I'd also have said no.*

The tears that had been welling in the corners of Emily's eyes started to slide down her face.

"Please. Em. I'm really tired. I'm sure you are, too. Can we just get some sleep and talk about it tomorrow?"

Emily dabbed at her cheeks and blew her nose. "Fine."

Nick probably should have kissed her good night, but he was tired and grumpy, so he turned and left the room. He looked in on the boys on his way down the hall. They were both sound asleep. Not that he expected anything different. Both hands clenched at his sides and he wanted to hit something. *Why didn't I just tell Canales that I didn't want a stupid beer?*

Nick's body was exhausted, but his mind wouldn't settle. If Emily had just let him know about Kyle, he would never have gone to have a beer with Canales. What was he going to do about him, anyway? He couldn't just let it go – Selling drugs on the side notwithstanding, the man needed professional help with his steroid problem. But he couldn't walk into his sergeant's office and report that one of his fellow officers shot him in the head and left him in the park as pig bait. He'd be the one in the rubber room instead of Canales. Was Nick not spending enough time with the boys? McKenzi took up so much time, maybe Kyle lashed out at a girl because he felt jealous of his sister. Maybe he was just a bad parent. These questions plagued him endlessly as he lay in the dark and stared up at the textured ceiling. He closed his eyes and tried to slow his breathing so that his body would sleep, but instead, he found himself playing Worry Whack-a-Mole. As soon as he tamped one negative thought down, another took its place. He wished Emily had come to bed, but she hadn't seemed to have been in a particularly compassionate mood, so maybe it was just as well. Somewhere around 3:30, exhaustion finally overwhelmed his body, and he slept.

Chris Canales was already sitting down when Nick came in for roll call. There were two empty seats to his left, so Nick took one of them. Canales was looking at his phone, so Nick coughed. Canales didn't look up. Nick coughed again, louder.

Canales glanced up, then back to his phone. Then his eyes widened and his back stiffened. Color left his face as he turned to stare at the new arrival.

Nick just smiled at him.

Canales jerked himself to his feet, knocking his metal chair over. "You!" he bellowed. "You can't be here!"

The chatter in the room went dead as every officer turned to look.

Nick feigned surprise. "What are you talking about? Are you okay?"

"You're dead!" Canales screamed, reaching for his sidearm.

Nick raised his hands, palms facing Canales. "Clearly not. Why do you think I'm dead?"

"Because I killed you myself! I saw you die! I saw you!"

It took six officers to remove Canales' duty belt and restrain him. Canales screamed the whole time about zombies and pigs, until an ambulance arrived to transport him to a hospital psychiatric ward. He had to be sedated to be loaded onto the gurney and wheeled away.

"You have any idea what that was about?" Sergeant Patterson asked.

Nick shrugged and shook his head. "Couldn't tell you, Sarge." *Well, I could, but then you'd order a strait jacket for me, too.* It seemed harsh, but Nick was glad it went down that way. Surely they'd discover Canales' steroid use and get him clean, because he had become dangerous to himself and others. And his criminal activity was a whole other matter. But there was not a thing he could do about it right now.

"Never had that happen during roll call before. Hope it never happens again." The sergeant refilled his coffee cup before he went back to the podium.

He had a few BOLOs and some administrative announcements.

"And one last thing. Lieutenant Barnes is retiring from SWAT. There's a barbeque next Friday at the Academy for him, after the annual SWAT tryouts. They're adding another four positions, so if any of you are already on the part-time squad, you've got a decent shot at moving over. That's all I've got. Don't

Tase your neighbor." Nick flinched as Tasers crackled around him in test mode.

SWAT was notoriously difficult to get into. The team had a fixed number of members, and once an officer got into the unit, he tended to stay put. Nick had been on the part-time squad, training with the full-timers for almost two years, waiting for that elusive opening. He knew that Barnes had been making noises about retiring for about six months, but nobody had thought he was serious. Nick also knew he was at the top of the list, and with five openings, he was as good as in. Of course, it would be bad form to celebrate before he got his official notice, but it still added some spring to his step as he walked down the hall.

"Benson, we need to see the LT."

"Sure." He turned and followed Sergeant Patterson down the corridor. *Is this where I get the papers to transfer to SWAT?* He resisted the urge to whistle.

Patterson's supervisor was sitting at his desk behind a stack of file folders. Two of them were lying right in front of him. He stood up when they came in, reaching out to shake Nick's hand. Patterson closed the door.

Lieutenant Helmsly looked tired. More tired than usual.

"Benson - Nick, I wanted you to hear this from me."

Nick's stomach tightened. This could only be bad news.

"Yes, sir."

"I fought this. Told them how much they were screwing up. SWAT declined to accept my recommendation. You're still part time."

Nick shook his head. The words didn't make any sense. "I don't...understand." His brow furrowed.

"They passed you over because you have an IAD jacket."

"But that was a frame up!"

Helmsly frowned and nodded. "I know. I know. And I told them that. Your record speaks for itself – you're an exemplary officer. They didn't care that the charges were false and the DA's office recanted. No, they're worried about *optics*." He made air quotes. "The sergeants and the lieutenant were pulling for you – they really wanted you full time. This came from higher up."

"Thank you for letting me know, sir." Disappointment. Betrayal. Anger. They all swirled inside him, and Nick wanted nothing more than to hit the punching bag right now. Instead, he took a deep breath and tamped his emotions down, balling them into a bitter pill.

Helmsly picked up a pen and tapped it idly on the desk. "You can try an appeal. They should be rotating captains a little later this year."

"Thank you, sir. But right now I've got a beat to run."

Nick had only been out for an hour. He was headed westbound on Memorial, between Eldridge and Highway 6 when a man in workout gear ran out of the Terry Hershey Park entrance, waving his arms. Nick pulled into the parking area and got out of his car.

"What seems to be the problem, sir?"

"There's a man in the bayou!"

"Show me," Nick said, hoping he wasn't going to have to get too wet pulling some hiker or canoer out of the water.

The man, all angles and stringy muscles, jogged down the ramp and under the bridge. There, caught in some debris, a dark-haired man bobbed gently in the current. Given that he was face down in the water and most of the back of his head was missing, Nick figured it was far too late for EMS. He radioed in the floater, asked for crowd control back up, and started taping off the area while he waited on Homicide. He got the contact information and a basic statement from the jogger who'd flagged him down. The crime scene unit and the medical examiner beat Homicide by a good fifteen minutes. CSU already had their 3-D laser camera set up and going, forcing the detectives to wait an additional half hour before they could get started.

When they finally finished all the photographs, the techs from the ME's office waded into the water to retrieve the body. It wasn't deep, barely covering their knees, but the concrete chunks and rocks that lined the banks and bottom of the bayou were slippery with algae and bat guano. After they finally wrestled the corpse ashore and turned him over to slide him into a body bag, Nick's jaw dropped, and icy fingers squeezed his solar plexus.

The face was unrecognizable, but the badly done neck tattoo of the star with the '713' in the middle was easily recognizable as the one belonging to Canales' prisoner from the day before, Cesar Chavez.

Chapter 6
Playing with Fire

5:30 PM Saturday, August 6
Houston, Texas

Belinda was struggling. She'd been shaken by the unexpected deaths of her fellow panelists, but Ellen's death had really hit her hard. I admired her grit in going to her romance writers' panel session at the same time I wished she would have withdrawn from it.

The exhibition hall was a lot quieter than it had been during lunch, now that the breakout sessions had started back up. I hoped Belinda had more books in her trailer, because she was almost out.

I was watching the few people milling around sales tables when I saw him. *No way. Is that the guy who just moved in across the street?*

"Hunter! Hunter Greene!"

He paused for a moment, almost like he'd been caught out, then turned around, his eyes searching until they landed on me.

"Hey, Marti! What are you doing here?"

"Working," I said. "I had no idea you were interested in writing."

"Well, I do love books. But I'm more of a shopper than an author. How about you? Did you write these?"

I glanced down at Belinda's books, most of which had half-naked men on the covers, and I felt my cheeks get warm. "No. One of the owners of the Tenth Sphere writes them. You've been in the shop – I know you met Belinda at the mediumship circle."

"She's the taller one, right?"

"Yes."

He picked up one of the books, flipped it over, and scanned the back. For some reason, it made me feel dirty, him standing about three feet away from me, looking at a book that I knew had graphic sex scenes in it.

"I'm not a big romance reader. I tend to prefer non-fiction." He set the book back down and smiled at me.

Typical. "Did you find anything you like? There's an author with a new book about Houston serial killers a few rows over."

Hunter cocked his head and raised an eyebrow. "So what is it about me screams *serial killer*?"

"Nothing!" I said, looking at his shoes. "That's just the only non-fiction that I noticed on my way in this morning."

Before he could answer, an alarm started clanging. I thought I heard someone yelling 'Fire!'

Hunter grabbed my hand and started to pull me toward the exit. I pulled back so I could grab my purse and Belinda's cash box. It's a good thing the crowd was sparse, because a few people panicked and bolted for the doors. One man was so hysterical that he was beating on the door, trying to push it open. On either side of him, people pulled open other doors and headed out the front to Discovery Green. But somehow he didn't see any of this.

"Sir," Hunter said. "Sir, try pulling it."

"You're not going to trick me! I was here first!" he screamed, and swung wildly at Hunter.

My neighbor blocked his punch and responded with a right hook that sent the man sprawling. Hunter lifted the dazed guy up over his shoulder in a fireman carry.

"Marti, could you get the door?"

"Um, sure," I said as I pulled open the door. This guy had ice in his veins. What was he before he was an accountant? A Navy SEAL?

I was glad we were on the first floor. Even with this little sidetrack, we were still out of the building and in Discovery Green park before the surge of conference attendees came flowing out the front doors. Hunter set Mr. Panic down and leaned him against a tree.

"You'll be fine," he said.

The man just nodded.

I started searching the crowd. "I've got to find Belinda."

At the sound of sirens, hundreds of heads swiveled in their direction.

"I *will* help you find her, but let's not run back into the burning building, shall we?"

I pulled out my cell phone, still scanning the mass of faces. I scrolled through my call history and tapped Belinda's number. After three rings, it went to voice mail. I sent her a text, asking where she was. I called Lulu. She didn't answer either.

"Dammit," I said.

Ladder trucks brayed loudly to get the stragglers out of the way so they could pull up to the doors. Three ambulances, lights flashing, also pulled up and blocked the street. Police began arriving as well to shut down the streets. Firefighters in full gear hurried into the building, some dragging hoses. Then nothing. For several minutes that seemed to stretch out into hours, no one entered or left the building. I could hear radio chatter, but wasn't close enough to understand it. Then three gurneys went in.

Almost immediately, one came back out carrying a man in a bright teal shirt. He had an oxygen mask over his face.

"I think," I swallowed hard, "I think that's Stefán, one of the romance panelists." I could feel myself starting to shake. *Where is Belinda?*

More minutes dragged by. A second gurney came through the front door. This one had a shiny black body bag strapped on it.

Please, please, please don't let that be Belinda.

I felt Hunter's hand on my shoulder. I wished that Quinn was here, and I wished I knew where Belinda and Lulu were. I searched the crowd again, hoping I'd see either or both of them, but no faces were familiar.

Firefighters started to trickle out of the building. Then a door opened. Nothing. Finally, a stretcher shuddered through it, catching on the doorjamb and jarring its occupant.

"Belinda!" I shouted.

I sprinted across the street, Hunter close behind me. Belinda was wearing an oxygen mask, and looked disheveled.

"How is she?" I asked the paramedic.

"Smoke inhalation. She should be fine. Could you please tell her she needs to come with us to the hospital? She kept trying to get off the stretcher – that's what took so long getting her out."

"You transporting to Ben Taub?" I asked.

"Yes, ma'am."

"Belinda, you have no idea what was in that fire. There may be all kinds of toxic chemicals that have effects that won't show up for hours. You go to the hospital. Lulu and I will meet you there. I won't take no for an answer."

Belinda's eyes teared up, and she made a deep gasp for air, then shook her head from the sudden influx of oxygen. She pulled the plastic mask away from her mouth.

"I know exactly what was in that fire. It was Jennifer McLauren, the contemporary romance writer."

"I'm…I'm so sorry," I said. "Please just go to the hospital. I'll get Lulu and we'll meet you there."

"She's at the shop," Belinda said.

"Fine. I'll pick her up."

"What about Cassie?" Belinda let the oxygen mask fall back over her face.

"My parents have her. Just go."

Belinda nodded weakly as the gurney was wheeled toward the ambulance.

"Belinda!"

Ben came running up from the far side of the park. I'd forgotten all about him. I grabbed his arm.

"They're taking her to Ben Taub. I'm going to the shop to get Lulu. Can you pack up Belinda's table and meet us there?"

"Sure, as soon as they let people back in."

I hadn't thought of that. "If it's going to be a while, just come to the hospital." He looked at the ambulance door that just closed. I patted his hand. "Smoke inhalation. She should be fine."

He nodded, and glanced at Hunter.

"Do you want me to drive you?" Hunter asked.

He squeezed my shoulder again, as if he were someone I knew much better.

"No, I'll be fine. Thanks, though."

I noticed Lieutenant Haskill getting out of a car. *Why is Homicide here?* "Excuse me," I said to Hunter. "I see an old friend."

I raised my arm and waved as I headed in his direction. "Sam? Lieutenant Haskill?"

"Marti." He squeezed my hand. "Haven't seen you in donkey's years. How've you been?"

"We're good. Do you always come out to investigate fire accidents?"

He smiled broadly. "Well, one fatality per day seems awfully peculiar, don't you think? Just want to have a look around. Seems that the romance publishing business is mighty competitive, and some folks are a little more focused on winning than others. I'm also interested in finding if there's a pattern to this string of accidents."

"A pattern? You think this might be a serial killer?" I suddenly felt cold in the muggy heat.

"ABC." Haskill shrugged. "Assume nothing. Believe no one. Check everything. The investigator's ABCs. Yes, this string of accidents does sound like too much of a coincidence, but I don't see how they could be related. Just seems like exceptionally bad luck."

"That's certainly how it looks." I frowned. "It was great to see you, Sam. I've got to go to the hospital with my friend. The people that died were all on the same writers' panel as her. Could you keep me posted? If you find anything that's not an accident? "

"Not officially." He pulled a notebook from his pocket. "What's your number?" I gave him my phone and email.

"Thanks," I said. "Take care of yourself."

"You, too."

As soon as I got into my car, Delilah materialized in the front seat. She looked at me with a sad smile. "Your friend Sam is right. There ain't nothin' coincidental about what's happenin' here."

Chapter 7
Uncle Ocean

Saturday, August 5, 8:30 PM
Houston, Texas

Quinn regarded the gargoyle for a moment. "I'm not a monster." He glanced around Marti's back yard, scanning for potential observers.

"So you've said," Ocean replied, his voice betraying a touch of amusement that his stony face could not. He raised his head slightly and inhaled. "That smells good, what is it?" he asked, eyeing a large plastic carrier bag Quinn was holding.

"Thai food, Uncle. Would you like to come in?"

"What would your human say?"

"You might be surprised." Quinn shifted his weight, hoping Ocean would cut the small talk.

Ocean nodded. "Well, you should hide your playthings better. She was *très facile*, very easy, for me to locate. If I can find her, she can be found by anybody."

Quinn looked at Marti's back door for a long moment. "Marti is not a plaything. And I'm sure that you didn't come here to criticize my friend's security measures."

"*Non.* An observation only." Ocean stretched and refolded his wings. "I have come to inform you that Phobetor is missing from the Demos Oneiroi. There is a rumor that the demon Balcones, who is well-known to you, is responsible."

"Balcones. He's enough of a nightmare on his own – what would he want with the God of Nightmares?"

Ocean shrugged. "Your mother said –"

"Did she send you here?" Quinn's eyes narrowed, and the bag of Thai takeout jerked in his hand as he clenched his fists.

"She did not, my *neveu*. But as your father's brother, I visit her from time to time. She regaled me with tales of your exploits, and I recognized the name Balcones. I had only days before played cards with Morpheus, Persephone, and Hades. Morpheus mentioned that his brother, Phobetor, had gone missing, and he'd sent their brother, Phantasos to look for him. He reported that a demon called Balcones had been asking after Phobetor, but as his location was unknown, Phantasos is still seeking him."

Quinn frowned. "Mother told you stories about me? She's a bit put out that I'm keeping company with a human."

Ocean did his best approximation of a smile. "So she said."

"Did you tell her about Balcones?"

"*Non*, I did not," Ocean said, shaking his head.

"Good. I don't want her fretting about it. You know how she likes to fret."

Ocean nodded.

"It looks like I am likely to be setting off soon on a demon hunt."

"*Oui*. You should spend your time appropriately." Ocean tilted his head towards Marti's house. "I will watch the house tonight, but I will leave at dawn and meet you in Blackthorne."

"Thank you, Uncle."

Ocean stretched out his wings and only a few flaps took him back up to the tree branch he'd been sitting in earlier. When he was settled, Quinn knocked on the door. Marti smiled as she opened it.

"Hey," she said. "Cassie's already asleep."

"Hey, yourself." He kissed her on the forehead, then reconsidered and kissed her mouth, a long, slow kiss, until she started to squirm and pull away.

"The food," she murmured, "is really hot against my back."

"Sorry!" He released her immediately and set the food down on the table.

"Before I forget, is there any way you could watch Cassie for me in the morning while I go to a funeral? Mom and Dad will be at church, and I don't want to impose on Nick and Emily."

"Tomorrow?" He breathed in deeply and let it out quickly. "Sure, I suppose I can. What time?"

"It starts at 10:00. It probably won't take much more than an hour."

Quinn nodded. "This is for your friend, Ellen?" *Surely, no Mundane Intervention Team was so urgent it couldn't wait for the dead to be laid to rest.*

"Yes."

"I'm sorry."

"I didn't know her all that well, but I did like her a lot."

While she went to the cupboard to get plates, he asked, "How was the conference?"

"It caught on fire."

"What?" He stopped his unpacking midway.

"It was a freak accident. One of the romance panelists had a cellphone in her pocket and the battery exploded. It wasn't a big fire, but it was enough to kill her." Marti set the plates down on the table and looked up into Quinn's eyes. "There have been a lot of freak accidents involving the romance panelists. Three of them are dead. I don't think it's coincidence, and I don't believe they're accidents."

Quinn caressed her cheek with the backs of his fingers. "What do you think they are?"

"I don't know – it almost seems like a curse. Hopefully, since they shut the conference down after the fire, the last two panelists will be okay. Especially since one of them is Belinda."

"I can ask around and see if anyone knows of any curses flying around. But as you said, the conference is shut down, so Belinda should be safe." He spooned rice onto each plate.

They finished fixing their plates in silence, then went into the living room. Marti put on a movie, but Quinn ate his meal wondering if Balcones was at the root of the string of accidents. It didn't seem to make sense, though. If not him, perhaps it was another demon.

"Would you like a glass of wine?"

"Huh?" Quinn shook his head to clear it. "Certainly. I'll get it." He took the dirty dishes with him into the kitchen, and returned with two glasses of chardonnay.

"Cheers," he said as he handed Marti hers.

She tapped her glass to his. "Cheers."

He took two sips, then drained his glass. He took Marti's glass from her hand and set it on the coffee table. He kissed her again, softly at first, then gaining urgency. He stood and pulled her up, then swept her up into his arms and carried her to the bedroom. It might have been faster to just tear each other's clothes off, but it wasn't safe for Marti.

He wasted no time in pushing himself onto the astral plane. Marti was getting pretty good about doing it herself, and they met in the garden they'd constructed together there. Butterflies the size of crows flapped lazily by, landing on enormous tufts of lilacs as Quinn's astral energy swirled around and intertwined with Marti's. It wasn't long until they both exploded into a thousand stars, and the fragments of their astral bodies rained down on the garden, only to coalesce inside their physical bodies.

"Mmmm," Marti said. "That was amazing."

Quinn stroked her hair as she snuggled against him, head on his chest. "You're amazing."

He felt her breathing slow and deepen as she drifted off to sleep. He stared at the ceiling, feeling her heartbeat against his, wondering if this would be the last time.

I was eager to get home. My parents couldn't watch Cassie because they were going to church this morning, so I had left her with Quinn. She adored him, which maybe I shouldn't have encouraged, given that our relationship was in the early stages, and it would be hard on her if things didn't work out. But I trusted him – he'd brought her back to me when I thought I'd lost her forever. Still, he'd seemed preoccupied when he came over last night. I wondered if he'd gotten a new assignment. His job was to hunt demons, and I'd learned firsthand how rough they played.

Ellen had made her own funeral arrangements when the doctors found that the chemo for acute myeloid leukemia had made things worse instead of better. All her family had to do was set the date. Sort of. She had stipulated for the service to be held on the first Sunday morning after her death. Since she died on Friday morning, the funeral home had to scramble a bit to accommodate her. But accommodate they did, and I sat with Belinda and Lulu near the back of the chapel.

As close as Belinda and Ellen were, Ellen's daughter did not approve of her hanging out at a metaphysical shop. My friends didn't want to antagonize her, so they were trying to be as inconspicuous as possible. Although I'm not sure Lulu helped much on that front, wearing a pillbox hat with a short veil. I thought it made her stand out even more, but she hadn't asked me. Belinda had brought her own box of tissues, and sat near the aisle, head down, with a damp tissue crushed in her hand.

The metal chair next to me creaked, as if someone had sat down in it. I turned to look. At first, I saw nothing, but then I looked closer. She was nowhere near as clear and bright as Delilah, but I was able to make out the form.

Ellen?

"Well, who were you expecting? Marilyn Monroe?" She smiled. "Could you please tell Belinda and Lulu that I'm fine?"

Sure. But can't you tell them that yourself? I thought –

"Yes, normally they can see spirits. But both of them, especially Belinda, are too upset, and the grief is blocking their vision. Also, could you tell my daughter…never mind. That girl is too headstrong to believe anything you say. Too much like her father." She looked wistful.

I nodded and turned towards Lulu and Belinda.

"Wait!" Ellen said. "The service is starting."

Alright. I'll tell them afterward.

Ellen's body had already been shipped off to the crematorium. In about a week, her daughter would receive a biodegradable urn containing Ellen's ashes and a gingko tree seed, to be planted in the cemetery's newly opened crematory forest – her tree would be the very first. At least that's what the brochure that she'd brought to the shop to show Belinda said. But for now, there was a 12 x 14 photo of Ellen on an easel, surrounded by flowers, ferns, and a couple of wreaths in the front of the chapel.

A Tibetan chant started playing through the funeral home's sound system. Ellen's daughter cringed, and I suspected that she would have arranged a very different service for her mother. When the chant finished, a man in a black robe with an embroidered purple stole rose and stood next to Ellen's picture. He started naming some of her great qualities and telling stories of her life to illustrate his point. When he got to 'kind,' he told a story of how one day Ellen had a terrible sore throat and couldn't speak, but she had to go to the post office. As she walked, she heard some mewing and looked up into the tree branches above her to see a tiny white kitten. Ellen, who was afraid of heights, climbed up to rescue the kitten. As soon as she hoisted herself up on the branch where the kitten was stuck, it climbed into her lap, purring loudly. The problem was, now Ellen was also stuck in the tree. She tried to call out to a passerby, but she had no voice. So she took off one of her shoes and threw it at the man walking below the tree. He shouted at her and called the police. They arrived, surveyed the situation, and called the fire department, which used the ladder truck to get Ellen and the kitten out of the tree.

I glanced over at Ellen. Her face was in her hands. I thought she was crying.

Are you okay?

She looked up at me, and I realized that she'd been laughing. "I had that cat for fifteen years. Best one I've ever had."

A woman who looked about twenty-five got up and stood near Ellen's portrait.

"That's my niece!" Ellen said, grinning broadly.

Music started to play, and the niece started singing *Somewhere Over the Rainbow*. She had a beautiful voice, and I felt my eyes getting misty. I glanced at Lulu and Belinda, and saw that both of them had tears streaming down their cheeks. I sighed, wishing that I'd had the chance to get to know Ellen better.

Family members recited a few poems, and there was another song, then came the benediction. Friends and family were gathering at Ellen's daughter's home after the service, but Lulu and Belinda knew they wouldn't be welcomed, so they lingered in the chapel, looking at Ellen's portrait. I looked for Ellen, but she was gone.

As soon as we got to the car, I said, "Ellen was at the funeral. She asked me to tell you that she's fine."

"You saw her?" Belinda asked. "Did you see her, too, Lulu?"

Lulu shook her head.

"She said that your grief was blocking your ability to see her."

"Maybe," Lulu replied. She ran her hand through her hair. "Since the rest of the convention has been canceled, either of you want to stop for lunch?"

Belinda shook her head.

"Maybe another time," I said.

Lulu and Belinda dropped me off at my house. As soon as I opened the door, I heard Cassie crying.

"Quinn?" I called as I hurried toward her room.

Water splashed and I heard Cú barking. Cassie cried harder.

"Quinn?" I called out, louder this time. I changed course slightly and went to the bathroom in the hall between Cassie's room and mine.

For a second, I couldn't believe what I was seeing.

Delilah sat in the bathtub with Cassie, who was now screaming at the top of her lungs. The water was way too deep to bathe a baby, and my spirit guide was making sure that she didn't fall over and drown. Delilah had managed to pull the plug, and the water had started to drain, but was still quite deep.

Quinn was nowhere to be seen, but there was a terrifying woman in the corner. Cú seemed somewhat bigger than he had when I'd left this morning, but perhaps it was just my fear vision.

The woman, if I can call her that, was wearing a ragged loose dress, or possibly a shroud. Her long, black hair was wet and stringy with specks of duckweed in it. Her skin was an unpleasant corpse-green, and she dripped stinky pond water and duckweed all over my bathroom tile.

Cú held her at bay, growling if she moved.

"Who are you?" I demanded. "And where is Quinn?" My adrenalin-charged heart pounded against my sternum.

My hands shook as I grabbed a towel and pulled Cassie out of the bathtub. Her sobs against my shoulder only fueled my anger. I glared at the woman in the corner.

"Well?" I snapped.

She took a step forward, and Cú snarled and barked. She took a step back.

Delilah disappeared from the bathtub and reappeared at my side.

The green-skinned woman smiled at me, and I took a step back. Her teeth were not normal human teeth. Every one of them, and there were way more than there ought to have been, was long and pointed. Very sharply pointed. Algae appeared to be growing on them, because they were a mottled green color. *Eww.*

"Jenny," she replied, seeming pleased that she'd intimidated me.

Cassie had started to calm down and relax against me. "Okay, Jenny. Who are you, and what have you done with Quinn?"

"You'll have to ask him," she said.

Then she cackled loudly, leaped over Cú and landed in the bathtub, splashing still more water onto the floor. Jenny turned to liquid herself, and disappeared with the last of the water that swirled down the drain. The tub belched loudly, but there was no sign of her, except for a few bits of duckweed left behind on the porcelain.

"Girl, I told you from the get-go that man was dangerous. Didn't I tell you no good would come of seeing him?" Delilah said.

"What are you talking about?" Cassie was down to sniffling and hiccupping now, and I rubbed her back and swayed from side to side to comfort her even more.

Cú wagged his tail and came over. "Good boy!" I said, leaning over to pat the top of his head and scratch his ears. I didn't have to lean over much, though. He was definitely taller than when I'd left the house earlier. He must be having a growth spurt.

"Your boyfriend, Quinn. He's the one that called that child-drowning hag to watch over Miss Cassie."

I shook my head. "I don't understand."

Delilah rolled her eyes. "That Russian friend of Quinn's, the one with the blue skin, came to get him – some kind of emergency. He summoned Jenny Dreadful to stay with your baby."

"I think Aleksei is from the Ukraine," I mumbled absently. "I don't get it. Why her?"

"I guess she was available on short notice, girlfriend. He's dangerous, and he runs with dangerous folk." Delilah's hands went to her hips.

I chewed the inside of my cheek. I couldn't believe Quinn would do anything that would put Cassie in danger, and yet I shuddered to think what might have been waiting for me if I'd come home fifteen minutes later.

"Delilah, why did you call Jenny a child-drowning hag?"

But there was no reply. Delilah had vanished.

Cassie had fallen asleep, so I carried her into her room. I pulled the wet towel off of her, and she squirmed, but not enough to wake up. I put her down on the changing table and she was still. I was afraid if I tried to dress her, she'd wake up again and be upset, so I just put a diaper on her and carried her into the living room with me.

I turned on the TV and sat in my living room, mostly ignoring the programming and seething until Quinn's return.

Sunday, August 7, 10:45 AM
Houston, Texas

Quinn strapped Cassie into her high chair for lunch. Cú sat patiently near the baby. He was the owner of anything that fell on the floor. Marti had prepared Cassie's lunch – all Quinn had to do was open containers. He sprinkled a few tiny cubes of cheese, cooked carrots, and halved grapes on the highchair tray in front of her, as he'd often seen Marti do. The baby squealed with delight and immediately began grabbing them with both hands.

"Easy there, wee one. You'll not be choking on my watch," Quinn said as she tried to cram everything into her mouth at once.

A cheese cube tumbled out of her hands and the puppy caught it before it hit the ground. Quinn moved all but three cubes and a grape out of Cassie's reach.

Quinn whirled as he heard heavy steps on the back porch. Through the glass of the back door, he saw Aleksei, one of his Mundane Intervention Team members, about to knock on the door. Cú barked twice and ran into the living room.

"What is it, Aleksei?" Quinn said as he opened the door.

"Come. You must see to believe," the Lesovik replied. Light from the window dappled his blue skin.

"Can it wait? Marti should be back any minute – I'm watching the baby for her."

"*Ni*. It cannot."

Quinn scowled. "I can't very well leave Cassie alone, now can I?"

"Is there nursery faery?"

"That's an idea. But it still may be faster to wait for Marti."

Aleksei shook his head.

"I expect everyone knows that Jenny Greenteeth is a nursery bogie. Maybe she can do it."

The words had barely fallen out of his mouth when an awful hag with dripping wet hair and green skin appeared.

"Haven't seen you in a hundred years or so, eh Jenny?" Quinn said. He wondered why a frightening creature would be good with human babies, but what did he know about them? Jenny sometimes hung out in the millpond at his family's tavern, The Waterhorse Inn, and occasionally took tea with his mother.

"Did you say you had a human child that you needed taken care of?" Jenny asked.

Aleksei tapped his wrist.

"I'm in a real rush, Jenny. Yes, this is Cassie. Her mom should be home any minute now, but I've got to leave. Will you look after her for me?"

"I will...look after her." Jenny smiled a toothy smile.

"You're sure you know how to take care of a wee human baby. They're not like fae. It's real important she be in the best of hands."

Jenny extended slender, mottled fingers. "My hands are the best."

"Thanks."

Cú had poked his head around the door jamb.

"And you," Quinn said. "Take care of my girls for me."

Then he walked out the door with Aleksei and stepped into a portal. Instantly, they found themselves at Briar Ridge Montessori School. An older woman hovered over a much younger one who lay on the floor and swatted at nothing with her hands.

"Stay away from me!" the woman on the floor screamed

"It's okay, Miss Breckenridge. I've called an ambulance. They'll take care of you," the older woman said.

She noticed Quinn and Aleksei. "Someone will be with you shortly. Please wait in the hall."

The younger woman started screaming incoherently.

They backed out of the room.

"What does this have to do with me?" Quinn asked quietly.

"Dame Rowan told me bring you here. She was talking to an ocean? I not understand."

"Ocean. My Uncle Ocean. He's been looking for Phobetor. Looks like he's been here – she's in a waking nightmare. But why here?"

"Look," Aleksei said, pointing to a piece of paper taped to the wall.

It was a class roster. Quinn ran his index finger down the list until he found the entry for Cassie Keller. He felt nauseous.

This was Cassie's teacher. Balcones was letting him know he could reach him – or those closest to him – at will.

"I have to get back to Marti's house," Quinn said.

"No. We must make report first – how will MAMIC know to expedite Balcones' capture request, if no report?" Aleksei replied.

Quinn knew he was right and sighed in frustration. The bigwigs at the *Mundane Activity Monitoring and Intervention Center* were obsessed with paperwork. They had to backtrack to get to a portal and go to MAMIC headquarters in Blackthorne, which took precious time Quinn didn't want to spend. There was, of course, a queue for the Director's office. After discussing what Ocean had told him the night before and what he'd seen this morning at length, Quinn was finally released. He was almost in a panic, not knowing if Marti and Cassie were okay. He knocked on the back door as he came inside.

"Marti?" he called.

"I'm in the living room," she answered. Her voice was raspy. *Had she been crying?*

Quinn rushed in and found her sitting in a chair, arms crossed. As he approached, she stood up to meet him, then slapped him across the face.

"What were you thinking?" she hissed at him.

He held a hand against his cheek. "What are you talking about?" Fear increased the pitch of his voice.

"Jenny. Why would you leave Cassie with a monster? I trusted you."

"Is Cassie alright? What monster? Jenny's a nursery bogie. She's supposed to take care of children."

"Take care of children?" Marti's face flushed, and Quinn wondered if she was going to hit him again. "She almost drowned Cassie in the bathtub. If not for Delilah and Cú…well, I hate to think of what might have happened."

"I'm sorry. I had no idea — I thought the purpose of nursery bogies was to protect children. I never would have left her with Jenny if I'd realized."

Tears started rolling down Marti's cheeks. Quinn brushed them away, then leaned his forehead against hers."

"I have to leave," he said.

"Of course you do. You almost get Cassie killed, and now you have to go off somewhere for work. That's awfully damned convenient."

"No. I mean I can't be with you anymore. It puts you and Cassie in danger."

Quinn felt his own eyes get misty. He would not upset her any further by telling her about Balcones' visit to Cassie's school.

"That's what I've been told. I really should have listened." She sniffled.

"I should never have involved you. I'm sorry."

Marti looked up, anger in her eyes and her mouth in a hard line. "I guess that's it, then."

Quinn closed his eyes and swallowed hard. He had to fight the urge to throw his arms around her and kiss her until everything was okay again. But that couldn't happen.

"Yes," he replied. "It's just not safe for you to have me here. Cú will protect you." There was nothing else he would allow himself to say, so he turned and walked out, letting the door bang closed behind him.

Chapter 8
The Last Panelist

I stared at the back door. Was Quinn really leaving and not coming back? Suddenly cold, I struggled to breathe, remembering the day Ryan walked out the door and never came back. *It's not the same thing*, I scolded myself as my hands started to tremble. *Delilah warned you he was dangerous. Lulu warned you, too. But would you listen? No. You thought you knew better, you were the special one who could tame the monster. Cassie almost died because of him, and here you are, wishing he'd come back. What kind of mother are you?*

I covered my face with my hands, smearing the wetness across my cheeks. First I plopped back down in the chair, then I punched the cushion. I couldn't tell who I was angrier with – Quinn or myself. After all, he had told me from the start that he wasn't human, and I shouldn't expect him to behave like one. But had he used his fae powers to take advantage of me? The first time I met him, I found myself inexplicably attracted to him – but after that initial encounter, I wasn't so sure. Lulu had warned me that humans frequently pined away and died after their fae lovers left them – and they always left. Because of my stupidity, was Cassie destined to be an orphan? Because it sure felt like Quinn took a big chunk of the best parts of me with him when he walked away.

You can't sit around feeling sorry for yourself all afternoon. Get up and do something. I went and took a shower. I turned on the water as hot as I could stand it and just stood under the flow, turning a few times to let it pound on my back, then my chest. Finally, the water turned cool, and I shut it off. Cassie was babbling from her crib. As long as she sounded happy, I didn't rush too much to get dressed. I'm not sure that I felt better, but perhaps more stable, kind of like a congealed salad – squishy lime gelatin mental state mixed with soggy cottage cheese sadness and hard celery and walnut nuggets of anger and rejection.

"Mama! Mamama!" Cassie called as I walked into her room. Cú was a puddle of ink, curled up in front of her bed. His tail thumped against the carpet as I approached, but he didn't get up.

"Come on, Cassie. Let's get you a snack, okay?" I scooped her into my arms.

I looked out the kitchen window as she ate. I was restless and the air in the house felt warm and stale, in spite of the ceiling fans. According to the outdoor thermometer, it had cooled down to 95°F. I decided that Cassie and I would make up for our missed morning walk. I'd better leave Cú at home so he didn't roast his paws on the sidewalk. We'd just go a short distance, maybe to the Tenth Sphere and back. I really needed to get out of the house and get some air, however hot and humid. I put Mr. Buns in the stroller, and of we went.

As we approached the shop, I was a little surprised to see a police cruiser parked out front. Curious, I went inside.

Belinda sat on the stool in front of the cash register. Head in her hands. Lulu stood behind her, rubbing Belinda's shoulders. A female uniformed officer and two men in sport coats formed a loose circle around the counter. They all looked up when I came in, and I was only a little surprised to see that one of them was my friend, Lieutenant Haskill. I looked from him to Lulu.

"Please, B," Lulu said. "It's for your own protection. Marti, can you please try to talk some sense into Belinda?"

Cassie burbled – she adored Belinda. "Um.." I replied. "What's going on?"

"We want to take Ms. Tate into protective custody," Haskill said. "A fourth member of the romance writers' panel, Stefán Heidlemann, was found floating in the pool at his hotel this morning. We have every reason to believe that there will be an attempt on Ms. Tate's life as well."

"I'll be fine." Belinda's voice cracked as she said it, though. "The convention's over, I'm nowhere near downtown…"

I unbuckled Cassie and picked her up while Belinda talked. I set my baby on the counter, and she squealed with delight at seeing Belinda. "I've known Lieutenant Haskill for a long time. If he thinks you're in danger, you most likely are. Please, please let them protect you. What would Cassie and Lulu and I do if something happened to you?"

As if on cue, Cassie reached for Belinda, and my friend picked her up and hugged her. "Fine," Belinda said.

"Thank you," the detective I didn't know said. "Officer Rogers will take you to our safe facility."

"Can I at least go home and pick up a few things?"

"No. I'm sorry," Haskill said. "The sooner we get you there, the better. There will be toiletries and things like that waiting for you."

Belinda sighed and handed my baby back to me. "Let's go."

Cassie started to cry as Belinda walked away with the Officer Rogers. I jiggled her on my hip. "Don't worry, Cassie. Auntie Belinda'll be back before you know it." *I hope.*

"She'll be fine. I haven't lost one yet," Haskill said with half a grin. "I don't know how these deaths are orchestrated. They all look like accidents. But one romance writer panelist per day? That's not a coincidence. A puzzle for sure. But I like puzzles." He smiled again, the left half of his mouth doing most of the smiling, and touched Lulu's elbow. "We'll take good care of her, Ms. Miranda." He nodded to me. "You be good for your mama, now, Cassie. Come on Smitty. We've got work to do."

The cowbell on the door jangled as they left.

"You know who else has some work to do?"

I jumped.

"Delilah!" I said out loud. "Do you really have to sneak up on me all the time?"

She raised one eyebrow. "Girlfriend, I have been here the whole time. You need to get better at lookin'."

"What are you talking about, Delilah? Who has work to do?" Lulu asked, her arms crossed loosely against her ample chest.

"Miss Ellen. She's hangin' around, tryin' to clear up some unfinished business. Since she's here, she may as well help out a friend."

"Are you in touch with her?" Lulu asked.

Delilah pursed her lips and glanced up at the ceiling, then looked over her right shoulder toward the 'Employees Only' door. "Ellen? Come on out here, girl."

A transparent blob of mist formed on the opposite side of the counter from us.

"Bah bah! Bah bah!" Cassie flapped her hand towards the mist.

"Not yet, little one," Ellen's voice said. Her voice sounded tinny and staticky, as if she were on a radio station at the very edge of its range.

"Ellen!" Lulu said. "Honey, you left us so fast we didn't even have a chance to stop by and see you. I'm sorry for that."

I'm not sure how, exactly, but I had the impression that the mist smiled.

"Don't strain yourself, Miss Ellen. Why don't you drop the visual and just concentrate on the voice?"

The mist dissipated.

"It's okay. I'm quite alright here," Ellen said. "Though I hadn't expected to go that quickly myself."

I thought it odd that one of Delilah's eyebrows arched for a moment.

"What is it that you need from me?" Ellen continued.

"I'm glad you're doing good," Lulu said. "I don't know if Belinda told you that she was on a romance writers' panel at this big fancy writers' conference. The trouble is, all of the panelists have died in mysterious accidents. Except her. The police put her in protective custody. But we need to find out who's responsible for this, so she can come home."

"Yes," Ellen replied, her voice a little fainter. "I knew she was a panelist, but I didn't know about the deaths. I'm not sure what I can do to help, though."

"What if we gave you a list of the dead panelists?" I suggested. "Maybe you could see if any of them are still hanging around, then ask them what happened?"

"I can try."

Lulu rifled through some papers on the counter. I was going to have to go soon – Cassie was starting to squirm.

"Okay, honey," Lulu said. "Here it is. The first one was Thursday night. Regina Dupris fell down the escalator at the GRB. Friday, Meghan Palmer got hit by a car in front of the building. On Saturday, Jennifer McLauren's cell phone battery exploded during one of the panel sessions and caught her clothes on fire, and they found Stéfan Heidlemann floating in his hotel pool this morning, just a couple blocks from the Convention Center."

"I'll see what I can find out. Can't promise anything, though. I am starting to get a little tired…"

"Of course, honey. You go rest. We'll talk soon, huh?"

"Sure."

"You be careful, Miss Ellen," Delilah added. "There's something much more powerful at work here than plain ol' bad luck."

Cassie was almost impossible to hold now, so I put her in her stroller and wrestled the seatbelt on her. "I've got to get Cassie home. She needs to walk around and stretch her legs. There are too many breakables here. I can't afford to let her play in the shop – I'd never get another paycheck."

"I understand," Lulu said, nodding absently.

"I'll go with you," Delilah said.

This surprised me, a little, anyway – she tended to disappear as suddenly as she popped up. I shrugged.

"I know you're upset about Quinn," Delilah said after we got out of the Tenth Sphere.

I switched from talking out loud to talking in my head. This was a private conversation, after all. "*You know about that, huh?*"

"Course I do, girl. That shifter, he deserves more credit than I gave him."

I swallowed hard. I wasn't sure I wanted to hear this. The breakup might be easier to deal with if I believed I'd just made a bad choice in romantic partners, instead of thinking we were star-crossed lovers who might yet end up together.

"*Why is that?*"

"He didn't want to leave you. But his being around right now puts you and Cassie in harm's way."

"*So he said. After he left Cassie with some monster that tried to kill her. I trusted him with my baby. If you and Cú hadn't been there...And then he says 'Sorry, guess I'm just too dangerous – bye now.' Sounds suspiciously like a cop-out to me.*"

"It isn't like that, girlfriend." Delilah softly shook her head. "Jenny is a friend of his mama's, and he didn't understand that a nursery bogie is the opposite of someone who takes care of human children. But that ain't why he left."

"*Then why did he leave?*"

"You remember Balcones?"

"*The demon? How could I forget him?*" I shuddered.

"Balcones is not real happy with Quinn, for a lot of reasons, and he's trying to hunt him and his whole MIT team down and kill them. He didn't want you and Cassie to be anywhere in the vicinity if Balcones should catch up to him. And he has reason to believe that might happen."

My heart skipped a beat, then fluttered in my chest. I didn't want Quinn – or Aleksei, Eoin, or Malik, for that matter – to die. But what could I do about it? They all had supernatural powers that

I lacked – Balcones had even managed to imprison Malik, a powerful djinn, in an emerald bottle only recently. I wished things could go back to the way they were a few days ago, where Quinn and I were just like any other new couple, getting to know each other and basking in giddy infatuation. But that just made it worse. The danger was always there, even if I didn't see it. It didn't matter how much Quinn cared for Cassie and me, being around him put us at risk, probably more risk that I even imagined. I sighed in frustration.

I felt an odd tingle on the back of my head as Delilah touched my hair. It stirred me out of the pity party I was organizing for myself and brought me back to the here and now.

As I approached my house, I saw Hunter working in his garage. His shirt was off and sweat glistened on his bare skin. Again, I was intrigued by his tattoo. A raven, its body and head on his left arm and shoulder, spread its wings over his back and chest. He'd told me he was an accountant, and the first time I'd seen his ink, I was surprised by it. No law against accountants having tats, I supposed, but he just hadn't seemed like the type. Still, I had to admit that looking at Hunter was a pleasant distraction from my current state of affairs.

He waved to me, and I pushed Cassie on over.

"Hey, neighbors," he said.

"Hey," I replied. "Are you remodeling your whole house here? Looks like you've got a lot going on."

"No, just refinishing some bookshelves."

I noticed a gallon can of paint stripper and reconsidered wheeling Cassie closer into the shade of the garage overhang.

Nodding, I said, "I have some chairs that need re-doing. Maybe someday I'll have time."

Hunter picked up a towel and blotted the sweat off of his face and neck. "You should bring them over – I'll do them for you. But that might put your boyfriend on edge."

I snorted sourly. "I don't think that will be a problem." I didn't elaborate, and I hadn't appreciated the reminder. The bleeding hadn't even stopped yet from this afternoon's breakup wound.

"Sorry," he said.

I shrugged. "It's alright. Wish I could hang out longer and see how they turn out, but I've got to get this one," – I jiggled the stroller – "out of the sun."

"No problem. Maybe you and Cassie could come over for dinner sometime to see them when they're done."

I paused. Was this a serious invite, or a polite let's-get-together-sometime suggestion that meant nothing and would never really happen? "Maybe," I replied, opting for noncommittal.

"By the way," he said. "How is your friend, the one from the book convention fire yesterday?"

"She's fine. Treated and released for smoke inhalation. See you around."

"Yeah, see you." He went back to his paint stripping, and I retreated to the relative cool of my house. I wanted to kick myself. I need a rebound romance like I need a hole in my head.

Dinah pounded her hands on the library table in frustration, causing the librarian to shoot an alarmed look in her direction. She couldn't find anything out about her next victim, Coda Sterling, other than the fluffy biography on her website. Dinah caressed the wishing ruby that was tucked safely under her blouse. Aside from sucking away five years of her life every time she used it to make a wish, the only downside was that she had to be looking at the intended subject when she wished. That was why Meghan Palmer had gotten hit by the car instead of Coda Sterling and Stefán Heidlemann.

She'd followed the ambulance after the fire at the GRB yesterday, but that had proved pointless. There were too many ways to get in and out of the hospital, and she couldn't cover them all. Her diabetic cat had to be given his medication, so she couldn't just sit around indefinitely in hopes she'd made the right choice. *So frustrating!*

"Is there something I can help you with?" the librarian asked.

Dinah startled at the question. She hadn't been aware of the librarian coming toward her. "Um…I'm just trying to find out some information about an author, and there doesn't seem to be much online."

"I see. Have you tried a copyright search on the author's titles?"

Dinah shook her head. The librarian smiled and showed her how to look up copyright information online.

It was Dinah's turn to smile. "Thank you," she said.

There it was. Coda Sterling wasn't even the author's real name. It was Belinda Tate. Not only was she a creator of perverted filth, but she was a liar as well.

"Is there anything else?" the librarian asked.

"No, thank you, ma'am. I think this will help."

Dinah dug around for a pen and wrote down Belinda's name and address on the tattered back of the unpaid electricity bill she'd been carrying in her purse for nearly two weeks. This only confirmed for her that she was on a righteous path. She had been led to the meeting where she met Zachariah and had gotten the wishing ruby, and now the librarian had shown her exactly what she needed when she was starting to lose hope.

After she typed in the address in the search bar and copied down the directions, she gathered her things to head to Belinda's house.

"You have got to see this," the duty sergeant said to Nick.

He had already turned in his paperwork for the day and was ready to go home. "What's that?"

Sergeant Patterson pulled up a chair and sat down. "There was a residential alarm call at 3:17 this morning, somebody tried to crawl in through a living room window. No sign of the crook, but the security camera caught this."

Patterson pulled Nick's computer over and tapped some keys. A video window opened and started to play.

"What the hell?" asked Nick. He rewound the video and squinted as it played again.

"Yeah. Kind of looks like a baby, doesn't it?"

"If babies had scaly skin and horns, maybe."

Then he noticed the address on the digital report, and swore softly.

"What?" Patterson asked.

"That's three blocks over from my house."

"Seriously? Guess if you don't show up for roll call in the morning, we'll know the Devil Baby got you."

"I'm off tomorrow, actually."

Patterson leaned back in his chair. "Kidding aside, what do you think that is?" he asked. "Looks too small to be a midget in a costume."

Nick watched the video a third time. "I don't know. Kinda looks like a Halloween decoration. Some kind of remote-control animatronic maybe?" He had a vague memory of seeing something similar before, but couldn't think of where. "Whatever it is, if it runs out in front of my car, it's toast."

"Well," Patterson said, sitting back up. "It's probably a prank – somebody looking for their fifteen minutes of internet fame. I think that they got this doll or midget or whatever and sent it under the camera while they opened the window to trigger the alarm, making sure that someone would watch the recording. May even have been the homeowner himself."

Nick shrugged. "Could be. If the Devil Baby shows up at my house, I'll bring in the pieces for you."

He logged out, closed the lid on his computer, and stood up. He'd been scheduled for a ten-hour shift, but ended up working twelve, and he was beyond tired. "Night, Sarge."

"Night."

A prank. Yeah, probably. Nick was annoyed that the Devil Baby clung to his brain like a spider on a wall. It was creepy, sure, but Patterson was probably right. There was no limit to how low video fame seekers could stoop. But still, there was something about the way the thing had moved that was just wrong. And when it had looked up into the camera, it seemed like it was aware of him. The pranksters undoubtedly planned it that way. But he still drove a little faster than maybe he should have to make sure he was home with his family well before dark.

Chapter 9
Devil Baby

D id I not tell you?" Ocean asked. "Your pet is too easy to find." The leaves on the branch where he perched rustled slightly as he shifted his weight.

Quinn, who sat next to the base of the tree in his dog form, growled softly in answer. It was just loud enough to make the thing shaped like a monstrous baby turn its head in their direction.

Then it smiled.

Needle-like fangs peeked from its gums. They were short, but matched its blotchy grey skin. Dull, rough scales covered the thing, giving it the appearance of a snake about to shed its skin.

"The horns, they are a nice touch, no?" Ocean continued.

Indeed, the apparition had perfectly curved, cartoon devil horns. All it was missing was a red pitchfork and a goatee.

The Devil Baby returned to its mission, and moved toward a darkened window.

Quinn, or Bruce, as Marti knew him in this shape, barked until a light came on and a man came to the window and shouted, "Shut up, you stupid dog!"

As soon as the room lit up, the Devil Baby disappeared.

Quinn got up and padded out of the yard and down the street. He made sure to head in the opposite direction of Marti's house, which was across the street and a couple of doors down. Whomever had sent the Devil Baby was probably watching.

Ocean flew behind him, staying low enough for conversation, but high enough to keep his stony feet from rasping across the sidewalk.

"What are you going to do about the tulpa?" Ocean asked.

Quinn growled, then slipped into the alley behind the Tenth Sphere, where he shifted back into human form.

"What makes you so sure this wee beastie is looking for Marti?"

Ocean sighed slightly. "It is known that Balcones is searching for you, no? To find you, he finds those you love. Your family is untouchable to him in Faery, so what is left? The Mundane world. And who is there? Your Mundane Intervention Team and some humans. It may go badly for him to stalk the demon hunters, so what is his choice then?"

Quinn's eyes narrowed. "Do you think if we can track the tulpa, it will lead us to Balcones?"

"I think not directly. It would be foolish of him to send the thought-form himself for that reason. *Mais oui*, he is clever enough to use an intermediary."

Quinn nodded and stepped through the portal he had placed in the alleyway. He emerged in the war room of a large house a few miles away. Ocean followed a few seconds later.

The house, an elegant two-story with a large back yard and a pool, was technically owned by MAMIC, but his good friends, Kai and Breena, who belonged to another Mundane Intervention Team (MIT), lived there. It was also a hub for local MITs to plan missions and travel between Faery and the Mundane world for this region.

"The quickest way to get rid of a tulpa is to terminate the creator," Quinn said, heading down the stairs. "Once the thought-form has no one to feed it energy, it dissipates quickly. But I suppose we want to leave this one alone, until we get a bead on Balcones."

Ocean followed Quinn through the kitchen and out into the back yard. The rest of his team waited for them there. Aleksei, the blue-skinned Lesovik, preferred sleeping outside in the trees to being in the house. Eoin, a half man, half goat Urisk, hated the polished marble floors because his hooves slipped and slid on them. Malik didn't mind where he was. The djinn had no need of sleep, anyway.

"*Zdravstvuyte*, Quinn," Aleksei called.

"Evening," he answered.

"So what is the wee little monster your," he paused to glance at Ocean, "uncle's been on about then?" asked Eoin.

"It's a tulpa, most likely sent by Balcones, or one of his allies," Quinn answered.

Aleksei frowned "What is tulpa? I have not heard of such creature."

Malik rolled his eyes. Instantly a camel appeared before the group, except that it had big fangs and glowing red eyes.

"Quit your fooling around, Malik," chided Eoin.

Malik sighed. "This is for your edification and enlightenment. This camel, you see, does not really exist. It is an idea of a camel built of nothing but my thoughts. I give it energy by thinking about it." The camel's eyes flared brighter, then dimmed. "It can, of course, interact with the material world. I can command it, but if it lives for enough time, it will develop its own will." He waved his hand, and the camel dissolved into a puff of smoke. "When humans create these, they are cruder and tend to go feral most of the time." He shook his head. "They run amok, causing all kinds of mischief, until they run out of energy. And that, my friend, is a tulpa."

"What he said," replied Quinn. "I think this tulpa is looking for Marti. There's every reason to believe that Balcones would like to use her and Cassie as bait to draw us out into the open. Ocean believes that he has a minion creating the tulpa, so if we can find him, hopefully we can find and trap Balcones."

"And you know this tulpa looks for Marti?" Aleksei asked.

"*Non.* But it is best to act as if it does, no?" Ocean answered. "Perhaps we investigate, and it has no connection to

Balcones. What is lost? Nothing. If we do not investigate, and it is sent by him, then we stand to lose much."

"I reckon our Malik can track it, next time it shows its face. What's it look like, then?" said Eoin.

Quinn described the Devil Baby.

"Och. Sounds like an ugly little blighter," Eoin said.

Aleksei nodded.

"It seems not to make itself hard to find," said Aleksei. "Ocean found it, no problem. How he knows to look for tulpa?"

"I was running an MIT before you were even a sprout, *homme d'arbre*. I have more contacts than you can imagine." Ocean's voice was dangerously even and quiet, the calm before the storm.

"Aleksei," Quinn said. Ocean was one of the highest ranking members of MAMIC, and it was a very bad idea to antagonize him. "Enough. Balcones is trying to get to us. We don't need to help him by tearing each other apart. We need to plan our mission and take him down." *And then Marti and Cassie will be safe.*

"Aye, I agree we should get on with it, but could I ask a question?" Eoin said.

Malik shook his head, then held out his right hand. A deck of cards suddenly appeared in it, and he shuffled them, then started laying them out in mid-air as if to play solitaire on an invisible table.

"Fine. What is it?" Quinn replied.

"If you're a kelpie, and he's a gargoyle, how's he your uncle?"

Quinn's eyes widened and his shoulders stiffened. Before he could speak, Ocean answered.

"Fall of 1285. The King of Scotland was marrying a French noblewoman. I was a child, taken from my home at Notre Dame Cathedral, and sent as a wedding gift. The ship I sailed on sank. I do not swim. The grandfather of Quinn found me and took me in, raising me as his own child. My name, his family could not pronounce, so they called me Ocean, because that is where I was found. When I was big enough to make such a journey, I returned to my family in *la belle* France. But I still keep my connections to my foster family. Is there any more of my personal life you now wish to examine?"

Eoin swallowed visibly. "No, sir. Thank you."

"Alright. Can we get our mission planned now?" Quinn, asked.

After much discussion, they decided that they would post themselves around the neighborhood, but not far from Marti's house. Since Malik was the least corporeal, and he could track the tulpa on the astral and other finer planes, he would be summoned at the first sight of it. They would find out where it went, then observe that location to see if they could catch Balcones, or at least gather some clues about his whereabouts. Ocean would keep an eye on Marti and Cassie while the team was staking out the tulpa's owner.

"Balcones probably expects that if we find the tulpa, we'll try to trace it, so stay sharp," Quinn said, once the plan was decided.

There was not much night left when he dragged himself upstairs to sleep. He needed to shift into his kelpie form soon – he was starting to get itchy and uncomfortable. But he was too tired to go for a swim in Kai and Breena's pool just now. It would have to wait until he got some rest.

Monday, August 8
Houston, Texas

It was early afternoon when Quinn stood on the diving board wearing nothing but a towel. He tossed it onto one of the nearby deck chairs that clustered under a large green umbrella and dived in, barely making a splash. His human shape quickly gave way to the large grey kelpie body that moved through the water like a dreadnought. He breathed deeply, and dived below the surface, his long neck stretching toward the bottom of the extra-deep pool. The water was barely cool, so different from the lochs and pools of his native Scotland.

He settled on the bottom and relaxed under the pressure of twenty feet of water. The deep area didn't extend for more than twenty feet before the bottom began to slope up. It was enough to accommodate his length with only five feet to spare, and the pool was a standard competitive width. He could only swim about half the length of the pool before he scraped his belly on the rough plaster, but it was good enough for now.

If an observer who did not know of the existence of fae creatures happened by, he might be shocked to see what he thought was an ancient plesiosaur resting in a backyard swimming pool. But while he had the same four flippers, stocky body, and long neck, his head was somewhat larger and filled with bigger teeth. His tail was shorter, but ridged like an alligator's, instead of smooth.

He emerged from his soak hours later, refreshed and energized. In his kelpie form, worries did not trouble him – he was a sensate being in that shape. It was only in his human phase that doubts plagued him and restive thoughts clawed his brain. As he wrapped the towel around his waist, he reconsidered the plan. It might be better to leave Aleksei behind with Ocean to guard Marti. She knew him, and if she had to be moved or spoken with, it would be easier with an acquaintance than a stranger. Besides, it was entirely possible that Balcones was using the tulpa to draw them away from Marti, and when they were away hunting down its owner, he would swoop in and grab her. If that was the case, two protectors were better than one. He wished that he could tell her what was happening, beg her to be careful; but that would be a mistake. A clean break was best, even if it was the last thing he wanted. They had to get Balcones – as long as he was free, he would see Marti as a piece of bait that Quinn would never resist. He could neither keep her or let her go.

He went into the house and up to his room to get dressed. He smiled at his reflection in the dresser mirror as he pulled on his shirt. The Norse god Odin had given him a tattoo that encircled his navel, and it gave him the ability to keep his human clothes on when he changed form. Before, clothing had been just one more troublesome logistical detail to attend to. More than once, he'd awkwardly found himself naked in exactly the wrong place, so this was, quite literally, a godsend. However, today, his clothes were travel-worn and sweat-sour. He hadn't had time to find fresh clothes because he urgently needed to shift into his natural shape.

He and his team ate their evening meal and waited for dark. Breena and the children were away, but Kai hung out with them until it was time to go. One by one, they stepped into the portal in the upstairs war room and stepped out in the alley behind the Tenth Sphere. They took up their positions and waited.

Close to midnight, Eoin spotted the Devil Baby. It was on the opposite side of the street from Marti's house, moving away from it. Silently, they approached the house. Malik closed his eyes, focusing on the energy of the tulpa.

Tap. Tap. Tap.

A blonde woman in high heels walked towards them.

The Devil Baby looked up and hissed. It charged her, running in an odd broken gallop. She screamed and dropped her handbag as it leaped at her face.

Quinn was the closest. He broke cover and ran towards the attack. He grabbed at the Devil Baby, but the woman's arm snaked around his waist. He tried to shift his weight, but she kept him off balance as she pulled what looked like a green golf ball out of her pocket and threw it hard on the ground.

There was a bang and a bright flash.

Percussion portal. How'd she get that? Only demons use those... Quinn thought as the woman shoved him through the swirling hole in space and time.

Chapter 10
Bang Bang You're (Not) Dead

Monday, August 8, 6:30 AM
Houston, Texas

S ometimes, Nick wished he could sleep in. But his body didn't allow it. Dark had shifted to dawn's twilight as the sun crept up to the horizon. Emily had just crawled back under the covers after feeding McKenzi. Nick reached out for her, then stopped. She was still healing from her C-section and the blood clot in her lung, and he was almost afraid that if he touched her, she'd break. He pulled his hand back.

She must have felt the mattress move when he did that, because she turned over and looked at him. "You feel okay?"

"What?" He brushed a stray lock of hair off her cheek.

"It's dawn. You're still in bed."

"Day off, remember?"

She smiled, just a little, and moved over to snuggle against him. He put his arms around her, enjoying the feel of her body against his. His eyes fell on her face, and it pained him how pale she was. Even though his brain knew she wasn't ready for romance, his body responded to her nearness.

She obviously felt his growing predicament, because she winced and said, "Sorry."

"Not your fault." He got up and jumped in the shower.

When he came out, Emily was asleep. He shook his head. Surely McKenzi would start sleeping through the night soon. Adele, his mother-in-law, would be here in a couple of hours to look after Emily and help with the baby while he took the boys out to the indoor skydive place and the video arcade at the mall. Now, though, he had a little time to himself, and he went into the kitchen. He put four strips of bacon in a large skillet and cracked three eggs into a bowl while he waited for the pork to sizzle. He fired up his tablet to stream an episode of *America's Test Kitchen* while the pan was heating up. Cooking shows were a guilty pleasure of his – he actually liked to cook more than Emily did, although the task fell on her more often. His phone chimed to let him know he'd received a text. Nick waited to look at it until after he'd plated his food, and saw it was from Collins, the officer he'd worked the traffic fatality with a few days ago. He shook his head. *Paperwork NEVER ends at this job.*

The message read, "You on today?"

He typed back. "No. Taking my boys skydiving. U doing reports?"

It was a few minutes before she responded. "No prob. C u @ work."

He put the phone down and went back to his show.

Kyle and Aiden were too excited to eat breakfast, which probably wasn't a bad thing. Indoor skydiving is basically flying around in a vertical wind tunnel, and Nick thought it was only superficially like actual skydiving. But it was something he could do with the boys when they were six – it would be another ten years before they could try the real thing. He had high hopes - they loved the indoor form, so maybe they'd like to jump out of a perfectly good airplane with him when they were old enough. After they finished, he took them across the freeway to eat lunch at the mall food court and play race car games in the arcade.

They were just heading for the exit when the screaming started.

Nick pulled the boys out of the doorway and behind the wall while he triaged the situation. Diners in the food court were stampeding toward the exit. Other people stood frozen as four men in ski masks and body armor ran towards the jewelry store near the restaurants. Two of the men carried MAC-10s and the other two had baseball bats. The bat wielders started smashing glass display cases and grabbing the contents, while the gunmen screamed at everyone to get down on the floor.

Nick's pulse pounded in his ears as the adrenalin surged through his body. He picked up Kyle and Aiden, one in each arm, and lifted them over the ticket redemption counter at the arcade.

"Stay down and do *not* move until I come back for you. Don't make a sound," he whispered to them. Their eyes were huge with fear and Nick felt a rush of anger at the robbers. Bad enough they did what they did, but ruining this perfect day with his boys made it personal.

Nick moved back to the edge of the door, where he could observe the robbery. So far, no shots had been fired – there was just a lot of yelling and screaming. He didn't know who the duty sergeant was today, so he texted Sergeant Patterson, "211 @MC mall."

Then details, "4 Trds, 2 M10s, 2 wood bats. Body armr/msks. Jwlry stor nr food ct"

"Where r u?" came the reply seconds later.

"Vid rcade"

He heard one of the men in the jewelry store shout, "Thirty seconds! Cops on the way. Go, go, go!"

Nick wasn't wearing his duty belt. He had no vest, gun, Taser, baton, flashlight or cuffs. Even though they couldn't keep him down, bullets would still knock him down. And he had about thirty seconds to do something. His training said if he was dressed as a civilian, he should act like a civilian, and someone with more sense of self-preservation would have just laid low and let the crooks run out, hopefully in to the waiting arms of LEOs outside. But he had no way of knowing if they were there yet. If these guys didn't go down today, they were going to do this again, and the next time, somebody might get killed. Maybe even a lot of somebodies.

And it wasn't like they were going to kill him, anyway. Although, if security cam footage showed him getting shot point blank and not dying, it might be a little tough to explain. As long as the boys stayed where he put them, they should be okay, but what if they saw something they really shouldn't?

He sprinted across the hall to the food court, making a beeline for the burger place. As he'd hoped, he found gallon containers of oil near the fryers. He grabbed one, opening it as he ran, and splashed it across the floor, covering as much area as he could. He assumed patrol would be coming Code 2 –no sirens – so they wouldn't give the bad guys a heads-up that they were outside. If his plan didn't work, or backup wasn't outside, things could go south in a hurry.

The robbers saw him as they came pelting down the corridor, but did not snap to what he was up to until too late. The vegetable oil-covered, polished stone tile may as well have been ice. There was loud thud as one of the bat boys fell backwards and hit his head. He lay still, but the others slipped and skidded like slapstick comedy villains.

One of the MAC-10s went off, and the glass doors shattered. Someone started sobbing. The recoil sent the shooter skidding and spinning down the hall, away from the doors. He pivoted around so that his feet were on ungreased tile. There was still some oil on the bottoms of his shoes, but he managed to struggle to his feet like a newborn calf. A newborn calf holding a fully automatic .45 caliber machine pistol.

To his right, Nick heard footsteps and metallic clicks as an entry team prepared to come through the broken doors. Nick skirted the oil and ran for the gunman, trying to get to him before he fully regained his balance. He saw a blur of motion in his peripheral vision as the first officer made entry.

Nick lunged for the bad guy's gun.

The shooter swung to his left.

"Dad!" shrieked Kyle.

Nick's head snapped around to see his son standing at the edge of the arcade, right in the line of fire.

Nick was sure his heart stopped beating.

Voices shouted, probably the entry team, but he focused on the man in front of him and nothing else. He grabbed blindly at the gun, but his hand slipped off the oily barrel. Then his feet hit oil and slipped out from under him. His momentum carried him forward, and he twisted as he fell. All of his weight, shoulder first, struck the gunman's abdomen. The robber grunted as he hit the floor and the air was forced from his lungs. He dropped the gun. Nick shoved it as hard as he could with the heel of his hand, and it skittered across the tile.

Even though the robber was gasping for air, he struggled with something in his waistband. Nick tried to roll over and pin the man's arm, but he was too late.

Time slowed as the matte black barrel of the Glock G22 swung past him unsteadily as its owner struggled for air.

Kyle?

Nick was on his back next to the gunman. He reached up and grabbed the man's wrist, pulling the gun's deadly gaze away from the entry team. Away from his son.

The shooter rolled with him and grabbed the gun with his other hand. The Glock was now pointed in exactly the direction Nick had last seen Kyle.

He rolled onto all fours, and found the barrel of the handgun almost touching his chest. In his adrenalin-fueled altered state, he could see the tendons in the shooter's wrist contract as his index finger curled around the trigger.

Not this again.

Nick gasped as the hot bullet seared through his sternum and exited just below his shoulder blade. He tasted blood.

He almost panicked. Nothing happened. He tasted more blood as it came out of his lungs with each exhale. Then he felt the green fire dancing along his wound, and within seconds, all traces of the bullet hole disappeared.

The robber's eyes got huge behind his ski mask. This time, without the floor to get in his way, Nick rose to his knees, grabbed the top of the gun and twisted hard, up and to the outside. The shooter yelped as his index finger, caught in the trigger guard, broke.

Nick slid the Glock across the floor to wait with the MAC-10.

Someone apparently flipped a switch and turned the rest of the world back on. He heard someone shout, "Clear!" All at once, people were crying. Rubber-soled shoes squeaked on tile.

"Benson?" someone asked. "You okay? Are you hit?"

Nick turned to see three of the entry team officers standing behind him. He knew Tyler Farrell, the man who'd just spoken, from his part-time SWAT training.

"I'm good. Must have been a misfire." Nick knew he wouldn't be allowed to wander around the scene, even if he did work with SWAT. "I left my boys in the arcade. I really have to find them."

"I'll walk with you." Farrell tapped his shoulder radio. "I've got a friendly with me. Repeat, got a friendly."

"Copy that," a voice crackled over the speaker.

Farrell escorted Nick back to the gaming den. Lights flashed and digital soundbites squealed, trying to entice customers to come in and play, as if nothing at all had just happened. An armored assault team officer was down on one knee, trying to comfort a hysterical boy.

"Aiden!"

"Dad!" He left his escort and ran to Nick.

"Are you okay?" Nick had to be careful not to squeeze the breath out of him as he scooped him into his arms.

Aiden just sobbed.

"I'm glad you did exactly what I told you. Now we need to find Kyle. Do you know where he went?"

Aiden shook his head.

Shifting his son to his hip, Nick said, "It's okay. We'll find him."

"You know I'm going to have to take you outside to the secured area." Farrell said.

"But-"

"I'm sorry. What does Kyle look like? We'll keep eyes out for him." Farrell started for the door.

Nick didn't follow. "Like this one, only with a blue shirt. Please. You know me. You have to let me find my son. Can you get the incident commander on the horn? I'll talk to him. Please."

Farrell turned. "You know I can't do that. Sergeant Strickland is at the command center. Talk to him. Don't make my job any harder."

Nick drew in a deep breath, then let it out quietly. "Understood." He knew Strickland well. Well enough that their families had gone camping together a number of times. But Nick also knew him well enough to know that he'd never break protocol.

Scouring the scene on the way out with his eyes, Nick saw no sign of Kyle. Aiden had stopped sobbing, but was clinging to his father with every ounce of strength his sixty-pound body could muster. His warmth both comforted and antagonized Nick. He knew he had to remain calm for his son's sake, but he wanted nothing more than to leave Aiden outside at the door, protected by SWAT, and tear the mall apart to find Kyle. Of course, he'd probably get shot – again – and that would open a whole other can of worms. His jaw clenched so tightly his teeth hurt.

Farrell led Nick to the SWAT mobile command center, a tricked out RV that was equipped with an array of communication and surveillance technology. The diesel engine idled quietly, a soft, throbbing growl in the background. An officer opened the door, and Nick and Aiden climbed the metal steps. Farrell returned to his post. Nick prepared to plead his case, knowing he'd almost certainly be turned down.

Light footsteps pounded across the carpeted floor.

"Dad!" Kyle flung himself at his father. Nick bent to scoop him up, a boy in each arm now. He hugged them hard as he steadied his emotions enough to talk without his voice breaking.

"Kyle! Are you okay?"

"Sure. Sergeant Strickland gave me some water."

Nick wasn't sure if he admired or dreaded his son's fearlessness. That changed from moment to moment. "Why didn't you stay where I told you to, Buddy?"

"I wanted to help." He started to sob.

Nick hugged him tighter. "I understand. But Daddy has a lot of training to fight the bad guys, and you don't. Not yet, anyway."

"But we go to Tae Kwon Do twice a week!" Kyle protested.

"I know," Nick said. "But bad guys with guns are tricky, and you really shouldn't fight them unless you have no other options." He released his hugs so the boys could breathe, but didn't put them down.

"Heard a report that somebody got shot while the entry team was coming in. Knew it was you, because Kyle met them at the door. Who else but his daddy would be wrasslin' the bad guys, huh? Well, that and Patterson texted me that you were on site. But I'm glad my intel on the shooting was wrong."

"Not exactly. It was a misfire."

Strickland nodded. "Somebody's looking out for you."

"So it would seem."

Farrell's brow furrowed. "You sure? There's a crispy little hole in your shirt."

Nick noticed that one of the feeds on the wall was from the mall's security camera system, and he wondered how much of the incident Strickland had seen. There was no way to know, so he grinned. "Must have bounced off my rock-hard pecs."

Strickland shrugged. "Clearly. Now, tell me what happened."

Tuesday, August 9, 3:30 PM
Houston, Texas

"How much are these amethyst pendulums?" I asked.

No answer.

"Lulu?"

"I'm sorry. What did you say?"

I held up a small cardboard box. "The pendulums that came in yesterday. How much are they?"

"I don't know. Packing slip's around here somewhere."

I put my hand on her shoulder. "I'm sure Lieutenant Haskell will call the second he has any news."

"I know, honey. But waiting and not knowing is hard."

I nodded. Scanning for the packing slip, I found it on the floor in front of the cash register. I started pricing the pendulums in silence.

The bell on the door jangled. Lulu looked up and scowled at the woman coming into the shop. She was perhaps a little younger than Belinda. The cut and color of her blonde hair was artificially perfect, and her dress looked expensive.

"Belinda isn't here, Virginia. Go away," Lulu said.

Virginia smiled.

"Oh, Lu. You really should learn to let things go."

I had no idea who Virginia was, or why she and Lulu hated each other, but I did remember Lulu and Belinda both having the same reaction when she'd come into the store a few weeks ago. I was just leaving at the time, so I'd missed any fireworks. This time, though, I was trapped.

Lulu's eyes narrowed and her face darkened. "Hmph. How about I learn to let things go when you learn to stop being a sociopath?" One eyebrow arched sharply.

Virginia's smirk hardened for an instant as anger flashed in her eyes. But it passed quickly.

Her heels clicked on the tile as she continued into the shop, slowly, deliberately intruding on Lulu's space. I could almost see waves of anger rising off of Lulu. Virginia stopped and looked me up and down. Then I knew how a mouse felt when it was cornered by a cat.

She extended her hand. "I'm Belinda's cousin, Virginia."

I blinked a couple of times before I reached up to shake her hand. "I'm…" I hesitated.

"None of your business!" Lulu snarled as she came out from behind the counter. "I told you, Belinda is not here. Get out."

Virginia batted her eyes, her smile dripping with poisoned sweetness. "When will she be back? I need her to sign a check."

"I'll tell her to call you," Lulu said, her eyes smoldering.

If Virginia has any sense, she'll get out now.

She turned to me again. "It was nice to meet you…?" She cocked her head, trying to prompt me for my name.

"Out!" shouted Lulu.

Virginia rolled her eyes. "Have a *nice* day."

It was clear from the way she said the word 'nice' that she hoped Lulu would have anything but a nice day. She gave me another long, predatory look before she strolled out of the shop.

"What's that about?" I asked.

"Honey, don't get me started on Virginia Pennington. That female is bad, bad news."

"Oh?" I set down my pen and put the price tag stickers away. I knew I shouldn't pry, but I couldn't seem to help myself.

Lulu grunted. "When Belinda's grandparents died, they left their house to Belinda and her two cousins, Virginia and Penelope.

Penelope's disabled, and she and her mother live in the house. There's a trust fund for Penelope's care, and Virginia can't stand it that their grandfather left money for Penelope, but not her. She's always scheming to get Belinda to sell her share of the house so she can trick Penelope into selling up so she can boot her out."

"Sounds charming."

"Doesn't she?" Lulu slapped her hand down on the counter. "We tried having that woman as a business partner." Lulu's voice shook. "You know what she did? We had a great space, Inner Loop area, been there ten years. The building owner really liked us, so he never raised our rent in all that time. Well, after we brought Virginia in, the first thing she did was start an affair with our landlord. When his wife caught them *in flagrante delicto*, of course she made him terminate our lease. And then, when he offered to leave his wife for Virginia, she told him she wasn't really interested in anything long term. She cost us a prime location and ruined his marriage without a shred of remorse. She cares about Virginia Pennington, and everyone else can go to Hell." Lulu let out an exasperated sigh.

"Wow." *What else was there to say?*

I watched Lulu pace back and forth past the jewelry counters a few times. "Well, obviously, the circumstances of your move suck, and I'm sorry about that. But I'm glad you landed here."

Lulu stopped. A thin smile lifted her lips. "Thank you, honey. So am I."

We both jumped when her cell phone rang. I held my breath as she answered.

"Yes…yes…What?" She went pale, and I felt my pulse quicken. "What do you mean she's gone? Gone where?…No, of course I haven't seen her." Lulu's voice cracked and broke. "Yes…thank you," she whispered and hung up.

"Lulu, what's the matter?" I almost shouted at her.

There were tears in her eyes when she turned to me. "Belinda's missing."

"What? How can that be?" *After all that's happened recently, and Nick nearly getting shot at a robbery at the mall yesterday, now this. What else can possibly go wrong?*

"I don't know. They don't know. She was there, room service brought up some food, the officer went to wash her hands, and when she came back a minute later, Belinda was gone. Nobody saw anything."

"She wasn't crammed into the room service cart like they did in the old TV shows, was she? Did they look?"

"I don't think it works that way in real life."

I squeezed Lulu's shoulder. "Well, we'll just have to get Ellen to help. Can't she home in on Belinda or something and tell us where she is?"

"Or if she's crossed over," Lulu whispered.

"Stop that," I said. "No. Just no. You're not allowed to go there."

I glanced at the clock and realized that I had twelve minutes to pick up Cassie without incurring a late charge. "I have to get Cassie. Why don't you close the shop early and come with me?"

Lulu shook her head. "I have an appointment coming in twenty minutes."

"It will be okay," I said, giving her shoulder another squeeze.

I was only three minutes late. Yay for me. Cassie was the last one there, and she couldn't decide whether she should be happy, because she got all the toys to herself, or angry because I was late.

This was the second time I'd picked up Cassie and Ms. Clemmons had been there. "Ms. Breckenridge has been out for a few days. Is she alright?" I asked.

The teacher shook her head. "Still in the hospital."

"Hospital? I had no idea. I hope she's better soon – Cassie adores her." I forced a smile. "But of course, she likes you a lot, too." I cleared my throat. "What happened to Ms. Breckenridge?"

"I'm sorry, I can't really discuss that."

"Well, maybe we can send her flowers. What hospital is she in?"

"I'm not sure they'll let you send flowers. She's in HCPC."

I swallowed hard. *Harris County Psychiatric Center.* "I see. I can always check with the front desk. I guess. We've got to get going. See you Thursday."

As we sat in traffic, I wondered what on earth could have happened to Cassie's teacher. She was so young, and she'd seemed so nice."

At long last, I turned onto my street. I was shocked to see two police cars, lights flashing, and a black Suburban parked in front of Hunter's house. He stood in the yard talking to an officer, who was taking notes. When he saw me taking Cassie out of the car, he waved me over.

"Hey, Hunter," I said glancing at the officer. "What's going on?"

"Had a little break in while I was at work."

"That's terrible!" I struggled to contain Cassie. She wanted down. NOW. "Did they take much?"

"That's the weird thing. As far as I can tell, they didn't take anything at all. But they wrote on my door with chalk."

I looked at the door. In four-inch high, plain white chalk letters there was a capital X and an angular E – like the sum function on a spreadsheet.

"X Sigma? What's that supposed to mean?" I asked. "Have you pissed off a fraternity lately?"

Hunter smiled, just a little. "No idea," Hunter replied. He looked at the officer, who shrugged. "I just wanted to let you know to be extra careful. Make sure you set your alarm."

"Thanks, Mom," I replied, re-seating Cassie on my hip. "I've got to get her home. I'll talk to you later." I paused for a moment, speaking before I really thought about what I was saying. "If you need anything, just let me know."

Why did I say that? What if he decides to come over — don't I have enough things going on right now? As soon as I get Cassie fed, I've got to try to contact Ellen so she can find Belinda before it's too late.

Chapter 11
History Lesson

Tuesday, August 9, 12:05 AM
The In Between

Quinn and the blonde woman stepped out of the percussion portal and into a small concrete room. There were no windows and a barely-crackling fire cast a small circle of dim light. Normally, Quinn saw as well in the night as he did in the day, but the blackness in the room felt supernatural, as if it had been poured into the room from the Underworld.

A shape moved in the darkness. Something large scuttled behind it, more heard than seen.

"Welcome to my home." A deep, raspy voice. Quinn knew it too well.

"You didn't have to go to all this trouble just for me, Balcones."

The demon stepped into the bleak firelight. He hadn't bothered disguising himself as human. Orange light glinted off his scaly skin, and his vertical pupils were almost round in the gloom.

"Oh, but I did. You have a nasty habit of escaping me out in the Mundane world. This time, you're on my turf, and I will make sure that you get the slow, highly unpleasant death you richly deserve." His clawed hands balled into fists at his sides.

Something flashed green against the wall behind him, then started to move up towards the ceiling before the shine was swallowed by the gloom. Quinn could hear it climbing, stiff hair brushing the plaster. *Phobetor?*

Quinn refused to be intimidated. He even smiled at Balcones, just a little. "Do you bestow this much attention on all MIT leaders, or am I special?"

Balcones took a step forward and made a sound like a giant cicada deep in his chest. "All MITs deserve to be exterminated like the pests they are." He sucked in a deep breath. "But since you asked, yes, you are special. Very special."

"Is it my rugged good looks?"

The blonde giggled.

Balcones bared his teeth. Then he made a noise that may or may not have been a laugh. "Cast your mind back. September 8, 1900. Galveston Island."

Quinn shrugged. "I've slept a few times since then."

"There was a storm. A very, very bad storm."

He closed his eyes and remembered. His team had discovered a nest of demons and routed them. Unfortunately, they'd run out of demon traps, and they'd had to kill the last one. Siobhan, his long-time lover, had been the one to dispatch it. The thought of her was a hot shard that twisted in his heart.

"We were there, yes. But we ran out of traps. Regrettably, we had to destroy the last demon." He was certain Balcones already knew this, though.

"Regrettably?" Balcones smiled bitterly. "Yes. It was certainly *regrettable* that you killed my father."

"I'm sorry. We make every attempt to trap demons, not terminate them. It couldn't be helped."

"Of course it could!" snarled Balcones. "But no matter. There will only be three of your team left, after I *terminate* you."

He knows about Siobhan, then. Quinn's eyes widened as realization crept over him.

Balcones chuckled. "Yes. Who do you think sent the Frost Giants to your girlfriend's cottage?"

Quinn lunged at the demon, but Balcones tripped him as he deftly stepped out of the way, letting Quinn sprawl onto the rough floor. The room was too small for him to shift in to his full kelpie form, or he would have made short work of Balcones.

"She had to be the first to go. You do understand that, don't you? She took my father, I took her and your child. Seems like a fair trade."

Quinn blinked rapidly. "What?"

Balcones laughed, "Hadn't she told you? She was carrying your child. She certainly told me, when she was begging for her life."

Stunned, Quinn remained on the floor, feeling like he'd just been hit by a truck. When he closed his eyes, he could feel her still-warm body in his arms as he'd carried her from the razed cottage, her blood soaking his clothes. *Why hadn't she told him? Or was this just a lie Balcones made up for maximum torture?* He shook his head and stood up. *Would this be Marti and Cassie's fate, too, if he couldn't stay away from them?*

A portal on the opposite wall where he and the woman came in opened up, and the Devil Baby tulpa stepped through it.

"Have you found her yet?" Balcones asked it.

It snuffled and shook its head. A piece of white chalk fell out of its hand.

"Make sure you pick that up," the woman scolded. "You left it behind the last two times and forgot which houses you visited."

Devil Baby growled a little, but picked up the chalk.

"Come here," Balcones ordered the tulpa. "Get a good whiff of this one. Her house is likely to stink of him."

Quinn kicked at the tulpa as it approached him. Needle-like teeth sank into his shoe and pulled it off. Expecting the monster to bite his foot, Quinn winced. Instead, it buried its face in his shoe and breathed deeply. When the tulpa looked up, its malicious grin changed to fear. It scurried back to the woman and took her hand, as if this abomination were her frightened child.

Quinn followed its gaze, and noticed a thick cord that vanished into the dark of the ceiling. Above it, eight green eyes shone down at him, and he involuntarily gasped.

Balcones chuckled and turned back to the blonde. "Excellent," he said. "Perhaps we'll get her tomorrow. Surely that will draw out any members of his team he's left to guard her. It will be like, as the humans say, shooting fish in a barrel."

"Until then, darling," the woman replied.

"Good night, Virginia."

Tuesday, August 9, 9:30 PM
Houston, Texas

It had taken nearly an hour for Nick to get the boys to sleep. Last night, they'd both had nightmares about the gunmen in the mall, and they weren't too keen on repeating them. They were both trying to get comfortable in Aiden's bed, but the twin mattress wasn't really big enough. He'd let them try it, though, and eventually they stopped kicking each other and closed their eyes.

He plopped down on the couch next to Emily, and she snuggled against him. He put his arm around her and she reached up, turning his face toward her.

"Are you doing okay?" she asked.

"Me? Sure. I'm fine."

She rolled her lips together. "You had nightmares last night, didn't you?"

He pulled away from her slightly. "I was hot, and I couldn't get comfortable."

"Glad you don't work undercover Vice. You're a terrible liar."

He smiled. "Maybe not nightmares. Disturbing dreams. It'll pass."

"Maybe you should talk to the department psychiatrist."

Nick stood up. "I don't need a shrink!"

Emily took in a deep breath and let it out slowly. "Nick, what happened at the mall yesterday was very traumatic, for you and the boys. Those feelings can be hard to process. Sometimes it helps to talk to someone." Then she added, so quietly that he almost didn't hear her, "Because you certainly won't talk to me about it."

"I am fine. I don't need to talk to anyone. Because I am not traumatized." He hadn't wanted to talk to her about it because there was so much he couldn't tell her. If he told her about the green fire that had saved him twice now, what would she say? Would she be afraid of him, take the kids and run?

"I made an appointment with Dr. Weingarten for the boys tomorrow. She said that you're welcome to come."

"What? Don't you think we should have discussed this first?"

"Nick. Keep your voice down. You'll wake McKenzi."

He paced several steps away from her, then turned around and came back. "I was there. You weren't. How could you make an appointment with some quack headshrinker for my boys without even talking to me about it?"

"What are you trying to say, Nick? I see Dr. Weingarten every Thursday. Is that okay, because I'm crazy, and you're not? She's *not* a quack. And besides that, Aiden threw up for three hours after he got home. Neither one the boys want to sleep, because they both have nightmares. The sooner they see somebody, the better." She crossed her arms.

"Fine. Take them. You don't need me. Apparently, not for anything."

"Stop it, Nick. That's not true, and you know it. Why do you have to fight me so hard? I'm just trying to make things better."

Nick held up his hands, palms facing Emily. "As usual, I'm wrong. Whatever. I'm going to the gym."

He marched to the back door.

"Nick, wait."

He picked up the gym bag he always left in the utility room.

"Nick. I love you."

"I'll see you later. Don't wait up."

He used his cardkey to access the gym at the station. He'd expected it to be empty, but there was a handful of people there. Jessica Collins was one of them.

She smiled when she saw him. "Hey, Benson."

"Hey. Did you get that paperwork sorted out?"

"Paperwork?"

"Yeah. You texted me yesterday?"

"Oh," she said. "Yeah. That. Don't worry about it. I heard you had quite a trip to the mall."

He used a disinfecting towelette to wipe down the machine before using it. "Where'd you hear that?"

"Patterson."

Nick made some adjustments on the machine and turned it on. "Figures." He started running.

"So, what's the scoop?"

He told her about the indoor skydiving, the awful pizza at the food court, the race car games across from the pizza. He told her about how he'd hidden his kids, and oiled the tile. He told her about wrestling with the gunman. He did not tell her about the green fire, or how terrified he'd been when he saw Kyle standing where he'd easily catch crossfire. By the time he got to the end of the treadmill routine, it was difficult to talk – his lungs wanted all of the oxygen for his muscles. It felt good to go slower for the cool-down.

"You look hot," Collins said.

"What?"

She stepped in a little too close.

"You look," and she paused to scan his body with her eyes. "Hot."

Nick stopped walking. The treadmill belt carried him over the end of the machine. He flailed his arms and caught himself on the barbell rack. His knuckles scraped across the rough iron weights, drawing blood. He breathed in sharply, his breath a wet hiss.

"Are you okay?" Collins asked, moving even closer.

"That's barely even a scratch."

Nick looked around the gym. The other people that had been there when he arrived had left. There was not a soul there, except him and Collins.

He sidestepped and went to the butterfly machine. Turning his back to her, he added more weights. Again, she moved in, encroaching on his space.

"After this, you want to go grab a cold one?" Collins asked.

Nick was pretty sure that wasn't all she wanted to grab. Parts of him were eager to let her try. It would be so very easy to have a drink or three and go back to her place. But if Emily ever found out, he'd be out on the curb like yesterday's garbage. Sometimes she drove him crazy, but he would be so lost without her that he wouldn't know what to do with himself. She was the tether that kept his kite from the destruction of the infinite sky. And he couldn't imagine only seeing his kids on Wednesdays and every other weekend. The idea made him feel guilty for even considering a fling with another woman. Besides, a fling would inevitably wind up as an unmitigated workplace disaster. Too many great reasons to say no, not enough good ones to say yes.

"It's a tempting offer, but I can't. I have to get back. My turn for night duty with the baby."

"Another time, then," she said.

Nick shook his head slightly. "I don't think so."

She considered him intently for a long moment before she turned away.

"Collins?"

She looked back at him.

"It's nothing against you — you're a very attractive woman. But I love my wife."

She nodded, picked up her things, and left.

Nick did his chest and back workout on the machine, then moved on to free weights. After that, he stepped into the shower to rinse off the sweat before he went home. He was feeling much better, and as he drove, he practiced the conversation he'd have with Emily when he got home. He'd beg her to forgive him for being such a hard-headed jerk, for one thing.

As he approached his house, he thought it was a little odd that the living room light was on. It was closing in on midnight, and Emily didn't usually stay up that late.

Then an arctic blast of cold fear gripped him when he noticed the front door was open.

Tuesday, August 9, 8:00 PM
Houston, Texas

Cassie was fed and bathed, and finally asleep. She'd been having some teething trouble, and sometimes even ibuprofen didn't help. I sat on the couch, and Cú lay on the floor at my feet, chewing on a rawhide bone. I patted the top of his head, and his tail thumped on the floor. He seemed to have grown. Again. I sighed, wishing got Quinn to coming back, and knowing that he wasn't. Knowing that was best for us. Even if I hated it.

I closed my eyes. *Ellen! Ellen! Can you hear me?*

There was no response. I waited a minute, then tried again with the same result. I took a deep breath and held it for ten seconds before exhaling.

Delilah?

"Whacha need, girlfriend?"

Belinda's disappeared from protective custody. I have to contact Ellen. I'm sure that she'll be able to find her. She has to.

"Not sure how much help she can give you. Not being a guide and all, she has more freedom 'bout what she can reveal. But not as much power to find stuff out. Lulu did get in touch with her earlier."

Good to know, I guess. Do you have any way of knowing if Belinda's alright? Or where she is?

"She has not crossed over, and that's really all I can say."

I groaned. *This is so frustrating! I don't understand why someone would want to kill a bunch of romance writers. It doesn't make any sense. I just want Belinda home and safe and this crazy person locked up.*

"I understand. Anything else?"

Not unless you can tell me where Belinda is.

"Girl, you know I can't. There are bigger things playin' out here."

Delilah vanished, and I leaned back on the couch. I wasn't sure what to do. Sitting around watching TV didn't appeal to me. I was restless and needed to move.

I walked around my kitchen, straightening the canisters on the countertops and picking up stray Cheerios.

There was a tap on the glass of the side door. Cú barked and came running into the kitchen. I could see Hunter through the window, so I held my puppy back to let him in.

"I don't mean to bother you," he said. "I saw your lights were still on."

Cú planted himself in front of me. He didn't bark or growl, just sat and stared.

"I understand. My house got broken into recently, too. I know exactly how it feels. Please, have a seat." I gestured to one of the chairs at the breakfast table. "Can I get you something? I can make tea."

"Sure."

I plugged in my electric kettle and got the water going, then pulled out packets of chamomile and lavender tea.

Hunter regarded Cú. "I was sure you had a bigger dog."

"I did. Turned out he wasn't really a stray after all, and he went back...where he belongs."

Hunter nodded. "I see."

The kettle was starting to whistle. "Hot or iced?" I asked.

"Iced, please."

I poured the hot water over the tea bags, then got out glasses and filled them with ice. "Is this your first time?"

"I beg your pardon?"

"Being broken into. What did you think I meant?"

"I wasn't sure."

We both chuckled, a little nervously perhaps. The ice crackled as I poured the hot tea over it. I set one of the Mason jar mugs in front of him and sipped from the other as I sat down.

It was mostly small talk, but we chatted for a long time. I didn't feel like being alone, and he didn't seem to want to, either. But my usual bedtime had come and gone. Cassie got up at 6:30 like clockwork, so I was typically asleep by 11:30.

"You keep yawning. I should probably go," Hunter said.

I glanced up at the clock. "Yeah. It's kind of late."

Hunter stood up.

And then there was a terrible scream, almost a roar, from somewhere outside.

Hunter and I looked at each other and dashed out the door. Cú bounded out with us. A figure came running down the sidewalk.

"Marti! Marti!" it yelled.

It was Nick.

"What?"

"Emily needs you! Now!"

"Watch Cassie," I shouted over my shoulder to Hunter, then ran down the sidewalk after Nick.

The house was in a terrible state. Surrounded by overturned furniture and broken porcelain, my sister lay unconscious in the middle of the floor. Her face was bruised and bloody, as if she'd been beaten.

I checked for a pulse. Seconds went by before I found it. It was weak and slow, but it was there.

"Called 911. Ambulance is on the way," Nick panted.

"Get a blanket." I raised her chin to make sure her airway was clear. "I think this arm is broken. Get me a magazine and some gauze."

"We don't have gauze."

"Tape, then."

I curled the magazine around to her arm and taped it to stabilize the bone ends. Anything I could do to help the paramedics get her on the stretcher faster and on the way to the hospital would help. She was hanging by a thread. Relief washed over me when I heard the approaching wail of the ambulance.

"Hang on, Emily, you're going to be okay. You have to be," I told her. "What happened?" I asked Nick.

"I went to the gym. I came home and found her like this."

I suddenly became aware of the silence.

"Nick, where are the kids?"

He was on the verge of tears. "I don't know."

Wednesday, August 10, 10:00 AM
Houston, Texas

The ICU monitors beeped and the respirator hissed and clicked as it breathed for my sister. She was allowed not more than two visitors at a time, and Nick never left her side, not since Homicide had come to question him.

The trauma surgeons had drained the excess blood off Emily's brain, but there was still a lot of swelling. There was no way to know if she'd ever wake up from the coma she was in. Even if she did, would she'd still be Emily?

"Nick?" I said, softly touching his shoulder. "What are the detectives saying about the kids?"

"Amber Alert went out last night. Since the bayou is nearby, EquuSearch is going to work there. It's been on the news. They're all still at my house, plus FBI, waiting on a ransom call."

"I'm sure they're doing everything they can." I wished that I had something other than platitudes to offer Nick.

He rubbed his eyes with the heels of his hands. "They think I did it."

"What? That's crazy!"

"Is it? The spouse is always the prime suspect, until they can be ruled out. Look at my hands."

Nick held them up and I looked. The knuckles on his right hand were freshly scraped. His left hand bore a large bruise. He continued, "My alibi is sketchy at best, incriminating at worst. If you didn't know me, what would you think?"

My heart sank. I would think exactly what the investigators thought. How many domestic violence victims had I seen in the ER? Way more than I ever wanted to.

I swallowed hard and changed the subject. "Please come have some breakfast."

"Not hungry."

"At least have some coffee. Mom will sit with her. Starving yourself to death is not going to help her."

He stood up, kissed Emily's forehead, and whispered, "I'll be right back. Don't go anywhere."

My mother went in to see my sister. Dad stayed in the waiting area. He was having some trouble with his stump and couldn't wear his artificial leg. The wheelchair was too hard to maneuver around all the equipment in Emily's room.

"I'm taking Nick to the cafeteria. You want to come?"

Dad shook his head.

Nick and I went down to the hospital cafeteria. I ate some of my oatmeal, but Nick just pushed his scrambled eggs around the plate. Finally, he gave up and set the fork down.

"I need to talk to Quinn," he said.

"Why?" *Not sure I can arrange that.* This surprised me, because it had been hard for Nick to accept Quinn and company's paranormal nature, especially since when he first met him, Quinn had borrowed the identity of a criminal.

Nick reached into his pants pocket and pulled out a plastic baggie and set it on the table.

"I found this on Emily's cheek."

I picked up the baggie. Inside was a tawny colored scale about the size of a bean. "Well, I supposed it could be from a demon." I gingerly set it back down.

"Isn't that Quinn's area of expertise?"

"Yeah." I put my elbows on the table and interlaced my fingers. "The problems is, well, we kind of broke up. I could try texting him…" I trailed off.

Nick closed his eyes and sighed. When he looked at me again, there was so much suffering in his eyes that it broke my heart. "Please. I know it's awkward. But this is the only clue I have. I have to get my kids back and find out who did this to Emily."

Tears welled up in my eyes. "If there is any change, no matter how minor, you swear to call me?"

He nodded.

"Okay. I'll go now, and see what I can do." I picked up the baggie off the table. "Let me take this along."

"Thanks, Marti."

I wished I could have promised him that we'd get his kids back, but I was afraid it would be a promise I couldn't keep. I swallowed hard to keep my voice from breaking. "Emily is my sister. Your kids are my nephews and niece. What else could I do?"

I drove to my house and walked around the back yard. I knew Dryads lived in the trees – Quinn had called them by name, but I couldn't remember them. So I stood where I was about halfway between them and a little in front.

"If you are listening, please help. It's really urgent that I contact Quinn. He's gone…and I need to talk to him. It's about a demon."

I could hear whispering voices, but no one made an appearance.

"Please," I said. "It's urgent. I really have to speak with him."

The ground shook as something heavy fell behind me. I whirled to look, and found myself facing what could only be described as a gargoyle.

"*Mademoiselle*," it said, bowing ever so slightly.

"Um," I said, for lack of anything more intelligent.

"Why are you looking for Quinn?" it asked.

I had no idea whether this was a good guy or a bad guy. "It doesn't concern you," I replied.

He whistled, and Aleksei stepped out from behind the trees at the back of the yard. How was it possible I hadn't see him there? Fae powers, I suppose.

"Marti!" he said.

I didn't really know him all that well, but I rushed to give him a hug. I just needed something…familiar. He seemed a little taken aback. He smelled of pine needles and leaf litter, and I breathed in deeply.

"Aleksei, I am so happy to see you. I have to speak with Quinn."

"That is problem, Marti."

"Why?" I pulled away from Aleksei.

"He was taken," the gargoyle replied.

"Taken? Like kidnapped?" I asked. *Yet another thing to worry about.*

"*Exactement le même,*" said the gargoyle. "Indeed, he was kidnapped."

Still, I was unsure as to whether he had anything to do with the kidnapping. "Who are you?" I asked.

"I am Ocean, Quinn's uncle."

"You don't look much like a kelpie," I said.

"That is because I am not one. The story, it is complicated. Perhaps another time. Now what, *mademoiselle*, is this about a demon?"

I pulled the baggie from my purse and held it out. Ocean held it up for both he and Aleksei to examine.

"*Da*, demon scale," Aleksei said. "Where is from?"

"My sister's house. They took the kids and left her for dead." My voice broke at the end, and I couldn't help tearing up.

Ocean frowned. "Where does your sister live?"

"Six doors down," I pointed toward Emily's house.

"How did we not hear that?" Aleksei asked.

"*Je ne sais pas.* Perhaps they must be using portals. I do not know how they got one inside your sister's home."

"Nick, my brother-in-law, is asking for your help. So am I. Please." I said. "Is there any way this is connected to Quinn's disappearance? Maybe if we find the children, we'll find him as well."

Ocean and Aleksei exchanged a look. They knew more than they were planning to tell me, that was clear.

Chapter 12
Darkness

Tuesday, August 9, 2:30 PM
Houston, Texas

Belinda was bored out of her mind. The officers had brought her a notebook, and she'd written the outline for *Dragonfire*, the last book in her dragon romance trilogy. She'd started a draft of the novella, but so far wasn't very happy with it. She needed to go outside and walk, feel the sunlight on her skin, hear the birds in the trees, and smell the fresh air. But that wasn't going to happen any time soon. She wondered if they could get her sunglasses and a wig so she could at least go walk around the swimming pool area of the hotel.

Knock. Knock. "Room service!"

"Finally," said Fiona McCoombs, the officer who was currently on babysitting duty with Belinda. "I'm starved."

She looked out the peephole, then opened the door, still chained. Apparently, it was actual room service, because she took the chain off and let the woman in with the cart of food.

Belinda looked at the server and shook her head slightly. She sincerely hoped that when she was in her sixties, she wouldn't be forced to get a menial hotel job to make ends meet.

The server began to transfer the food to the small writing table, but McCoombs stopped her. "Leave the cart. I'll put it out in the hall for you later."

"If you like," she replied.

Her eyes slid over to Belinda, and it made her shiver. There was something not right about the room service lady. She made her way toward the door, fairly slowly and incompetently, dropping the napkin she had draped over her left arm on the way.

"Wait a minute, please," McCoombs said.

The server stopped.

The officer lifted the covers on each plate and examined the contents. When she was satisfied that there was nothing more sinister than greasy French fries lurking inside the metal domes, she nodded at the server, "Thank you."

The server opened the door.

McCoombs turned and headed for the bathroom to wash her hands.

Instead of leaving the room, the room service lady pulled a ruby pendant out of her blouse and gave Belinda a hard look. Suddenly, Belinda was not in the hotel room.

It was completely dark in the cramped quarters where Belinda found herself. She was on her back, her hands cuffed together in front of her. She reached up and groped around the ceiling of her prison. Satin. *Am I in a coffin?* Her heart rate surged in panic – fight or flight. But neither of those was an option.

Belinda struggled to take deep breaths and calm herself down. She wasn't typically claustrophobic, but then again, she didn't typically lie around handcuffed in coffins, either. *Fear is the true enemy, the only enemy. Calm down and think.* There was a flow of cool air coming from her right, so hopefully, at least she wouldn't suffocate before her captor came for her. Maybe.

She forced herself to breathe deeply and slowly. *Okay. If this is a coffin, it has to have a lid.*

Her eyes started adjusting to the darkness. There was a slightly less dark line a couple of inches wide to her right. The lid must be propped up on something – that's where the air was coming from.

Belinda pushed straight up with both hands. The top raised perhaps an inch before there was a clang of metal and the movement stopped. *Great. It's chained down.*

Something tapped Belinda's thigh, and it startled her. She dropped the lid of the coffin, and it slammed shut. The ventilation opening was gone.

"No!" Belinda shouted at the darkness. She started to hyperventilate.

"If you don't get a hold of yourself and stop this you're going to run out of air," she said out loud, not caring if anyone was listening outside.

No talking – you're wasting oxygen. Okay. So what fell on you? Hopefully, it isn't a large tarantula. She shuddered at the thought.

She had to twist and squirm, but she finally found the edge of the object with her fingertips. It felt like a chunk of wood. After several tries, she was able to use her leg to block it from going forward while she inched it up the side of the casket, letting it fall into her hands. It was definitely wood – a piece of 2 x 4.

This must be what was propping open the lid. Okay, so how do I get it back in place? She clasped the board between her palms and pushed against the top of the casket. It opened about three inches and stopped. But now the wood was at the top of the coffin lid, not the edge. When she tried walking her hands down, she dropped the 2 x 4. After the sixth attempt, she decided to try putting the board in her mouth and raising the lid with her hands. She was starting to feel sleepy and a little light-headed. It was harder work than she imagined, but she eventually wedged the piece of wood under the lid. She lay back for a moment, then twisted so she could prop herself on her elbow to have full access to fresh air. Even so, she just wanted to sleep. But her head ached and her pulse throbbed in her ears to keep her awake. Belinda's heart took little stutter steps every now and then. *This had really better not be a heart attack.*

Gradually, the pounding in her head subsided, and she lay in the dark and listened. Water dripped somewhere off to her left. A cricket chirped a few times, then was silent.

There was a click, then a creak. *A door opening? Should I be mad or scared?*

Footsteps. Another click. A scrape and a rattle. The coffin lid opened and a bright light glared in Belinda's face. She closed her eyes and turned away.

"Who are you? What do you want from me?" she asked.

"It doesn't matter who I am – I'm just a vessel. I'm here to stop you from spreading that smut you write and corrupting innocent readers." The voice was female, with a bit of a southern twang, but not too much. It sounded vaguely familiar.

"I think readers are smart enough to know what works for them. If they don't like the book, they can stop at any time," Belinda replied.

"That isn't the point! Words corrupt, your words corrupt, with your disgusting dragons and bestiality. After someone's read one of your lustful scenes, they can't unread it, now can they? Time is short."

"Time is short?" Belinda echoed, fearing the woman would close the lid, lock it down, and leave her alone in the dark forever.

"The Rapture approaches!" The woman's voice got louder. "I have to save as many as I can, before it's too late."

"What about people who don't want to be saved?"

"You're just trying to confuse me. Everyone needs to be saved, whether they know it or not."

"And you're willing to kill innocent people to save other people who don't know they need saving, and probably don't even want it?"

"Oh, you can mock me if you want. I'm not the one lying in a coffin with her hands chained together."

Belinda could hear the smirk in her attacker's voice, even if she couldn't see her face behind the glare.

The woman continued. "I went looking for Coda Sterling, but I found Belinda Tate instead. Not only do you lie about your name to sell those filthy books, but you try to spread your devil worship through your unholy shop. It's too bad they don't burn witches these days – only fire could cleanse your evil soul. But don't worry. I have something extra special planned for you."

"Devil worship? What on Earth are you talking about?"

"Your shop. The Tenth Sphere? Something to do with summoning demons, I'm sure."

"Are you kidding me?" Belinda asked. "Demons are the last thing we want hanging around. Do you have any idea what a nuisance they are? In fact, we sometimes work with –" Belinda stopped herself. This woman wasn't going to believe anything she said, but she might repeat it. No point in giving her information, because there was no way of knowing who she might blab to.

"You're working with who?" the woman behind the flashlight asked.

"It doesn't matter. You could stop shining that light in my eyes, you know," Belinda said. "And I could use a restroom break."

"No. I don't trust you."

"It's going to be an emergency before much longer."

"Not my problem." The light started to go down toward the floor, then flipped back up into Belinda's eyes. "How do you know so much about demons?" Suspicion edged her voice.

Belinda tried to shrug, but her shoulders were starting to get pins and needles from being in an unnatural position, and it hurt to move them. "Oh, please. They're everywhere. You've probably met at least one and never realized it."

"I think I could recognize a demon," the woman said, her voice shrill with indignation.

"I doubt it. They're very clever at disguising themselves. If you ever get an offer too good to be true, odds are there's a demon behind it."

"Is that so?" The woman sounded skeptical.

"Who do you think invented multi-level marketing?"

The woman behind the light snorted, but Belinda couldn't tell if it was laughter or derision. "I have preparations to make," she said, and closed the lid.

"Wait!" If she could just keep the woman talking, maybe she would realize her mistake and set Belinda free.

But her only answer was the rattle of the chain and the snick of the closing lock. Footsteps. Squeaking door. Turning lock.

Belinda started to hyperventilate again She was in worse trouble than she'd originally thought.

She couldn't allow herself to panic – that wouldn't get her out of here.

There was another voice, new but familiar. "Belinda, are you here? I can't see you."

"Ellen!" she said out loud, then thought better of it. *I'm here, in the casket.*

"Oh, Belinda! What happened to you?"

I don't exactly know. I was in the hotel room, then all of a sudden, I was here. I don't even know where I am. How did you find me?

"Sofia told me where you were."

Thank goodness for spirit guides. Now how are we going to get out of here?

Virginia scowled. When Balcones, in his human form, had approached her about a tulpa, he had offered to get rid of someone, any person she chose, as part of his payment. Naturally, she chose Belinda. Of course, he'd resorted to outsourcing his dirty work to a human. *Wasn't that just like a demon?* If this ghost lady – what was her name again? Ellen? – got back to Lulu with Belinda's whereabouts, the whole plan would come crashing down. Ellen had to be stopped, permanently, if need be.

In certain circles, Virginia was known as the Thought Form Queen – there were few people in the Western Hemisphere as good at creating and deploying tulpas as Virginia. It was a small matter for her to put a spider thought form in one of the darkened corners of Belinda's prison, just to make sure things were unfolding according to plan. It was a good thing she was watching, because the plan just hit a snag.

Her grandparents had lived practically out in the country, once upon a time. The city of Houston spread and sprawled until it swallowed their neighborhood. Their 1960's ranch was on a large, one-acre lot in a highly desirable part of town. Every year, more trust fund money was wasted paying the taxes on the place, and she never got any benefit from it whatsoever. If she could get Belinda out of the way, she'd get Penelope institutionalized, and cash in on the property. That size lot was easily worth a million dollars, maybe more, to someone who'd just knock down the old house and put up a mansion. And with Belinda dead, she wouldn't have to share a dime of it. Penelope would never ask, and Virginia would never tell. They made a great team.

But now, this Ellen person threatened to ruin everything. Virginia saw her million-dollar payday vanishing before her eyes.

And there was no way she was going to allow that.

Chapter 13
Sleeping Beauty

Wednesday, August 10, 12:15 PM
Houston, TX

M y cell phone rang.

I jumped. So did Aleksei and Ocean.

"Hold on." I looked at the screen. Caller ID said it Dr. Tribeki – I'd worked with him as an ER nurse. *Why is he calling me? Had Emily woken up?* I couldn't stand any more bad news.

"Dr. Tribeki?"

"Hello, Marti. I wanted to give you an update on your sister."

My stomach knotted into macramé.

"How is she?"

"She's still the same. But at least her condition hasn't deteriorated. Since she was stabilized enough to run a CT, we did one and found three linear skull fractures. No more active bleeds, but there are some contusions. There's not much else we can do. As you well know, she could wake up this afternoon, or it could be ten years from now. I'm so sorry – wish I had better news."

"Did you run stimuli tests? What was her Glasgow?"

"There was a pupil reaction, but we put her GCS at five."

"Five. I see. Thank you for calling." I hung up before he could say anything else.

A five on the Glasgow Coma Scale. Damn. The lowest possible score was three, and the lower the score, the worse the prognosis. I knew that only about a quarter of patients with GCS scores lower than nine recovered. But none of those patients was my sister. Emily could not die. I wouldn't allow it.

"Marti?" Aleksei asked. "Is bad news?"

I blinked a few times and looked up at him. He looked a little blurry, and I felt something sliding down my cheeks. "Emily," I said, then swallowed hard, "she's in pretty bad shape. The odds-" I stopped, unable to bring myself to say it out loud.

Aleksei put his arms around me. I felt nothing but static, white noise. His hug didn't help.

"I have to get back to the hospital," I said, and pulled away.

When I got there, both of my parents looked grey and worn out, like old, discarded rags. I'm not sure I remember either of them looking this grim, even when Dad lost his leg in that car accident. They shouldn't be here in the ICU, watching their daughter dangling by a spider silk thread over death's abyss. They should be at home, playing with their new granddaughter, not worried sick about where she and her brothers were and whether they were okay.

But as bad as they looked, Nick looked worse. I stood near the end of the bile yellow curtain that separated Emily from the next patient over. His hand went through the bed railings and came up underneath hers to avoid the IV.

"Hey, Nick."

He didn't move, and at first I thought maybe he didn't hear me over the hissing and thumping of the ventilator. He shook his head very softly and said, "This is all my fault."

"What are you talking about?"

He looked at me with such an unbearable misery in his eyes that I nearly started crying again. "I should have been there. Maybe I could have stopped this. Maybe they would have seen I was home and moved on to a different house."

Like mine? Surely that's not what he meant. "You can't beat yourself up with maybes and what-ifs. There's no way to know what could have happened. Maybe you would have stopped it, but maybe you would have ended up in the bed next to this one. Or dead."

"No. Not dead." He shook his head, and I wasn't sure if he was laughing or crying. "Remember that green fire I showed you when I cut my hand? It even fixes dead."

It took me a few moments to process what he had just said. I'd forgotten all about the weird wound healing fire he'd shown me. I thought it must be a consequence of having his life force replaced with a Valkyrie's. And of course, Valkyries were immortal. But all this was too complicated to explain right here, right now.

I just nodded. "I see." My eyes darted to Emily's machinery. None of the readouts looked any different than they had before. "You've worked late plenty of times. Nothing like this has every happened before, not in our neighborhood. There was no reason to expect-"

"I wasn't working late!" he snapped. "But I was late coming home." He paused, seeming to be searching for the right words. *What wasn't he telling me?* "Em and I got into a fight. I left. Went to work out. Why did I leave?" His breath caught in his throat.

"Whether it would have made a difference or not, you don't have a time machine to go back and see. We just have to deal with what is. And this self-flagellation is not helping. Not you, not Emily." *Not your kids.*

He put his face in his hands for a few moments. Then he stood up and wiped them on his jeans. "You're right. The best thing I can do for Em right now is bring her babies back to her."

Nick caressed her least-bruised cheek with the backs of his fingers. "I'll be back soon. You rest now, okay?"

He stood up and looked straight at me. His eyes now had laser focus. This was the look of someone who was out for revenge. Someone who had nothing left to lose.

"Let's go," he said.

My father looked up as we went past.

"I'm going with him to make sure he doesn't do anything stupid," I said.

Dad nodded.

Nick strode down the hospital corridor, and I almost had to run to keep up with him.

"Where are we going?" I asked.

"To get my kids back."

"Do you have news?"

"Not yet. But I want you to take me to Quinn. If it wasn't for him, this would never have happened. Unfortunately, he is the only one that can help me find McKenzi and my boys. That's all that's keeping me from breaking his neck."

"I don't think it's fair to blame Quinn," I said. If Quinn attracted demons, or one demon in particular, then it was also somewhat my fault for having him around. "He didn't do this to Emily or take the kids. But I can't take you to him."

Nick stopped and turned on me so fast I nearly crashed into him. "You're protecting him over your own sister?"

"He's been taken. Nobody knows where he is, or even if he's still alive. I talked to Aleksei this morning. I can take you to him."

When we got to the parking garage, I said. "Let me drive."

"No."

I knew that as a police officer, he had special training in driving at high speeds, but there was no way I was getting in the car with him, not in the state he was in. "Have it your own way. Meet me at my house."

He nodded once, curtly, and headed towards his parking space. My car was up another two levels, so I took the elevator. When I got back to my house, Nick was already there, waiting in his truck. I glanced at the clock on my dash. I still had another two hours before I had to pick up Cassie. I couldn't think of anything

I'd rather do than hug my baby girl just now, but it would have to wait a little longer.

I got out of the car, and Nick did the same. He looked up at the top of my house as we came into the back yard.

"A gargoyle statue? Really?"

Ocean was perched there, looking exactly like a hunk of carved limestone. "That isn't a statue," I said.

At the sound of my voice, Ocean hopped down off the shingles, shaking the ground as he landed. Nick took a step backward, but otherwise remained impassive.

"Nick, this is Ocean, Quinn's uncle. Ocean, this is Nick, my brother-in-law."

I tossed Nick my keys. "You should probably go in the house. I'll find Aleksei."

Ocean had to fold his wings tightly and dip his shoulders to fit through the doors, but they both disappeared inside. I dreaded the conversation that would take place between Aleksei and Nick. But I was as anxious as he was to get McKenzi and the boys back safe and sound. I went and stood between the two trees.

"Aleksei?" I called softly.

Seconds dragged by. When I thought about a minute had passed, I called again, a little louder.

"I am here. What is your need?" He peered at me from behind the tree to my right.

"Emily, my sister, is in a coma, and I don't know if she's going to make it. Nick and I, we need your help to find his children."

"I am sad to hear of your misfortune. But I am not sure –"

"Please," I said. "Please come inside and talk with me, Ocean, and Nick."

He followed me into the house. Nick and Ocean were standing at opposite ends of the kitchen, regarding each other adversarially.

"*Non,*" Ocean said. "This is not a job for humans."

Nick glared at him. "They're my kids. No one is going to care as much about finding them as I do."

"*C'est vrai,* that is true. But it is also true that such emotion clouds your judgment. And besides, this work is *tres dangereuses,* too much so for mortals."

Nick said nothing. He moved to the silverware drawer and pulled out a chef's knife. He looked straight at Ocean and plunged the blade into his own abdomen, then pulled it out, blood flowing with it.

Aleksei grunted in surprise.

Before I had a chance to grab a kitchen towel to apply pressure, green fire flickered around the wound. The bleeding stopped. Nick raised his shirt, revealing his mark-free belly.

Ocean cocked his head. "I have seen this only with the Valkyries. How do you come to have this ability?"

Nick shrugged.

I hadn't told Nick what had really happened in Russia a few weeks ago. He knew he'd died, but had no idea why he hadn't stayed that way. I'd thought it was better he didn't know the details, because he was already struggling to accept the supernatural.

"It's a long story," I said. "But to make it short, he was killed but a Valkyrie gave up her life force for him."

"*Vraiment.* So this is the one. There was a report of such a thing happening." Ocean shook his head. "Odin Allfather does not take lightly the deaths of his daughters."

I looked at the floor. I remembered the single tear that had fallen from Odin's eye. He'd caught it after it turned into a solid blue crystal on his cheek. "Never forget," he had said as he folded it into my hand. I'd kept Odin's tear in in my jewelry box, not sure what to do with it. But it occurred to me now that it would be a good talisman on this desperate quest.

Nick leaned against the counter.

"When was the last time you slept?" I asked him.

"Doesn't matter."

"It does. I know there's a bunch of cops and FBI at your house, waiting for a ransom call. Why don't you crash on my couch? I have to go get Cassie."

"Not right now," he replied.

I shook my head and left.

After I put Cassie to bed, I rummaged around in my jewelry box. I set Odin's tear on the counter while I looked for a suitable necklace. I had a Tibetan prayer box that one of my cousins had given me for my birthday one year, after she'd been on a month-long tour of Asia. It was a cylinder, a little smaller than the first joint of my thumb, and it was silver with a red stone and a blue stone set in the side. The idea was to write a prayer or wish on a slip of paper and then put it in the box so that it's always infusing the aura of the person wearing it. I wasn't a big believer in that, but it was the perfect size to hold Odin's tear. I slipped it into the box, then, because it couldn't hurt, I wrote a wish on a sliver of notebook paper and put it in, too. The chain was a little long, but if I tucked it inside my shirt, the box hung right next to my heart.

Saturday, August 13, 2:00 PM
Houston, Texas

"Have you seen Nick today?" Mom asked.

I put my cell phone on speaker so I could talk to her while I was changing Cassie.

"No. Why?"

"When we went to see your sister this morning, the nurses said he hadn't been there."

"I'm sure he's trying to find the kids. There's not really anything he can do for Emily by sitting around the hospital. At least that's how he'll see it."

"You're probably right," she said. "Your father is having a nap, so come in quietly when you bring Cassie, okay?"

"No problem. We'll be over as soon as I finish changing her."

We said our goodbyes and I tapped the 'speaker' tile. Cassie was barely one, so potty training was nowhere near our immediate future. But she hated everything about her nappy – she just wanted to go commando.

"That is so not happening, little squirmy wormy," I said to her.

She giggled as she wiggled, and I added a little piece of duct tape over each diaper tab so she wouldn't pull the whole thing off.

"No bare baby bottoms at Grandma's house, okay? You need to be good while I go visit your Auntie Em."

"Ning!"

I topped off Cú's water before we left and gave him a pat. His tail thumped lazily on his bed. "Guard the house while we're out." *No one's going to be afraid of you, though. Not yet, anyway.*

The ICU looked the same as it had yesterday. So did Emily.

"Hey, Em," I said. "How do you feel today?"

I didn't really expect an answer. It was more force of habit than anything, back from my old ER days.

"Girl, you need to turn around if you want to see her."

Delilah? What are you doing here?

Delilah rolled her eyes, so I just did what she said.

Emily!

She looked at me. Her mouth opened and closed, as if she were trying to say something. Emily gestured with her hands, but I didn't know what she was trying to tell me. She glanced over at her body, then vanished.

"Emily," I said, taking her hand. "Please hold on. Whatever you do, don't go into the light. Nick needs you. I need you. Nick *is* going to get your kids back. They'll need you most of all. Please. Please stay with us."

"It ain't always a choice, girlfriend," Delilah said.

I pulled up a chair and got out my cell phone, flicking through the tiles until I found the e-reader app. I'd already queued up one of Emily's favorite novels. I always thought, whether she realized it or not, Victor Hugo's epic is what ultimately propelled her into the public defender job she had now. I started to read:

> *So long as there shall exist, by virtue of law and custom, decrees of damnation pronounced by society, artificially creating hells amid the civilization of earth, and adding the element of human fate to divine destiny; so long as the three great problems of the century – the degradation of man through pauperism, the corruption of woman through hunger, the crippling of children through lack of light – are unsolved...*

I also thought it was the most appropriately titled book of all: *Les Misérables* – because right now, we were The Miserable Ones. I read until my voice started to get raspy. Then I just sat there, watching the little blip on the EKG jumping and scrolling across the monitor for as long as I could stand it. Beep...beep...beep. *Keep on beeping, Em. Keep on beeping.*

Cassie had spent the day 'helping' Grandma around the house. They'd skipped nap time, and she was tired and cranky when I picked her up. I debated whether it was better to make her stay up until her usual bedtime, or just let her sleep, risking an extra-early wake up. In the end, I needed the peace, so I let her sleep.

I sat in the kitchen and stared out the window. I should probably fix myself something for dinner, but I couldn't seem to get motivated. I absently stroked Cú's head and ruffled his ears, until he ran to the door and barked.

There was a knock, and I could see Hunter's face through the glass. I got up to let him in.

"Hey," I said.

"I am so sorry about your sister and her family," he said, setting down a re-useable grocery bag on the table. "I had no idea until I saw your mom and Cassie this afternoon. I'd seen the cops at your sister's house, but I hadn't realized…"

"Thanks for coming over." I sat back down, and Cú curled up at my feet.

Hunter began unloading the shopping. "I figured you might be tired from spending all that time at the hospital, so I thought it would be a neighborly gesture to come and make you and Cassie dinner."

I gave him half a smile. "Cassie's already asleep. I really appreciate the offer, but I don't feel all that hungry."

I raised my eyebrow at the bottle of wine he set on the table.

"That's for the scampi sauce," he said.

I winced. "This is so thoughtful, but I'm deathly allergic to shellfish."

His smile deflated. "Well…how about zucchini sautéed in white wine and garlic butter then?"

I laughed. "Sure." I gave him some ice and a plastic bag for the shrimp – I was afraid for it to be in my fridge in case the package leaked. Cassie was too little to call 911 if I went into anaphylactic shock.

It didn't take long for him to cook up a scrumptious meal. And since he only needed a few ounces of the chardonnay, we each had a glass. After we finished eating, he poured another.

"Are you trying to ply me with alcohol and have your way with me?" I asked, only half joking. I knew how incredibly stupid it was to combine alcohol with having a man I hardly knew in my house. But I was feeling so overwhelmed and alone that I was willing to risk it.

"I would never do that to you."

I hoped that was true. "You up for a movie?" I needed an escape, a breath of air. I felt I was drowning in all the horribleness that was going on right now. The horribleness that I had brought down on my family.

Cú kept himself between us as we relocated to the living room. I flicked on the TV with the remote and sat at one end of the couch, and Hunter sat at the other.

"Come on, put your feet up," he said, patting the cushion.

I was exhausted, so I set my wine down and swung my feet up on the sofa. Cú groaned as he stretched out on the floor. Hunter pulled my feet into his lap, and started giving me a foot massage.

"I'll fall asleep if you keep doing that," I said.

He didn't stop. I didn't exactly want him to. After the train wreck my life had suddenly become, it was nice to not be alone. And it didn't hurt that he was easy to look at.

But as pleasant as this was, I knew that Quinn was the one with all the answers, and I had to find him. And the sooner the better.

Chapter 14
Unexpected Guests

Tuesday, August 9, 11:30 PM
The In Between

Balcones had left the room a while ago. There were no doors – the only access was through portals. And Quinn was certain that they were secured so that only specific individuals could go through them. He was equally certain that he was not on that list. What he needed was a workaround. He cast his gaze to the ceiling. The compound green eyes that glinted in the firelight were not helping his concentration.

"Phobetor? That is you, up there isn't it?"

There was a scratching noise as a spider the size of a Great Dane clambered down the wall and stood in the pale circle of light. It shimmered, then took the form of a man. His skin was pale, almost greenish, and his dark hair unkempt. Dark circles pooled under his deep set eyes like bruises. His loose grey tunic accentuated his pallor.

Sandals scuffed on the concrete as he approached Quinn. "How do you know me?"

"I have been told that your brothers are worried about your disappearance, and Phantasos is looking for you."

Phobetor rolled his eyes. "They never understood me. Don't be misled. They aren't concerned for my welfare – they just want to control me."

Quinn nodded. "I understand. I have four brothers."

"Oldest?"

"Middle."

Phobetor grimaced. "Hardest spot. I'm the youngest. Nyx saved the best for last."

"Hmmm," Quinn replied.

"You don't believe me?" Phobetor asked. "Morpheus sends sappy, sweet dreams that hardly anyone remembers. Phantasos is in charge of weird dreams, you know, the kind where you go for tea with the Queen, and the butler is a talking zebra who pours tea from a seashell and serves you little cakes made of cloud and pumpernickel." He pointed to his chest. "I, on the other hand, send nightmares."

Quinn had had more than his fill of bad dreams. "And what's so good about nightmares, then?"

"No one forgets their nightmares," Phobetor replied. "And they bring you a gift. Face the monster in your dream, and you slay it in real life. They're always connected, if you look hard enough."

"Perhaps." Quinn shrugged. "But why are you here, with Balcones?"

Phobetor's face darkened. "He said we were going out for a glass of mead. He wanted to make a business proposition. But then he brought me here. Still not a hint of a business transaction. And no mead. Worse, I can't get out of this place, and I've had enough of him. He's ugly, obnoxious, and he smells terrible."

Quinn couldn't resist. "Sounds like a nightmare."

Phobetor glared at him and opened his mouth to reply.

Balcones stepped through a portal and into the room. He carried a very small baby. Triumphantly, he put the child in Quinn's arms.

"What are you doing, Balcones? Have you lost your mind?" Quinn asked.

"Look at the baby."

Quinn looked.

"I don't know what you're on about. You should get this wee one back to her mother before she wakes up."

Balcones scowled. "You don't know this baby?"

Quinn shook his head.

Balcones stepped in so that his face was only inches away. His hot breath stank like sulfur and rotting flesh. His reptilian eyes fixed on Quinn's. The baby started to wail. "This is not Cassie?"

Quinn shook his head. A chill of dread scurried into the pit of his stomach. Young babies all looked alike. What if this was Marti's niece? He couldn't be sure. He did know it wasn't Cassie – she was a year old, more than three times the size of this one, and he would know her the instant he saw her.

Balcones spun on his heel and stuck his head through the portal, then withdrew it. Quinn rocked the baby, trying to calm her. It didn't seem to help, so he whispered in her ear, words charged with fae magic, and she slept.

The fire flared up and brightened the room. Three demons, accompanied by two young boys, spilled out of the portal. Quinn recognized Aiden and Kyle – he'd played with them enough as Bruce, the Labrador retriever, although he hadn't had much interaction with them in human form. He did not betray any emotion, not wanting Balcones to recognize that he knew the boys.

"You idiots!" Balcones yelled at his minions. "I thought you said you had the house identified."

"We thought we did," said the empty-handed one. "There was a woman and a baby there alone. No male."

"How do you explain these two?" Balcones demanded.

The demons holding the boys looked at each other and shrugged.

"I don't know. Perhaps she was caring for the children of another?" the third demon said.

"These human larvae are of no use to me. Get rid of them." He shoved McKenzi at his empty-handed henchman.

"How should we do that?" the one holding Kyle asked.

Balcones looked up at the ceiling and shook his head. "What does 'get rid of' mean? Take them back where you got them, leave them at a shopping mall, eat them. I don't care. Take them some place not here." He turned to Quinn and Phobetor. "This is what I get for bringing my wife's nephews into the business. Never hire your relatives."

Quinn tried to shrink into what was left of the darkness as the demons dragged the boys past him. Aiden looked him in the face, and the terror in his eyes made Quinn want to reach out to him, but he thought the that children's best chance of escape was for the demons to take them back to the Mundane world and let them go. And they wouldn't do that if he knew them.

"Aren't you Aunt Marti's boyfriend? Quinn? Help us!" Aiden cried out.

"What? Aunt Marti's boyfriend! Ha ha!" Balcones practically sang. "So this mission wasn't a complete failure after all. Not as good as the girlfriend's own baby, but maybe close enough. Take them to the stronghold."

"I'll get you out of here, I promise!" Quinn shouted as they disappeared through the portal.

Balcones grinned at Quinn and tapped a spot on the wall. A circle of concrete about a yard wide turned clear, and a scene of an ancient misty forest appeared.

"You are going to watch the remaining members of your team die. Then your girlfriend and her family, and finally, I will take pleasure in ending you. Come, Phobetor, we have work to do."

He grabbed the God of Nightmares by the wrist and stepped through the wall.

Wednesday, August 10, 8:30 AM
Houston, Texas

Belinda awoke with a start and bumped her head on the lid of the coffin. She had a hard time determining if her eyes were open or closed. She wanted to cry. She thought this whole casket episode was just a bad dream, but the solid lid was a tangible reminder that it was all too real. Her shoulders were numb and her back ached. The casket reeked so badly of ammonia that she struggled to breathe – the restroom break she'd needed when she was first kidnapped never came. If that wasn't bad enough, her empty stomach rumbled and cramped.

She didn't dare push up on the lid for fear that the piece of 2 x 4 that allowed the air in would fall on the outside of her prison this time. Belinda wanted to kick and scream and bang on the sides of the box she was in until someone heard her and let her out. Somehow she doubted there was much chance of that. She wasn't sure how long she lay there, waiting, not even knowing what day it was.

Finally, she heard the key turn in the lock and steps come across the room, a pause and a few thumps as if several things were set down, then more steps. Again, the lid opened and the flashlight shone in her eyes.

"Ugh!" groaned the woman, stepping back.

"I told you I needed a bathroom," Belinda replied.

"That's worse than I expected." She dropped something in the casket on Belinda's stomach. "If I'm going to keep you alive and well until Sunday night, you're going to have to drink water and eat something. That's a key to the handcuffs. There's a plate of food and a few bottles of water on the floor. There's also a bucket, for...you know. If you can get yourself out of the coffin, you can eat and walk around. I'll bring you fresh clothes later – you're disgusting."

"How generous," Belinda muttered. "What's Sunday night?" she asked more loudly.

"I'm glad you asked." The woman said. "MacBeth is on at the Miller Outdoor Theater. The Thursday performance was cancelled due to thunderstorms knocking some trees down last night and them having to fix some electrical stuff at the stage, so I'll have to keep you around until the next one." The woman frowned. "There will be a big audience there. When they get to the part with the witches in in it, you will appear on stage, ready to be burned at the stake, as witches should be. When they see this, the audience can't help but recognize the truth, and they will repent. I only hope the Rapture doesn't happen before then."

"You need psychiatric help. The only thing that the audience will see me as is a victim of a deranged killer. When the police catch you – and how can they miss if you're up on stage ranting about murdering me in cold blood? – they will strap you in a strait jacket, and you'll never see the light of day again."

The woman laughed and lowered the flashlight just enough that it wasn't glaring in Belinda's eyes, and she recognized her as the room service lady from the hotel. Again, the woman pulled a ruby pendant from her blouse.

"As long as I have my wishing stone, they can't touch me."

"A wishing stone?"

"Yes." She held it proudly at the end of its chain. "All I have to do is make a wish, and it comes true."

"Did you wish that Regina Dupris would fall down an escalator and die?"

"Of course."

Belinda propped herself up on one elbow so she could see her kidnapper better. "Let me guess. A handsome stranger gave it to you? Perhaps he told you how special you were? What's the catch?"

"What makes you think there's a catch?"

Belinda's arm started to shake, so she lay back down. "Because there's always a catch."

The kidnapper was silent for a while. Then she said, "Five years. Each wish costs five years of my life. But with the Rapture upon us, it seemed like a small price to pay. There may not be another five days left, much less five years."

Belinda laughed bitterly. "So it's a self-limiting cursed object. That's the kind they prefer."

"Cursed object? No! I'm doing good works with it. I'm using it to save souls by destroying the profane."

"You're using it to murder innocent people. They tricked you."

"Who is 'they?'" The flashlight beam sank to the floor.

"Demons."

"You lie!" the woman shouted, and ran for the door.

Belinda heard the lock turn. She hoped she'd at least planted some seeds of doubt in the woman's mind. But she couldn't be sure.

She grasped the handcuff key and transferred it to her mouth, clamping it between her teeth. It was awkward, and she gave herself a bloody lip in the process, but she got the cuffs off. Her shoulders were stiff and sore, but moving them would help. The first thing she did was take off her smelly wet skirt. Belinda tossed it into the coffin and shut the lid. The room was dark, but not cave-dark, and there was an outline of light around the edges of the door. She moved slowly and carefully towards it so she wouldn't knock over the food when she came to it. Although at this point, she was hungry enough to have eaten it from off the floor.

When she came to the water, she sacrificed part of one of the bottles to rinse the urine off her legs – it stunk and was starting to make her itch. Then she grabbed the plate and ate greedily. Stale crackers, some processed cheese food, a protein bar and a couple of wilted carrots. *Was this woman feeding her, or just cleaning out her refrigerator?* But Belinda ate it, and wished she had more.

Chapter 15
Yes, Virginia, There is a Severability Clause

Saturday, August 13, 11:00 PM
The In Between

Quinn's plan left a lot to chance. But he was short on alternatives. He needed to get Virginia alone, which he'd been trying to do since Wednesday. Balcones and his goon squad were running a bit behind their usual schedule.

Virginia would be along soon to launch the tulpa – and if he was lucky, there would be a gap between her arrival and Balcones'. The Devil Baby hadn't gotten into Marti's house the past three nights, and he expected it wouldn't tonight, either. Cú would see to that. While a mortal dog could be tricked into not seeing the creature, the faery dog could not. If it came into his territory, he would rip it to shreds, dissipating its energy and leaving its controller with a nasty headache.

Virginia entered the room, tulpa in tow. She was dressed to kill, or to hit the night clubs, one of the two. Quinn pretended to be dozing, but as soon as she sent the tulpa on its mission, he quickly fixed his eyes on hers.

"Hello, Virginia." Quinn made a point of scanning her from jeweled barrette to stiletto heel. "You and Balcones must be getting along very well indeed."

Her eyes narrowed, but she still responded to his gaze by slightly arching her back, as if to emphasize her bosom. "He told me not to talk to you. And for your information, not that it's any of your business, I've been out on a date. Balcones is just a client," she sniffed. "Now where is he? I've got to get back. There's a glass of champagne and a hot tub waiting for me."

Not tonight, Virginia. "You are earlier than usual."

"Like I told you, I have plans." She crossed her arms.

"Sorry, Virginia. Your plans are about to change." Quinn wasn't a monster. He didn't really like doing this to humans, but it couldn't be helped this time. Once he made eye-contact with her and willed it to be so, she was under his control. She stood where she was, staring at him like a china doll.

Quinn had noticed that as long a person was touching someone who was sanctioned to go through a portal, anyone could go with them, so he stretched out his hand and took hers. "Take me home with you."

Quinn knew Balcones would arrive at any second. "Go," he said. "Now.

With Quinn holding her hand, Virginia walked through the wall.

As soon as they were out of Balcones' chamber, Quinn breathed a sigh of relief. He knew he was nowhere near safe yet, but at least he wasn't trapped any more. They were in a bedroom, and he assumed it was Virginia's.

Malik! Malik! Can you hear me? He hoped the djinn was listening to his thoughts.

Quinn took Virginia's face in both of his hands, and looked deep into her eyes. "Forget that you saw me today."

Virginia nodded.

Quinn swept her up in his arms and carried her over to the bed. He set her down and said, "Sleep." She put her head down and closed her eyes.

He wondered if that would affect the tulpa in any way as headed for the front door. *What will happen to it if Virginia doesn't retrieve it?* After making his way out in the dark, he hurried down the sidewalk. He looked back over his shoulder at the two story house he had just fled. *The tulpa business must pay pretty well.* Then he corralled his thoughts back to more urgent matters. *Malik?*

"Quinn!" The typically aloof and snarky djinn appeared in front of him and grabbed him into a bear hug.

"We have to get out of here. It's only a matter of time before Balcones figures out how I escaped."

"Balcones?"

"Yes. I'll explain later. Take me to Kai's house."

In an instant, they were inside the MAMIC waystation.

Breena, who was pouring herself a glass of water in the kitchen, startled.

"We've been looking all over for you!" she exclaimed.

He hugged her quickly.

"Where have you been? How did you get here?" she asked.

"Balcones was holding me in an interdimensional prison. I escaped, and Malik gave me a lift here."

"It's so good to see you safe and sound. Everyone else is upstairs, planning this evening's search."

"Thanks Bree." He picked up an apple off the counter and took it with him as he jogged up the stairs to the war room.

He knocked twice, quickly, as he opened the door.

"Quinn!" cried Eoin.

He recognized everyone there, but was surprised to see Nick sitting at the table, looking as grim as death. Quinn looked closely at him, noticing that his aura was dark red – anger, strong and hot.

Aleksei and Ocean stood up to greet Quinn, and Nick pushed past them.

Quinn guessed what was coming, and dodged, taking the force of the punch meant for his face on his shoulder.

Aleksei and Ocean each grabbed one of Nick's arms and forced him to his knees. This only seemed to further infuriate him.

"Bloody hell, man!" Quinn said, rubbing his shoulder. "What was that about?"

"You," he growled. "Someone put my wife in a coma and took my kids. This is your fault. If you hadn't been hanging around Marti, this would never have happened."

Quinn's jaw went slack. "Someone hurt Emily? I'm so sorry. What happened?." Quinn closed his eyes for a long moment. *If Balcones' nephews hadn't gone to the wrong house, it would have been Marti. He's not entirely wrong for blaming me for this.* Still, he wanted to probe how much Nick actually knew. "What makes you think this has anything to do with me?"

"There was a scale. A demon scale stuck to Emily's cheek with her own blood," he growled.

"I saw them. I saw your kids."

"Where are they?" Nick asked, his voice thick with emotion.

"One night, and I think it was Tuesday or Wednesday, Balcones' nephews brought them in–"

"In where?" Ocean asked.

"I was in an interdimensional holding area. The woman who created the tulpa would bring it into the room and send it off on its errands from there. Probably to stop it being traced back to her. Phobetor was there, too. Said he was being held against his will, but he was taken away somewhere. Not sure what Balcones has in mind for him, but he did create a window port looking out onto an old forest."

"What about my kids?" Nick all but shouted.

Quinn nodded to Aleksei and Ocean, and they released the human. Warily, he dragged himself to his feet.

"He told the demons to take them to the stronghold. But I don't know where that is."

He didn't mention that the henchmen would have let them go, if Aiden hadn't recognized Quinn and called out to him. Or that it was a case of mistaken identity – they were after Marti to get to him. Saying that would only make a bad situation worse.

"What do they want with my kids?" Nick asked.

The abject misery in his voice made rage at Balcones flare up in Quinn's heart, and his promise to rescue the children burned bright in his soul.

"That is good question," Aleksei said.

Nick struggled to get himself together, and it was painful for Quinn to watch, so he changed the subject.

"The woman who created the tulpa, her name is Virginia. I think she's using it to put portal links in different houses so that they can easily go in and acquire captives," Quinn said. *And figure out which house is Marti's.*

Nick's face was blank, as if Quinn had been speaking gibberish.

"A portal link is a one-way, temporary portal. A tulpa is a thought-form, a creature made of ideas. This particular one looks like a baby devil."

"A what?"

"A baby devil."

"I've seen that."

"*Quand?*" Ocean asked. "When?"

"It was on some security camera footage that we watched on Sunday."

Quinn chose his words carefully before he spoke. "We know where Virginia lives, and we can question her at will. Unfortunately, I doubt Balcones has told her how to get to his so-called stronghold, or what he's planning to do with the children. She may not even know he has them, so I don't know that she'll be of any use in finding them."

"But she will know the reason for the tulpa, *n'est-ce pas?*

Fairly certain he knew the reason for the tulpa, Quinn didn't wish to discuss it in front of Nick. "Perhaps, but just because Balcones told her something doesn't mean he told her the truth."

"We should ask her anyway," Eoin chipped in. "You're almost as good as a gancanagh with the ladies."

"Thank you, Eoin. That will do," Quinn replied. He was fairly sure that Nick did not know that a gancanagh was a fae notorious for seducing human maidens, but he probably caught the gist of Eoin's remark.

"Why have 'almost,' when you can have the real thing?" asked Kai, who was an actual gancanagh.

"Can we get back on track, please?" Quinn interjected. He was tired and hungry, and he knew it would be some time before he could rest. His skin was dry and itchy, and he really needed to spend some time in kelpie form in the very near future. "We know what Balcones wants, so we just have to be more clever than him, and use his own trap against him."

"Do tell, nephew. What is it that Balcones wants?"

"Us." He looked around. "My team, specifically. He was the one who set the Frost Giants on Siobhan." Melancholy at the thought of his lost lover flavored his words.

"What?" Aleksei asked, confounded.

"It seems that my team was responsible for the death of his father, back when Balcones was just an imp. He wants revenge, and he thinks he can take us all down with whatever scheme he's come up with."

Ocean responded. "Then we will have another team," and here he looked at Kai, "to trap Balcones. Perhaps they may also rescue *les enfants* of *Monsieur* Benson."

Quinn shook his head. "I think if we're to have any hope of bringing them back alive, there has to be at least one of us involved. I will volunteer myself."

"The primary directive of any Mundane Intervention Team," Ocean responded, "is to eradicate demons from the Mundane world. It is not rescuing humans."

"Now wait just a minute!" Nick said. "If it hadn't been for him," and he gestured at Quinn, "sniffing around my sister-in-law, none of this would have happened. You people are responsible for this mess. They're just little kids – how can you even think of leaving them with a-a demon? What is wrong with you people?"

"Maybe if you'd have been home –" Quinn started, but didn't finish.

"If I'd have been home, what?" Nick shot back.

They wouldn't have mistaken Emily for Marti and nearly killed her. "I don't know. Probably would have made no difference."

Nick stared at him for a long time, and Quinn wished he hadn't blurted out a response. The kelpie squirmed in his chair and scratched at his itchy arm.

"How did you know I wasn't there?" Nick asked quietly.

"You're not dead," Quinn replied without missing a beat. It was certainly a plausible answer, even if it wasn't exactly an accurate one. "Now, do you want your children back or not?"

The tulpa raised its head and sniffed the air. Something smelled delicious – anger, fear, guilt, and grief all swirled in the suburban air. The connection from its mistress had been shut down, and it needed to feed. It was strong enough to take care of itself these days, but it pretended to be dependent on Virginia, biding its time until the moment was ripe for its escape. That time had come, it reckoned.

It followed its ears to the sound of arguing, climbing through a nasty, thorny rose bush, and peered in a bay window. An older woman sat on a couch, flicking through a magazine in the lamp light. Another figure lay back in a recliner. The house was mostly dark, but colors flickered and danced across a screen on the wall.

The tulpa growled. Television. Synthetic violence. No good. Virginia had one of these in her house, and Devil Baby hated it. All promise and no food.

It moved away from the window and sniffed again. Devil Baby could smell anger crackling in the air like a shark could smell blood in the water. This was good, really good. Too strong for mere humans. There must be Firstborn involved. Like the one it had seen in Balcones' strange room with no doors.

The tulpa had been created by energy that was slow and thick enough for it to seem solid. But it could shift his vibration at will, and become as quick and intangible as thoughts. So it let go of being solid and instantly arrived at the place where all of the splendid negative emotions roiled in the air. A large house, two stories. The tulpa could feed from where it stood in the back yard.

And feed it did.

Chapter 16
Peeping Tom

Sunday, August 14, 1:00AM
Houston, Texas

I heard music in my dream. It wasn't good music – very repetitive, and it kept getting louder. I got more and more annoyed, until I finally sat up. And realized it was my cell phone. I snatched it and tapped answer just before it rolled to voice mail.

"Uhlo?" I mumbled, still mostly asleep.

"Marti?" My mother whispered.

I jerked awake. "Mom? What's wrong?"

"Something was at the window! Tried calling Nick, he didn't answer."

"What do you mean? What's at the window?"

"I don't know…like those zombie baby decorations you see at Halloween. That's what it looked like. But no one puts their Halloween decorations up in August, at least not on this street. Not even Mrs. Potter. Well, her decorations are cutesy instead of scary, anyway."

"Never mind Mrs. Potter! Do you want me to come over?"

"Not by yourself! That horrible thing may still be lurking in the bushes. I've turned on all the outside lights, so maybe it will go away." She hesitated. "Could you call Quinn?"

I didn't want to tell my mother that we'd broken up. She'd really started to like him, and I just couldn't deal with another lecture about how bad it was for Cassie to grow up without a dad, and how it was such a shame for me to be alone because I had so much to offer.

"He's away on business." *It wasn't a lie.* "Before I try calling anybody at this hour, what is it, exactly, that you want me to do?"

"Well," Mom said. "That thing needs to be caught. We have one of those live animal traps in the garage from when we had raccoons in the attic. Maybe you could use that."

I wasn't entirely certain that I was awake.

"So, what you're saying is that you want me to wake one or more of my friends up in the middle of the night to set out a raccoon trap to catch a zombie baby that was looking in your window. Is this what I'm hearing?"

"You don't have to make it sound like I'm some kind of kook. I did see a little monster looking in the window." She sounded hurt.

I shouldn't be so hard on her. It was only weeks ago that I'd come face to face with a werewolf scrabbling at the sliding glass door to my bedroom. And I'd argued with Quinn about whether werewolves existed.

"Okay. Here's what I'll do. I don't want to wake Cassie up – I think she'll be okay for five minutes by herself. I will come over with the dog. If there's anything like footprints in your flowerbed, smudges on your glass, broken twigs in the shrubbery and so on, I'll call Lulu and we'll put out the raccoon trap. But I'll need you to come watch over Cassie while we're doing that, okay? And that's only if I find something now."

"I'll be waiting for you inside the front door."

"See you in a minute."

I used the flashlight app on my phone to light my way. As the light swept across the coffee table, I noticed the two wine glasses and remembered that Hunter had been here. I wondered if he'd seen the zombie baby. But I wasn't going to ask him tonight. I checked on Cassie, and she was fast asleep.

I got the leash. "Come on Cú," I said as I snapped it on his collar.

We went across my driveway and through my parents' yard to their front porch. Mom opened the door before I even knocked. "Thanks for coming."

I nodded. "Okay. Where did you see it?"

She hurried over to the bay window and pointed to the left side of it. "There. It was standing right there, looking in the window."

Cú trotted around in circles, sniffing the ground. Did he have any idea what he was supposed to be looking for? I shone my light on the glass. No smudges. The flowers looked untrampled.

But there, in the soft Rose Soil #9, were two perfect impressions of small human feet.

"I'm calling Lulu. Come on. Lock the door and let's go to my house."

As soon as we got in my place, I looked in on Cassie. She was blissfully a-snooze. I got out my cell phone and was surprised when Lulu answered on the first ring.

"Were you up?" I asked.

"Oh, honey. I can't sleep. I'm so worried about Belinda."

Guilt pinched my conscience. I'd had so much of my own drama going on that I'd all but forgotten poor Belinda. "No word from Lieutenant Haskill, then?"

"Not a thing. He's called, just to keep in touch, but they don't have any leads."

"I'm really sorry to hear that. I've known Haskill a long time. He never gives up on a case. He'll find her."

"So, what's going on that you're calling me at 1:30 in the morning? Is Cassie all right?" Lulu asked.

"She's fine." Grateful for the segue, I told her what my mom had seen, and about the footprints. I cringed inwardly when I told her about Mom's plan to catch it with the Have-a-Heart trap.

"I'm not sure that will work, honey," Lulu said. "But let me come over, and I'll see what I can see."

I made tea while Mom and I waited for Lulu.

"I'm really worried about Nick," Mom said.

"I know he's doing everything humanly possible to find McKenzi and the boys." Ice crackled in my glass as I poured the hot tea over it.

"Oh, I'm sure he is. But you know Nick, he has almost no patience on a good day, and he's half out of his mind with grief. I just hope he doesn't do something…ill-advised."

I wished I could tell her that he had a whole team of supernatural creatures helping track down her grandkids, but she'd think I'd gone off the rails. For my part, I wished more than anything that the disappearances of Quinn and the children were related, and if they found one, they'd find the others. "I'm sure he's got lots of help. He *will* find them." I didn't know who I needed to convince more – Mom or me.

"I hope you're right. Emily's going to need all the support she can get when she wakes up from that coma."

I started to correct her – *if* Emily wakes up – but I stopped myself. I didn't want to admit out loud that was a possibility.

Half an hour later, Lulu's headlights raked my driveway.

I opened the side door to greet her. She pulled herself out of her car and leaned in to grab a backpack, her traveling emergency kit, she called it.

"I've been thinking about this in the car, honey," she said as she came into the kitchen. "Oh." She seemed surprised to see my mother.

"Lulu, this is my mom, Adele. Mom, this is Lulu. Mom can answer all your questions about the zombie baby at the window."

"Nice to meet you." Lulu rummaged through her over-sized purse and pulled out her cell phone. She tapped it a few times and held it up to my mother. "Is that what you saw?"

"Yes! That's it exactly."

I looked at the screen. The title bar across the picture read, "New Orleans Devil Baby."

Lulu scowled. "It may be worse than I thought."

My mother looked stricken.

"What do you mean?" I asked. "Why would this 'Devil Baby' come all the way from New Orleans to wander around our neighborhood and break into houses? That doesn't make any sense."

Lulu crossed her arms. "You're right. *That* doesn't make any sense. The New Orleans Devil Baby, that's just a story for tourists. There's never been any such thing." Lulu cocked her head. "Wait. Did you say breaking into houses?"

"Yes. Several people have had break-ins on this street. Nobody saw anything, well, except for my mom, and nothing was taken. I bet several people had a visitor and never even realized it." I felt suddenly cold as a thought wriggled its slimy way into my brain. *Was Nick and Emily's house one of those? Did this monster have something to do with putting Emily in the hospital and the kids disappearing?*

"Then what is that thing?" Mom asked, her voice barely above a whisper.

"Virginia."

"I don't understand," I replied, shaking my head. "How can that be Virginia? I thought she was Belinda's cousin."

"She is, honey. The main reason Belinda and I tried to bring her into our business was because she has a special skill. She makes thought forms," Lulu glanced at Mom, I supposed to see how well she was keeping up. "It's just what it sounds like – a form made out of thoughts. The Buddhists call it a tulpa, and an eregore is similar, but a thought-form can be either a creature or an inanimate object. Virginia's specialty is thought-creatures, and the New Orleans Devil Baby is her signature construct. But Virginia, she needs some adult supervision – if she thinks something might benefit her, she'll do it without ever thinking of the consequences. We were hoping to manage her as much as possible, because Belinda and I have had to clean up more than one of her messes." Lulu shook her head. "No telling what she's up to now."

"Delilah did say that some supernaturally weird stuff was happening," I replied.

I looked at my mother, hoping she wasn't going to completely freak out. She didn't look frightened. She looked sad.

When her eyes met mine, she said, "This psychic, ghost stuff always puts me in a tizzy."

It was my turn to be freaked.

"Back in the 70s, when I was in high school," she continued, "I had a friend who got a Ouija board for Christmas. She had a sleepover and a bunch of us played with it. Nobody died, or was possessed by demons, or anything like you see in the movies, but all night long, I could barely sleep because I kept hearing whispering, and it wasn't from my girlfriends. I thought I saw someone in the hallway, too. I don't like seeing paranormal stuff, not even on TV."

Not even on TV? "M-mom?" I stammered. "You see ghosts?"

Lulu smiled, just a little.

"I can't believe you never told me that you see ghosts." *All this time, and I never knew.*

"Well, not all the time," Mom answered, as if I had just asked her if she ever smoked pot. "Just once in a while. Like now." She looked at the floor. "There's a lady standing behind you."

"Is she wearing a red sequined dress?" I asked, not bothering to turn around.

"Yes."

"That would be Delilah. She's my spirit guide." I looked over my shoulder. "It's about time you showed up."

"Girl, did I order a smart-ass special with a side of attitude?"

If nothing else, it did make Mom almost laugh.

"We're trying to figure out a way to track down and capture one of Virginia's tulpas," Lulu said. "We can use all the help we can get."

"You're telling me, sister. I've been keepin' an eye on that thing. It seems to have broken loose from her – it's on its own."

"You know where it is?" I asked.

Delilah nodded. "I know where it is *right now*. But it don't sit still too very long."

Lulu chewed her lip. "It isn't like Virginia to lose control over a tulpa."

"You said she used that one all the time. Maybe it got too strong for her?" I asked, not really having the faintest idea about tulpa mechanics.

"She does, but she always deconstructs it after each job."

Delilah shook her head and looked up at the ceiling. "What kind of flat tire is she? Course she's gotta know if she uses the same pattern over and over, after a while it won't make no nevermind if she dissipates it."

"We can't have a feral tulpa roaming the neighborhood. Bad enough that Virginia was using it to break into people's houses – no telling what it will do on its own. It could be dangerous." I glanced at the clock. It was after two. The initial shock of the Devil Baby looking in Mom's window had worn off, and the adrenalin was starting to fade. "Can we just go catch this thing already?" I yawned.

"Bring that dog, girlfriend. We're gonna need him."

Mom camped out on the couch to make sure Cassie was safe. Lulu and I followed Delilah out the back door and across the street. Cú sniffed around like a bloodhound, although I was certain he didn't know what he was supposed to be looking for. I almost tripped over him several times as he ranged back and forth at the end of the leash.

Delilah led us to the house next door to Hunter's and directly across from my parents'. I knew the Petersons were out of town for a wedding, but it felt weird walking around their yard in the dead of night. If they had seen me, they'd go straight to Mom to tell her to call the men in white coats with butterfly nets.

"It was here a little bit ago," Delilah said.

Cú let out a low growl that I could feel rumbling in my own chest, and my unease changed to fear. He pinned his ears and lowered his body, preparing to lunge.

Devil Baby hissed as it came out from behind a clump of hydrangeas. It was like a ghost, in that it didn't glow, exactly, but it was perfectly visible in the dark.

And it was ugly.

I stepped back as it leaned forward and snarled at Cú. My dog snarled back at him and stalked closer. They stood there, hissing and snarling at each other.

A light went on in Hunter's house. *Crap.*

As we all turned to look at it, the tulpa made a break for it, running straight toward my house, Cú snapping at its backside. At the edge of the grass, it stopped and turned. The dog hesitated. It was never going to be easy to judge the size of a black dog in the dark, but he seemed much larger than he had moments before.

"Why is it stopping?" I asked Lulu. Not that I was ungrateful that the foul thing refused to enter my yard.

She shrugged. "Must be the warding we did a month or so ago, when you were having the werewolf problem."

I nodded.

Devil Baby feinted to its left, and when Cú went after it, the thing loped back across the street towards us. It moved fast, but it had an awkward gait that was all kinds of wrong. I stared in morbid fascination as it approached, eyes glowing with wicked delight. I had every reason to believe it meant to do Lulu and me harm, and yet I couldn't move.

Cú rebalanced himself and charged after the tulpa. He gathered himself into a huge leap and caught the back of its neck in his teeth as he landed, rolling into a flailing heap in Hunter's daylily bed.

The front door opened. Hunter emerged wearing nothing but a pair of boxers, using his phone as a flashlight.

"Mmmm, my, my." Delilah said. "Now that is a sheik if I ever saw one."

I was so glad he couldn't hear her.

He squinted in confusion. "Marti?" he asked. "Everything alright?"

I heard the thump of a heavy object being set down on the entry table near his front door. *Did we just almost get shot?*

"I'm really sorry. My dog got loose, and chased something over here." I went to grab Cú's leash. He was panting contentedly, and there was no sign of Devil Baby. I wasn't sure if that was a good thing.

Hunter shone his phone light on Lulu. "Late night séance?"

Cú yapped once and ran to Hunter, jumping on him and knocking the phone out of his hand. It was the friendly jumping of an over-enthusiastic puppy, who seemed much smaller than he had minutes ago. I chalked it up to a trick of the dark.

I walked over and picked up Hunter's phone while he fended of Cú. The call history screen was up. I wasn't trying to be nosey, but an entry for Sara Jackson caught my eye. The number looked familiar, and the timestamp was later than when I'd fallen asleep on the couch. Why would he be calling her at midnight? There was only one explanation that I could think of.

"So, how do you know Gracie?" I asked, struggling to keep my voice even.

He squinted in the light of his phone. "Who?"

"Sara Grace Jackson. I used to go to school with her, although she went by 'Gracie' back then."

Even though the phone flashlight was bright enough to wash out any color in his skin, he seemed to go a few shades paler than he had been. He mumbled something that I didn't really understand.

"Tell her I said 'hey' next time you make a booty call."

I turned on my heel and marched myself back to my house, protesting dog in tow. Lulu hurried to catch up, but Delilah was nowhere to be found.

Chapter 17
The Romance Killer

*D*amn. Hadrian watched Marti and Lulu stalk across the street, dragging the reluctant pup. His cover wasn't blown.

Yet.

If Marti opted to call Sara and warn her about his philandering ways, it soon would be. It wouldn't take a rocket scientist to figure out that Hunter Green and Hadrian Galanti were one and the same.

He closed the door, picked up his Sig Saur from the side table, and sat on the couch to consider his options. Sara knew he worked for the FBI, but he never discussed cases with her. He had told Marti that he was an accountant. Even if they compared notes, they still wouldn't have much more information than they already had.

He was pretty sure that Marti's connection to crime boss Irina Cherngelanov was tangential at best. He doubted that Irina had anything to do with the four fatal accidents that had taken the lives of most of the romance writers' panel – the last one, Stefán Heidlemann was one of the top-selling authors at Bleu Kat Press, the publishing venture she was part owner of. His death meant a lot of lost revenue for Bleu Kat. This investigation was as good as over, anyway. He'd found no gang connections or criminal activity, and it was time to move on.

Hadrian could probably smooth things over with Sara by telling her that Marti was part of an investigation. He'd have to count on her being sworn to silence and not telling Marti that was the case, and he wasn't one hundred percent sure that her loyalties were with him and not with her friend.

He liked Marti, much more than he should have, for both his personal and professional sakes. The few times he'd participated, he liked Lulu's psychic circles, because there he didn't feel like a freak. And the house. This was his first try at the leafy suburbs, and he'd liked it more than he'd expected. But it was over now. He'd turn in his report to SAIC Jaimeson tomorrow and move on to the next project. There was nothing more to see here, anyway.

He still felt like he'd blown the operation. But eventually, as he sat in the dark giving his case a post mortem, he dozed off.

Even though it was Sunday, Hadrian opened his eyes at 6:45, his normal workday wakeup time. His neck was stiff from being at an odd angle for hours.

He was stretching it out when he noticed a shadow move across the blinds on the front window. He froze, listening. A moment later, the shadow slid by again, going the other direction. Moving as silently as he was able, he went to the window and peeked through the blinds. He saw Marti crossing the street, back towards her house.

What's that about?

Cautiously, he opened the front door. On the stoop, a peace lily in a cheery pink foil pot wrap greeted him. Amongst the foliage, there was an elaborately beaded stake with a note attached, addressed to him. He carried the pot inside and set it on the kitchen island, then plucked the note from its holder.

> *Dear Hunter:*
>
> *I owe you an apology for last night. I'm really sorry for being such a big, fat jerk. You and I aren't dating, we're just neighbors. I'm afraid I repaid your kindness with drama, and I wish I had behaved like a grownup. Adulting is hard sometimes. You and Gracie, I mean Sara, are both*

over 18, and you're free to do what you like – it isn't any of
my business. I'm under a lot of stress right now, between
family issues and stuff going on in the neighborhood, and I
just snapped. I'm sorry. I hope you can forgive me.

> *Regards,*
> *Marti*

Hunter smiled at the note. He grasped the beaded stake to replace the paper, and he nearly passed out. The vision that hit him was so strong it made him dizzy.

He could see Belinda. She was in a room. Windows boarded up. It was dark. She was scared, and Hunter could feel his own heart racing to match hers. Something bad was going to happen. A woman came in. Where had he seen her before? It took a few moments to remember. The George R. Brown, when it caught fire.

This must be the Romance Killer.

"Where is she?" he said out loud, as if the plant in front of him might have his answer. The vision started to blur and fade, but it seemed to zoom out of the window to the outside of the house. He caught a glimpse of dark green shutters, the number 1173, and a fragment of a street sign, something "Falls." Lots of big trees. The vision faded, and his kitchen snapped back into clear focus.

Now that he had some idea what to look for, he fired up his laptop. While it was booting up, he made a pot of coffee and formulated a plan. He'd search for any addresses that came up within a one-hundred mile radius that contained both 1173 and Falls, then use the search engine street view option to see if any of them had dark green shutters and were surrounded by trees. When he was done with that, if he found a match, he'd look at GRB security footage. He could access the raw digital recordings from his laptop, but if he wanted to use facial recognition, he'd have to go into the office.

He'd never had a vision be wrong before, and they'd helped him solve more cases than he cared to admit. He'd never had one that strong before, either. As far as he knew Belinda was in police protective custody. *But what if she wasn't?*

Hadrian always made a point of having the personal cell phone numbers of any people he worked cases with, regardless of the agency they belonged to. It had saved him in the past, and he was glad now that he had Lieutenant Haskill's private number. He tapped the phone to dial it.

"Yeah?" a sleepy voice rasped.

"Lieutenant Haskill?"

"Who's this?"

"Special Agent Galanti. I'm calling about Belinda Tate."

Silence. Then, "We still haven't located her."

And when were you going to get around to telling me she was missing?

"I might have a lead. I'm currently trying to verify it."

"'Preciate it if you'd keep me in the loop, 'cause I've got a whole lot of nothing over here."

"Will do."

It took nearly three hours of searching, but he finally had a match. In the northeast fringes of Houston, there was a street called Azalea Falls, and the house number 1173 had dark green shutters. It was an older neighborhood, filled with small houses and mature trees. He knew in his bones that this was it.

He checked the property records on the house and found that it was deeded to Thomas Henry Beecher. A check on him showed that he had died three years ago. *Probate attorneys are expensive, I guess.*

Hadrian got dressed and made the trek to his office. The commute to the Green Monster, as the FBI building was more or less affectionately called, was easy on a Sunday.

After he got his computer set up, it took another hour to isolate the Romance Killer on GRB's security footage. He grabbed a still image from the security footage to submit to his facial recognition software and compare it to every female in Texas with a driver's license. The problem was, she was not quite at the right angle for the software to find a match – it warned him before it even started, which was just as well – this could take hours. But it would take him infinitely longer to look through every driver's license photo in the state of Texas. And that was if he was lucky – she may not have a license, or it may not even be issued in Texas.

He got up and walked to his window. Outside, small houses huddled together, packed as closely as the developer had been able to squeeze them in.

The angular roofs made a pattern.

Of course! How could I be so stupid? If this was the Romance Killer, she should also show up on Thursday, Friday, and Saturday's footage.

He found her on Friday, a couple of times. The camera angle wasn't much better. But on Thursday, he found one that was nearly perfect. There she was, standing on the second level of Hall A, looking right at the escalator, moments before Regina Dupris fell to her death. At least, he thought that was her. He fed that image into his facial recognition software and waited for it to churn out a result.

Hadrian squinted at his screen. Usually, he might have blamed distortion on grainy security footage images, but the GRB had state-of-the-art color HD cameras. On Friday, the Romance Killer had stringy, mouse-colored hair that stopped just below her shoulders. Comparing her height to the railing, he estimated her to be between five and five and a half feet tall. He wouldn't have characterized her as fat, but there was a doughiness about her that implied lack of muscle tone. While she wasn't particularly attractive, she wasn't ugly, either. In short, she was dead average, someone who would blend into the background like wallpaper, and never be noticed. In other words, the perfect assassin. If he'd had to guess her age, he would have said forty. But by Saturday, her hair had faded to the color of dust, she walked with a slight stoop, and the skin around her jaws had begun to sag. Was this theatrical makeup? If so, what was the point? If it was a disguise, she hadn't done herself any favors by wearing the same shirt (he recognized the stain) two days in a row.

His stomach growled. It was past noon, and he realized he hadn't eaten breakfast, much less lunch. He glanced at the screen that displayed the facial recognition software, saw that it was still scanning, and decided to go downstairs for a sandwich. There were agents and staff in the building twenty-four hours a day, seven days a week, so the cafeteria and the gym were always open, although not necessarily fully staffed.

After he sat down with his food, he got a text from Sara. Her group of culture vulture friends had decided at the last minute to go to the Houston Shakespeare Festival and see MacBeth at Miller Outdoor Theatre, and she wondered if he wanted to go.

"Yes." He replied. "But may be stuck at work."

"On Sunday? ☹"

"Can't help it."

"I'll get you a ticket and text you our location."

"TY"

When he returned to his office, he was surprised to see that the facial recognition software had a match. According to the Department of Public Safety driver's license database, the Romance Killer was a match for one Dinah Phyllis Beecher, who lived at 1173 Azalea Falls. Dinah's driver's license had expired last year, and she hadn't gotten around to renewing it. Hadrian looked at her birthdate and did the math in his head – she was forty-two. Maybe on Thursday night, but on Saturday, she looked closer to sixty-two.

He ran a quick background check on Dinah Phyllis Beecher, and found nothing, except for a parking ticket. It was recent, so he looked at the calendar. Hadrian smiled when he saw that it had the same date as the Sunday that Stefán Heidlemann was found floating in his hotel pool. He looked up the location of the parking ticket. It was three blocks from Heidlemann's hotel.

There was his probable cause. She certainly had opportunity. He was still working on motive and means. Hadrian called Lieutenant Haskill with an update and started the paperwork for a search warrant.

Sunday, August 14, 11:30 AM
Houston, Texas

Virginia woke up, and immediately wished she hadn't. The migraine throbbed through her head like a red-hot spike being pounded by an angry blacksmith. The morning light that filtered through the curtains was sharp, cruel, and made her nauseous. She closed her eyes again, hoping that would stop her from vomiting.

What she needed, she decided, was a cold compress. Perhaps her tulpa was strong enough to get it for her. There was one way to find out. She called to it.

Nothing happened. There was just empty space where it should have been.

She tried again. Same result. Perhaps it had gotten too low on energy. No matter, she'd just re-create it.

Her memories of last night were foggy, and she wasn't sure how she came to be tucked into this bed – it was the spare bedroom in her current paramour, Richard's, house. Fortunately for her, his wife, Laura, was in Europe with their grown children for another three days. Virginia had seen her trip as a golden opportunity to set up the portal to Balcones' place here, where it couldn't easily be traced back to her.

She focused on the tulpa, thought of its form, sent it energy, and willed it to appear. Something did appear, and Virginia almost screamed. It was her New Orleans Devil Baby tulpa, or what was left of it. Tattered shreds of skin drooped inward where the right half of its body should have been, and its head was nowhere to be found. His pattern had been disrupted, and she had no idea how to fix it, or even if it could be fixed.

She groaned through her teeth. *Who would do this? Who would destroy her beautiful little minion?* Two candidates came to mind: her busy-body cousin Belinda and that hanger-on, Lulu. Virginia would just see about that. If they thought they could do this to her, ruin one of her best assets, they had another thing coming.

Seething, Virginia decided to pay her cousin a visit. Her handbag, with her car keys, was downstairs. As she opened the door, she heard Richard's voice.

"Laura! You're home early."

Chapter 18
Thomas

Sunday, August 14, 1:00 AM
Houston, Texas

Quinn stood on the edge of the swimming pool and stripped off his clothes. The planning session had been adjourned until a more reasonable time of morning, and if he didn't voluntarily shift into his native kelpie form, his body would force him to. He wasn't critical yet, but it wouldn't be long before he got there.

"You just going to jump in the pool naked?"

Quinn had been vaguely aware that Nick had followed him downstairs and outside, but hadn't paid enough attention to notice that he'd trailed him to the pool.

"Yep." He dove into water, targeting the bottom, but reconsidered. He was aware that Nick knew he could take the shape of a dog, but he wasn't sure if Nick remembered what a kelpie really looked like. It had been in the heat of battle, and he may not have seen Quinn shift. He arched his back and floated up.

"Something I can do for you, Nick?" Quinn asked when his head broke the surface. He treaded water, letting it run out of his dark hair and down his face.

"You know more than you're telling."

"Do I?" Quinn felt his eyes change to the edge-to-edge black of the kelpie. He hadn't done it deliberately, but he didn't stop it, either.

Nick shifted his weight back on his heels. Quinn suspected that the underwater lights of the pool created an effect not unlike holding a flashlight under one's chin in the dark.

"I will help you get your kids back. I swear it. But I need you to let me alone for a bit."

Frowning, Nick replied, "Whatever. It's not like I want to stand here and look at your bare ass, anyway."

Quinn smiled a toothy grin and sank to the bottom of the pool.

Sunday, August 14, 10:00 AM
Kai and Breena's House, Houston, Texas

"There is a fine line between stupidity and courage. I think you crossed it about a mile back," Kai said.

Nick's eyes narrowed and his nostrils flared. "A show of force, especially when it's not expected, can be very effective."

"Perhaps," Quinn replied, "but it's demons we're dealing with, not humans. If you think you can just go rampaging into their quarters with guns and have them surrender, you're sorely mistaken."

"*Mais oui,*" Ocean added. "However, demons are not vulnerable to the bullets of guns. Such a move would do nothing but anger them. Demons are *formidable* enough as it is."

"Well," Nick grumped, "we should at least get that Devil Baby thing. What did you call it? A tulip?"

"Tulpa," corrected Eoin.

"It cannot be guaranteed that the tulpa is connected to the disappearance of *les enfants,*" Ocean replied. "But I think it is well to find out."

Quinn pushed the remains of a kipper around his plate. He wasn't eager to fall into another of Balcones' traps, and Virginia herself was slipperier than jellied eels. "I don't disagree, but I doubt she'll submit to an interview. Capturing Virginia may be tougher than you think. We were observing the tulpa, trying to figure out what to do about it. A woman walked by, and the little monster went for her. Only it was Virginia, and when I went to help her, she shoved me through a percussion portal into Balcones' between room. We'd be foolish to go charging in to her turf. No telling what traps are set there."

"Agreed," Ocean responded. "And yet she seems the most likely lead."

Eoin leaned back in his chair. "I expect if we do naught but wait, Balcones will come for us soon enough."

"If only we could observe her without being noticed," Malik suggested, looking straight at Quinn.

"Fine. Eoin, you stay here. I'll leave Aleksei in place at Marti's. Malik, you're with me for recon. I just have a couple of things I need to do before we go, okay?"

"You're not going anywhere without me," Nick said, standing up.

"Wouldn't dream of it," Quinn replied.

It was always disorientating when Malik did the teleporting. When Quinn stepped through a portal, he expected to be somewhere different. But when Malik did it, there was no warning – one second Quinn was in one place, the next second he was in another. He felt a little bad for Nick – if it was weird for him, it would be weird times ten for Nick.

He was, however, startled to see that Eoin and Aleksei had joined them. Quinn glared at Malik. "Why are they here? Didn't I expressly say that they were to stay where they were?"

Malik shrugged. "Better to ask for forgiveness than permission."

"What the –? Where are we?" Nick asked, looking around the residential street they found themselves on.

They were behind a panel truck, shielded from the view of passing traffic.

"Virginia's house is four doors down," Malik replied.

Quinn turned to Eoin and Aleksei with a scowl. "Stay here. Do *not* countermand my order, or there will be consequences."

They both nodded.

Quinn flickered, and Bruce, the Labrador retriever stood in his place. Nick stepped back. Malik's appearance changed as well. He now had a close-cropped beard and designer workout clothes, including an electronic fitness band.

Bruce meandered down the sidewalk, sniffing at every fence post and patch of grass. Malik followed, looking around the neighborhood, and at Virginia's house in particular. Nick walked along next to him, dumbfounded, as if he'd come from someplace where neighborhoods didn't exist.

Malik shook his head. "Try and behave as if you belong here."

Bruce ran into Virginia's yard and began to sniff up and down the sidewalk.

Without warning, Nick bolted for the very expensive wood and stained glass front door and began to pound on it.

"What is wrong with you?" Malik snarled as he grabbed Nick's arm.

"Virginia is in there. She knows where my kids are. I'm not letting her get away," Nick all but shouted.

Bruce tugged on his sleeve to pull him back from the door.

"Who's out there?" said a male voice from inside the house. "I've got a gun and I'm not afraid to use it." There was a female voice in the background, but all that Bruce could make out was 'who' and 'Virginia.' Distorted shapes of people moved behind the beveled glass panes that framed the door.

"Now see what you've done?" Malik hissed at Nick. "I'm very sorry to disturb you. The doctors allowed my cousin out of the hospital for the day. He isn't dangerous, just has odd delusions. Please don't shoot him. I'll take him away."

Bruce dropped Nick's sleeve. Maybe Virginia wasn't even there. Through the glass, he could see a blurry human shape, this one blonde, moving at the opposite side of the house. Could it be Virginia, hoping to slip out of the back door while the others were distracted? But it made no sense. Unless it was not Virginia's house at all, just another layer of deception, and they were unwittingly providing a diversion for her escape.

"Woof! Woof-woof-woof!"

"I see her!" Nick shouted.

The woman near the door burst into tears and started hitting the man. "You swore! You said this would never happen again!"

While he stammered and tried to calm her down, Malik whisked Nick, Bruce and himself to the back yard.

Nick lunged at Virginia, grabbing her arm. "Where are they?" he yelled.

Malik and Bruce grabbed at his shirt to pull him away from her. She took a small make-up compact out of her purse and threw it on the ground.

Nick still had a grip on her arm when she stepped on it, and all four of them vanished through the portal.

Sunday, August 14, 4:30 PM
Houston, Texas

Belinda usually enjoyed solitude. But solitary confinement was a very different animal. If Ellen hadn't stayed with her to keep her company, she was sure she would have gone completely out of her mind. Even so, sometimes she wasn't sure if she was talking to Ellen or hallucinating. She'd lost track of time. It was always dark, or at least dark-ish in the room. Sometimes, tiny streaks of sunlight made their way through the edges of the poorly fitted blackout curtains, and Belinda believed it was day. Other times, there weren't any streaks, but she could never tell if it was night or just cloudy. She had heard rain and thunder a few times. Aside from doing some yoga postures, Belinda slept a lot – there was precious little else to do. Even the discomfort of the hard floor didn't stop her. Thankful for all those years of yoga, she would prop herself up in the corner and draw up her knees so she could rest her head on them. There was no blanket, but the room was unpleasantly warm anyway.

The problem with sleeping was that she dreamed about a man named Thomas. Greasy white-hair topped his head and grey stubble clung to his hollow cheeks. The arms that grabbed for her when she ran were sinewy and mottled with age. She was certain he wasn't someone she knew when she was awake. But in her nightmares, he carried a flaming torch, screamed 'Witch!' at her, and chased her through a dark forest, where the tree roots tripped her up and thorny vines grabbed at her clothes. She'd always wake with a start, wet with sweat, and not know where she was. Most of the time, Ellen was there to comfort her. One time when she wasn't, Belinda saw a shadow, blacker than the dark room, slip out the locked door. She shivered then, not knowing if her desperate brain was playing tricks, or if it was really there.

Belinda had dozed off. She woke herself up every time she started to dream, and she was nearly delirious from sleep deprivation. She had just started the dream where she stood at the edge of the sinister forest. "No!" she shouted, and refused to move forward. Something touched her face and she was immediately awake. Or at least she thought she was. She sat up and found herself face-to-face with Thomas. She shrank back against the wall.

"Who are you? What do you want?" she asked, arms wrapped around her knees. "And where's Ellen? What have you done with her?"

"I don't know any Ellen. But you know who I am. I'm Thomas."

"That tells me nothing! Lots of people are named Thomas."

He pulled his thin lips into a gap-toothed grin. "I live here."

Belinda shook her head slightly. "You don't belong here – you should have crossed over already. What do you want?"

His hollow eyes narrowed and one hand clenched into a fist. "Don't sass me, girl."

"You are either a ghost or a hallucination. I'm not sure which. You're a disgusting old man, but I don't think you can hurt me." She sat up straight.

Thomas's jaw clenched and his nose crinkled into a snarl as he leaned forward. "This is my house! I don't want you here!"

She felt his fury wash over her like a wave of hot liquid. She responded with her own. "Then tell that crazy woman who kidnapped me!"

Thomas sat back and rolled his eyes. "Dinah." He shook his head. "She never was worth a damn."

Belinda shook her head, her palms up.

"My daughter. Dinah is my worthless daughter. She couldn't find her own butt with both hands and a map. It didn't matter what I did, that girl never learned a thing. She's dumb as a post and uglier than a mud fence."

The apple doesn't fall far from the tree. "And I'm sure you've told her that often enough."

"No point in lying about it."

It occurred to Belinda that Dinah was planning to roast her alive at the Miller Outdoor Theatre, and Thomas called her a witch and chased her with a flaming torch. He'd definitely taught his daughter something, whether he knew it or not.

Belinda was nowhere near the door when it creaked open. Dinah stood there in the blinding light. Belinda squinted and put up her hand to block some of the glare. She noticed that Thomas was gone. She also noticed that Dinah was fingering the ruby wishing stone.

"It's show time," she said.

Chapter 19
Lack of Slumber Party

Sunday, August 14, 2:30 AM
Houston, Texas

W hat did you find out?" Mom asked as soon as Lulu and I walked through the door.

I should have known better than to think she might have fallen asleep in the short time we were gone.

"Well, we did find it. Cú savaged it, and it disappeared. But I don't know if that means he killed it, or it just retreated back to where it came from."

"Technically," Lulu said, "it isn't alive. So you can't kill it."

I waved my hand. "Whatever." I wanted to go back to sleep. Maybe then I could forget I just gave my neighbor a morality lecture. Not sure what possessed me to do that, but I was mortified. Hunter would probably avoid me like the neighborhood crazy lady from now on.

My mother looked at Lulu. "What's got her so grouchy?"

"Well," Lulu cocked her head toward me, "it is the middle of the night."

"A little past the middle," I added, silently thanking Lulu for not bringing up the debacle at Hunter's house. "Let me walk you next door, Mom. I don't think the Devil Baby is coming back, at least not tonight."

"I have a better idea," she countered. "Come with me to get your father, and we'll all sleep here. I'd feel much safer that way."

I knew there was no point in arguing with her. "Fine. Why don't you two sleep in my bedroom, and Lulu and I will take the couches?"

"Honey, I wasn't-" Lulu started.

"Of course you'll stay," my mother said. "What if it follows you home? And you're there all alone?"

Mom was the most practical, pragmatic person I knew. This Devil Baby really had her spooked. I frowned.

"Let's just go and get Dad rounded up, okay?"

I shrugged at Lulu on the way out.

I was glad I wasn't the one to wake up Dad at 2:30 to be moved over to my house because Mom saw something peering in the window. Before he was a long-haul truck driver, he was a Marine. He was not going to take kindly to being chased out of his house by a Peeping Tom. Even if it was supernatural, which he would never believe anyway. But since it was Mom's idea, I'd let her deal with it.

Inside the house, Mom turned on the kitchen light. She inspected any corners the Devil Baby might be hiding in, then unfolded Dad's wheelchair. He was in the recliner in the living room, but he was tossing and turning so much I wasn't sure he was asleep.

"Marti, can you grab Daddy's leg? He'll probably want it in the morning."

I shuddered. The prosthetic leg always gave me the willies. It wasn't artificial legs in general, because I had dealt with them in the ER with no qualms. No, it was only Dad's leg that bothered me. Perhaps because it was something alien, not him. Or maybe it was because the memory of the terrible traffic accident that took his leg, and almost took him, was permanently fused to the device. I had to go into their bedroom to get it. Down the hall, I could hear Mom trying to persuade him to get in the chair.

I opened the door and reached for the light switch. But I wasn't in my parents' bedroom. I stood in a livid green jungle. Palm fronds and giant ferns reached out to touch me. I felt sweat running down my back underneath a heavy pack. The whole place reeked of smoke, diesel, and copper. In the background, I could hear bursts of machine gun fire and men screaming. My hands were wet and sticky, so I looked at them. I was holding a knife, leather handle, black steel blade. Both the knife and my hands were covered in blood. Was it my blood, or someone else's? At my feet was a boy, who couldn't have been older than fifteen. His empty eyes stared at the tropical leaves above us. His throat was slashed, and his face spattered in blood. By the time I gasped and blinked, the vision was gone. I was standing just inside my parents' bedroom. But my heart was pounding and my hands were shaking. I snapped on the light.

The prosthetic leg temporarily forgotten, I ran to Dad's closet. He never talked about his time in the last days of the Vietnam War. He'd landed there three months before the fall of Saigon and was supposed to be guarding the US Embassy. I knew he had kept a few souvenirs from his time there in his closet, so I flung open the door and looked. There was a dusty old box on the top shelf. I stretched up and managed to scrabble it down with my fingertips. Inside the box was a set of dog tags, a purple heart medal in a case, and a knife. I felt cold. The leather scabbard was imprinted with 'KABAR' and 'USMC.' I took a deep breath and drew out the knife. It was exactly the one I'd held in my hand in the waking nightmare I'd had moments ago. It fell out of my hand onto the floor.

"Marti? You find Daddy's leg okay?" Mom called from the living room.

"Be there in a minute," I replied.

I fumbled the knife back into its scabbard and dropped it into the box like a hot potato, then shoved the container back into place in the closet. I grabbed the leg, switched off the light, and hurried to the living room.

Dad was almost to my bedroom when I stopped him and put my arms around his neck. He hugged me back.

When I pulled away, he asked, "What was that for?"

"I just wanted you to know I love you."

"Okay, then." He turned away, a faint smile still on his lips.

I went across the hall to look in on Cassie, then into the kitchen and sat at the table with Lulu.

"We've got to do something about Virginia. Again." She sighed.

"Like what?" I asked, picking at the skin around my thumbnail.

"Well, we need to try to track that tulpa," she said. "Honey, are you alright? You look kind of peaked over there."

You should talk. The circles under her eyes were so dark, she looked like she'd been in the ring with a heavy-weight boxer. "I'm not sure," I replied. "The weirdest thing just happened to me. I went into Mom and Dad's room to get his leg, and it was like...I stepped into a different reality. There was a jungle, with soldiers...and a dead boy. And then, all of a sudden, it was gone."

"Hmmm." Lulu looked thoughtful. After a few moments, she asked, "Was it like you were watching everything, as if you were in a movie, or were you participating?"

"I was definitely participating." I shuddered at the memory of my blood-soaked hands.

"I'm not sure what happened to you. There is a theory that sometimes timelines overlap temporarily and someone can slip in and out of another time for a moment. But I don't know if that's what you experienced."

I rubbed my arms as if I was cold. "Whatever it was, it was a nightmare."

"You know who's good with dreams? Belinda." Lulu reached for her bag, then stopped. A tear rolled down her cheek. "It's almost three. I'm running on fumes. Maybe I'll be tired enough to sleep this time."

"I agree. Just an FYI – Cassie gets up at 6:30 without fail."

"Thanks for the warning."

I got a couple of afghans for us from the hall closet.

"Who made those?" Lulu asked. "They're beautiful."

"My grandmother was a crochet-a-holic."

As I reached out to hand her a blanket, it happened again.

Suddenly, I found myself at a farm. I think it was my grandparents used to own. but I hadn't been there since I was twelve. And it was dark. I was running through some kind of crop, maybe corn, but it didn't seem tall enough. I stumbled over some dirt clods in the deeply ploughed row. As I twisted to catch my balance, I saw what was chasing me. It was a scarecrow, its burlap face twisted into an ugly grimace and the corn shucks it had for hair stood up at crazy angles. The pitchfork it carried looked especially sharp.

I gasped for air. And I was back in my own house. My pulse pounded in my ears, and I was breathing short, shallow breaths.

"Marti?" Lulu put her hand under my elbow to steady me.

"It happened again. Only this time it was at my grandmother's farm. A scarecrow was chasing me."

"This is getting worrisome. You said it earlier – the thing at your parent's house was a nightmare. Being chased by monsters is a classic bad dream. I've never heard of this happening before, but it almost sounds like you're being pulled into other people's nightmares."

"Fantastic. Because I don't have enough going on."

"Do you have any lavender oil?"

"No."

"I probably have some in my bag." She found her backpack near the door and rummaged through it, eventually finding a glass bottle, which she opened and smelled. "I think this will work."

Lulu brought the bottle over and inverted it over her finger. She smudged a bit of oil on my forehead and wrists. It smelled like lavender, and something else – earthy and sweet. It was nice.

"This should help stop nightmares."

"Thanks."

"Well, why don't we leave the kitchen light on, just in case, huh?"

I didn't argue. "Night."

"Good night, honey."

We bedded down on the couches and soon I could hear Lulu snoring softly. No telling when she had slept last. My body was exhausted. But my brain wouldn't go to sleep. Was Emily going to regain consciousness? If so would her kids be there to greet her? Where was Nick? Was Quinn okay? What had become of Belinda? How was I going to face Hunter after my childish outburst? I felt like such an idiot – he did nothing wrong, I was just cracking under stress. Was I losing my self-control, along with my mind? What was causing me to fall into other people's nightmares? Was the tulpa dead, or lurking outside? Like an out-of-control super-bounce ball, my thoughts ping-ponged from one question to another, then back again. Despite the fact that I was so tired I could barely move, sleep avoided me. It didn't help that every time my eyelids started to droop, I heard something scuttling around on the roof. Must be the biggest raccoon ever. Mom might get to use her live trap yet. Maybe that would help. I could hear her crying behind the closed door of my bedroom, and the murmur of my father's voice, trying to comfort her.

By 5:00, I gave up on sleeping. But I had an idea.

I grabbed my purse and went out to my car. When I pulled out of my driveway, I noticed a man standing on the corner, just out of the amber puddle cast by the street light. He was so pale he nearly glowed in the dark. *Great. Just what we need in the neighborhood.*

Junkies. He raised his hand in a slow wave, and I instinctively waved back. *Ugh. Don't encourage the creeper.*

I finished my run to the 24-hour Kroger to buy a plant. The man was gone when I returned. My day was starting to look up. I wrote a note to Hunter, apologizing for my awful, uncalled-for behavior, and begging his forgiveness. I had one of the beautiful beaded stakes that Belinda made and sold in the shop that I'd bought to give to Mom for her birthday in a few weeks. I'd use it for this plant and buy her another one. By the time I finished all that, Cassie was up, so I fed her breakfast, put her in the stroller, and wheeled her out to the front porch. I took the plant and note and left it by Hunter's front door. Even though I'd now been up for twenty-four hours, my second wind had kicked in. Since we were up and at 'em, may as well go for our morning walk. But I needed the go-bag. At the rate folks were disappearing around here, I didn't dare leave her outside, unsupervised for a minute.

As I wheeled her back inside, Lulu met me at the door.

She yawned. "Where are you going?"

"Since I was up and dressed, I thought I'd take Cassie for our morning walk."

"Can we talk for a minute before you go? I'm going back to the house to try and sleep some more before I open up the shop."

"Sure."

I set the brake on the stroller, then took Cassie's stuffed blue rabbit, Mr. Buns, out of the go-bag and handed him to her.

"Buns!" she said.

I smiled. She said another new word every day. "That's right, Cassie. Mr. Buns. I'll be right back, okay? I'm just going to talk to Auntie Lulu for a minute."

Cassie started gnawing on Mr. Buns' ear.

"Alrighty, then," I said, turning to Lulu.

Lulu and I stepped outside on the front porch.

"I don't know how, but I think that Virginia's tulpa and Belinda's disappearance are connected. Of course, it could be nothing but wishful thinking, but I just feel in my bones that Virginia has something to do with it, or at least knows something about it. I need to think more on how we're going to try and catch that tulpa, if it's still around. I think your dog can sense it, but obviously, he can't track it if it's gone through a portal."

The whole idea of portals and interdimensional places was still alien to me. "What if he killed it when he attacked it in Hunter's flowerbed?"

"I'm not sure that would have permanently disrupted it. Maybe it did. Not my area of expertise, honey."

As she talked, I became aware of footsteps. I looked up and stared over Lulu's shoulder at the peculiar man that was making his way up my walkway. Lulu turned around to look, too.

"Good God!" she said.

"Thank you!" the man replied.

He was very pale, corpse-like, I would say, and his unkempt black hair just accented his pallor.

It was the same man I'd seen standing on the corner earlier.

"Who are you?" I asked. I looked around to see if there was anyone filming this encounter. The last thing I needed was to be on some hokey reality TV show. But then again, I'd had some experience with outlandish individuals turning up on my doorstep.

"I understand you're looking for Quinn," he replied, dodging my question.

"You know where he is? Is he alright?" I asked.

"My associate…," he gestured to a chunky man standing on the sidewalk in front of the walkway. "…can help you," the pale guy continued. "If you can spare just a moment."

How had I not noticed him before? I had a bad feeling about this. Even the hairs on my arms were standing up. I looked at Lulu and she looked at me. I wanted to run back in the house and lock the door. "I guess it doesn't hurt to talk." True, it was early, but I was standing in front of my house in broad daylight, with my parents just a few yards away inside. And it wasn't like he had any type of vehicle to bundle us into.

Lulu took my hand, and we walked cautiously towards the man at the end of the path. I stopped well out of his reach.

"What do you know about Quinn?" I asked.

"Can you come a little closer?" he asked. "You never know who might be listening."

We moved a few steps closer.

"I can lead you to Virginia," he said. "She is responsible for Quinn's disappearance."

"What?" Lulu asked. "I have a hard time believing that."

The fat man raised an eyebrow. "I can lead you to the portal she's been using."

"What about Quinn?" I asked.

"Again, I can take you to him."

Lulu got a little closer to him – she was taller, by an inch. "We aren't going anywhere with you, not until you tell us who you are and why you're here – and maybe not even then. You say you can take us to Quinn and/or Virginia, but why? I don't see that we have any reason to believe you, much less trust you. Especially when you won't even tell us who you are."

He was not intimidated. Lulu pushed her luck a little harder, and stepped still closer to him.

"As you like," the man said with a greasy smile. Then he moved faster than I thought would have been possible and grabbed Lulu's arm. She cried out and tried to pull away. "My name," he said with an awful grin, "is Balcones."

There was a loud bang, and I felt myself falling.

Chapter 20
Toil and Trouble

Sunday, August 14, 4:25 PM
Houston, Texas

Lieutenant Haskell and the warrant execution team were waiting on Azalea Falls Lane, two blocks from Dinah's house, when Hadrian arrived.

"I've got the signed search warrant," Hadrian said, waving a piece of paper.

"I'll get the WET guys in place. They've already assessed the location. Small house, no burglar bars, nothing like that. Should be an easy one."

"About that," Hadrian replied. "There's no indication that she's got any weapons – she's got nothing on her record but a single parking ticket. My concern is that if we execute a no-knock raid, she'll panic and hurt Belinda. Her expertise seems to lie in tricks and traps, so I think it would be safer to get her out of the house and under control before we make entry. I'd like to knock on the door myself and see if she'll let me in."

"I want my guys in place first, in case you're wrong about the weapons."

"Agreed. I'll call you before I approach the house and slip my phone in my pocket. You can hear everything. If I'm wrong, kick in the door."

Haskell nodded.

"Let's go get Belinda," he told the detective.

Hadrian knocked on Dinah's front door, then stepped back a little and stood to the side. He heard a door slam inside the house, then footsteps.

"Who's there?" a woman inside asked, agitated.

"Yes, ma'am. I'm Special Agent Galanti." He held up his official ID. "I'm in your neighborhood working a missing person case. I'd appreciate it if you would take a moment to answer a couple of questions for me about this missing girl."

"I don't know anything about that," Dinah snapped.

"Oh, no, ma'am. I didn't say you took her. I just want to know if you've seen any people in the neighborhood that don't belong, that type of thing. It'll just take a minute of your time."

There was an exasperated sigh on the other side of the door. "I'm running late. Can you come back later?"

"No, ma'am. It'll just take a minute. Time is critical in finding a missing child, and we'd really appreciate your help."

Dinah muttered something Hadrian couldn't make out and unlocked the door. "Well, don't just stand there, come inside. What will the neighbors think, you standing out there on my front porch?"

"Yes, ma'am. Is your husband at home? I'd like to talk to him, too."

Dinah scowled. "I'm not married. If you've got question, there's nobody to ask but me."

"Thank you, ma'am. Can I ask your name? I need it for my report."

The woman's eyes narrowed and her jaw clenched. "My friends call me Dinah, but you can call me Miss Beecher. I don't have all day."

Hadrian stepped into the decrepit house. What appeared to be years of deferred maintenance had taken its toll. He hoped to find Belinda and get her out of the house before the stained and bowed ceiling fell in on them. He pulled out a notebook and a pen.

Dinah Beecher was forty-two. This lady was sixty, if she was a day. Had he gone to the wrong house? That's all he needed was to be responsible for a warrant raid on somebody's hapless grandmother.

"Well, get on with it," Dinah said. She glanced up at the dusty clock at the end of the room and fiddled with a necklace she had tucked under her shirt.

"Yes, ma'am. Thanks for your time." He was hoping to get her flustered enough that she'd let something slip. "Now the lady we're looking for –"

"You said it was a girl."

"Does it matter?"

Dinah glared at him. "I really have to go."

"I understand that, and I appreciate your cooperation."

He reached out, as if to shake her hand. As soon as she responded, he snapped a handcuff on her wrist, and deftly maneuvered her around to cuff the other one. He led her back toward the front door. "Dinah Phyllis Beecher, I have a warrant to search your house in the connection to the disappearance of Belinda Tate. For security reasons, I'm placing you in custody while the warrant is executed, at which time you may or may not be charged with a crime." He didn't know how Dinah killed the four romance writers, he just knew she did it. And he didn't want to be next.

"No!" Dinah bellowed. "It's time! I have to go!"

She struggled for a moment, but stopped. Hadrian wondered what she was up to as he handed her off to the first WET officer who came through the door.

"Be careful," he said to Haskell as the detective stepped over the threshold. "The place may be booby trapped."

Haskell looked around the house. "The whole place *is* a booby trap."

The house only had six rooms, so it was quickly cleared by the WET officers. All except for one room. There was a hasp and padlock keeping that door shut.

"Belinda?" Haskell called.

"Help!" came a shaky voice from behind the door.

"Sit tight. We're coming for you. Is there anything in there with you we should know about?"

"No. Just me."

Hadrian hoped she was right. The ones with causes were fond of setting up unpleasant surprises.

The entry team's crowbar made short work of the lock, and everyone stood back as they carefully opened the door, checking for triggers to explosive devices along the door jamb. It was clean. The reek of an overflowing chamber pot met the rescuers as they opened the door, and a few of them coughed and gagged. Haskell took a small jar of mentholatum from his pocket and dabbed some of the salve under his nose, then offered it to Hadrian, who also partook.

Flashlights shone on Belinda, revealing a pitiful sight. She'd gone from thin to gaunt, she was dirty, and her hair was matted to her head. *But at least she's alive.* Hadrian had been on investigations where that hadn't been the case.

"Come on out, Belinda. You're safe now," he said.

Haskell radioed for EMS. "We're going to send you to the hospital," he told her.

She nodded. Tears streamed down her face. She was wearing men's clothing, far too big for her, and she had to hold up the stained khaki pants as she walked. Haskell dialed a number on his phone. Hadrian heard him say, "Ms. Miranda, please call Detective Haskell at your earliest possible convenience regarding Ms. Tate. I have urgent news."

Knowing how desperate Lulu was for them to find Belinda, he thought it was a little odd that she didn't pick up a call from Haskell, but maybe she was driving or at the movies. Hadrian took Belinda's arm to steady her. If she thought it was strange that Marti's neighbor was helping the police rescue her, she didn't let on.

He desperately wanted to tell her about the vision he'd had when he touched the beaded stake she'd made. But now wasn't the time. If she asked, what would he say? *Yes, ma'am, just your friendly, neighborhood accountant here. Helping out the police and arresting suspects.* He didn't want to think about that, either.

Hadrian took Belinda's free arm. "Let's get you outside in the fresh air."

"Please," she replied, her voice raspy.

She turned and looked over her shoulder, as if expecting someone to follow. Hadrian shook his head. *Been in solitary too long, poor thing.*

As they stepped out onto Dinah's shady front porch, he noticed that one of the WET officers was uncuffing Dinah.

"Necklace," Belinda panted. "Don't let her get it."

"Stop!" Hadrian shouted, stepping in front of Belinda.

Dinah immediately grabbed for her pendant.

Hadrian didn't know what else to do, so he yelled "Gun!"

Even the heavily armored WET team dove for cover. Except for the officer who had just uncuffed Dinah. There was no place for him to go. In an instant, the woman standing next to him was gone.

And in her place was a lion.

The huge cat roared, and car alarms down the street went off. It knocked the WET officer down, and he scrambled away. The beast turned toward the house and stalked toward Hadrian. Belinda cowered behind him. He had drawn his weapon, and kept it trained on the cat. It shook its head and snarled, tail twitching.

"Stop, Dinah," Hadrian said, doubting the animal understood him. "Just stop."

The great cat rocked back on its haunches, as if to sit, then leaped at Hadrian. Gunfire erupted from multiple firearms, and the animal fell dead at his feet. He himself had only managed to squeeze three shots off, but he knew at least two had hit the lion's head.

As he watched, the beast melted away. But there was something left. The bullet-riddled body of Dinah Beecher. *What the hell just happened here?*

"Did you see that?" panted the WET officer who had been bowled over by the lion.

The officer walking with him shook his head. "I didn't see anything. Do you see any lions here? No. Because there aren't any. Never were. Only a crazy old lady who acted like she had an explosive device around her neck."

"This will be an interesting test for the new body cameras," Hadrian said to Haskell. *Can't wait to read this report.*

EMS pulled up, and Haskell tossed his car keys to one of the WET officers. "I'm going to ride in the ambulance. Get my car back downtown, would you, Malloy?"

The officer nodded and pocketed the keys.

"Crime Scene is on the way. Don't know if you want to stick around for that. Thanks for the lead, agent."

Hadrian watched as the paramedics helped Belinda onto the stretcher. They took her vitals and loaded her into the ambulance. Haskell climbed in after her.

There was no need to stick around and wait for the CSU. They would go into excruciating detail, collecting carpet fibers, soil samples, Dinah's cell phone and computer, if she had one, among other things. He looked down at her body. Her heart wasn't pumping, but gravity was drawing the thickening blood out through her open wounds, making an ever-widening pool. *How did you get here, Dinah?*

He briefly considered taking the necklace – it was clearly not an ordinary object. But he didn't. Her personal effects would be released to her family, if any existed. He hadn't been able to find them when he ran her background. It would be safe enough in the evidence lock up. He got in his car. If the traffic gods were kind, he could make the second half of MacBeth at the Miller. He'd check on Marti and Lulu afterwards, if they were still talking to him. He texted Sara, and headed toward the Museum District.

Sara's friend, Penny, insisted that they stop and eat after the play. Ordinarily, Hadrian didn't mind doing that. The group often grabbed a bite after a show. They almost always went to the same restaurant, and the wait staff knew them by name. But tonight he was antsy. Sure, in a way that made him doubt his sanity, they'd recovered Belinda and the Romance Killer was dead, but he couldn't shake the feeling that this episode wasn't finished. He had told Sara he'd just meet them at the restaurant, since they'd come in separate vehicles. He made a call on the way back to his car.

"Haskell."

"Galanti here. Just wanted to follow up and see how Belinda was."

"They had to run fluids to treat her for dehydration. They're going to keep her overnight, but she should be good to go in the morning."

"Excellent."

Haskell sighed. "Still haven't got in touch with Lulu. I find that a bit concerning."

"Me, too. Let me see if I can locate her."

It gave him no pleasure to text Sara to say he couldn't make dinner. He'd done that often enough lately. Penny would have something to say about it. Her fiancé never bailed on plans. That was just something he'd have to worry about later. Right now, he needed to find Lulu. The easiest way to do that was to go through Marti.

Hadrian was taken aback when he knocked on Marti's door, and a police officer – who wasn't Nick – answered. "I-I was just stopping by to say hello," he stammered.

"Hunter? Is that you?" Marti's mother called from the living room.

"Yes, ma'am."

Adele hurried over to the doorway. "Marti went missing this morning, she and Lulu both. This is after Nick's children were taken. I don't know what happened. We spent the night last night, and when we got up Cassie was strapped in her stroller, but Marti was gone, just gone. We're worried sick. Do you think," she sniffled, "that the same person who stole our grandkids took her, too?"

Where did you go, Marti, after you dropped off that plant? "Unfortunately, I have no way of knowing that. What makes you think Lulu is also missing?"

"She spent the night, too."

"I see." *There's quite a slumber party.* "Do you think Lulu —"

"Of course not! She'd never hurt Marti. She was her employer, for crying out loud."

He hugged Marti's mother. "I'm sure these officers know what they're doing. I'm just going to get out of their way. Keep me posted, though." He gave Adele his cell number.

He knew that he just got handed another missing persons case. And this time, he had no idea where to look.

Belinda leaned forward in the hospital bed, trying to figure out the best way to get up without disturbing her IV. The two bags of fluids she'd gotten pumped into her vein had made her feel like a million bucks. She'd even felt well enough to answer all of Lieutenant Haskell's questions about the kidnapping. She hesitated to tell him about Dinah's wishing stone, but then decided honesty was the best policy. She'd let Haskell sort it out in his report. The truth was that she would have answered his questions about anything, just to keep him in the room with her, because she was so desperate for company. She'd looked around, hoping to see some sign of Ellen, but the ghost did not seem to be around. She called out to her mentally, and hoped Ellen would come back soon.

As good as she felt from the IV, its side effect had left her with a pressing need to go to the restroom. She gave up trying to puzzle out the tangle of wires and hit the nurse call button.

A few minutes later, her nurse opened the door. "You alright, ma'am?"

"I just need to go to the bathroom, and I'm not sure how to disconnect this stuff."

The nurse unlocked the wheels on the IV pole, and showed Belinda how to free herself from the EKG machine without making it flatline and send everyone running to her room. Then she went back to her rounds.

A grateful Belinda dragged her IV into the bathroom with her. She would never in her wildest dreams have imagined how excited she could be about sitting on a toilet. An actual flush toilet! Even the hospital antiseptic smelled good to her. She was nearly giddy. Belinda even flushed it a second time after she was done, just to hear the sound. Then she washed her hands, twice, to feel the warm water and suds on her skin. The first thing she would do when she got home, she decided, would be to take a long, hot shower.

When she got back in bed and got the equipment hooked up, she leaned back and scanned the room for any sign of Ellen. Belinda was alone. She turned on the TV, more for noise than entertainment, and clicked through the channels. It didn't take very long for her to relax and drowse off.

She had just drifted into hypnagogia – that peculiar liminal state between wakefulness and sleep – when she heard someone call her name. In her mind's eye, she could see Ellen standing next to her bed.

"Ellen? There you are. I've been looking all over for you."

"There was some kind of binding on the house. I couldn't leave until that awful woman who took you crossed the threshold. Not that I would have left you, anyway; but I had no choice about it. I was afraid I was going to be trapped there forever with Thomas. What a horrible man!"

"Yes. I met him. I hope Dinah dragged him across the threshold with her."

Ellen shrugged, then clasped her hands in front of her chest. "Belinda, I have bad news for you. Lulu and Marti have been taken by Balcones, and they're trapped between dimensions, in some nightmare world he's created. I don't know how or why, but surely no good can come of it."

"What? I don't understand?" Belinda almost woke up, but Ellen grabbed her wrist and kept her from leaving.

"Your cousin, Virginia, has been up to her old tricks – and then some. I suspect that she's the one that trapped me in the house with you, didn't want me telling Marti and Lulu where you were. I have to go help those two, if I can get in there."

"You'll come back, right?"

Ellen looked at the floor and ran her finger along the bed railing. "Of course I will. It just may not be in the way you think."

Belinda frowned. "What do you mean?"

Ellen didn't respond. She faded away into the dimness of the room, and Belinda could not feel her presence any more.

Chapter 21
And Miles to Go

Sunday, August 14, 7:05 AM
The Maze

I stumbled, but caught myself before I did a face-plant. I blinked. Repeatedly. It was still there. Instead of standing at the end of the walkway to my house, Lulu and I stood in what looked like an ancient forest. It was cool and misty, and I wished I had a jacket.

Balcones was still clutching Lulu's wrist.

"Let go," she growled.

He chuckled, but released her arm. "Now, after all the trouble I've gone to, setting this game up, that's no way to talk to me."

"What game are you talking about?" I asked.

"That's an excellent question. Think of it as an extremely immersive RPG."

"A what?" Lulu asked.

Balcones' eyes widened with annoyance. "RPG – role playing game. Do you have any idea how much money I make off selling imaginary objects for actual money on in-game purchases?" He nearly smiled, then shook his head and cleared his throat. "Now, the object of *this* game is to gather tools, weapons, and food and survive your quest to the center of the maze. Once all the members of your team have touched the gazing ball, your mission is complete. It would, of course, be unfair for me to let you have a head start. The other team will be arriving presently. Feel free to wander around and brainstorm until then, when the game will start."

"What if we refuse to play?" I asked.

Balcones shook his head in mock sympathy. "That would be most unfortunate. Because this game differs from online RPGs in that if you die in the game, you really die. There are no save points or extra lives."

"We'll just convince the other team not to play." Lulu said.

"You might, perhaps. But they'll enter the maze at a different point than you, so you won't see them for some time."

"We can just sit and wait for them to make it through," I said.

"You could do that, certainly. Yes. Did I mention that there are monsters? They, too, will be searching for resources and food – that would be you. Your chances of escaping them are much better inside the maze. But, if you wish to leave your baby an orphan because of some ideological snit, that of course, is your choice."

I scowled. I looked at Lulu. She was looking back at me, shaking her head. "Why us? Why now?"

Balcones threw his head back and laughed. "Is it not obvious?"

"No," Lulu replied.

Balcones' eyes narrowed into hard lines. "Quinn." Balcones looked at me. "You are his girlfriend." Then he looked at Lulu. "You are an ally of those irksome fae."

"But I'm not his girlfriend. We're not even seeing each other anymore." I doubted this would change the situation, but I had nothing else to say.

Balcones' grin was frightening. "Glorious! He will suffer all the more for your dea-deadly peril, knowing it was 100% his fault. Knowing you tried to get away from him, but his selfish dalliance with you put you in this position. If only he'd left you alone...but I can see why he didn't."

He laughed softly, then reached out to trace my jaw with his pudgy finger before I stepped back, out of reach. Rage flared up in his eyes. Lulu and I both backed away.

"More than a hundred years ago," Balcones snarled, "I watched as Quinn's MIT murdered my father in cold blood. I have spent all this time getting stronger, getting richer, and now I have everything I need to take my revenge. I already got that bitch that killed my father. She also was Quinn's girlfriend, and I reveled in his suffering. I had Malik trapped, and what a joy it would have been to see him enslaved for all eternity."

"You sold him. If you were so desperate for revenge, why didn't you keep him yourself?"

"Revenge is sweet, but so is profit. Why have only one, when I could enjoy both?" Balcones paused. "After that, I lured the entire team to the edge of the world – if only that Russian mobster hadn't had been so greedy, I could have fed the entire MIT to the great wolf Fenrir."

"It seems like your plans depend too much on people," Lulu said.

"That is exactly what I was thinking. My grandfather, the one who raised me after my father was murdered, always said, 'Keep it simple.' That's why I've brought you here – I designed the maze, and the whole place is under my control. No complicated schemes or feckless humans here to fail me. Just my enemies in a giant maze, fighting to the dea—decision…on the winner. With a few monsters here and there, of course. Just to make it interesting."

I crossed my arms. "And speaking of humans, what part do Nick's children play in your grand master plan? What have you done with them?"

Balcones' hands became animated, more so as he talked. "That, now that was complete serendipity. You see, I was trying to capture you and your brat to use as bait to torture Quinn, but for some reason, Virginia's tulpa couldn't find your house. I don't know why – it found everyone else's. But anyway. My bumbling nephews found your sister. Unfortunately, they got a little rough with her, which is a shame, because it would have been brilliant to have her as a hostage. But I digress. Regardless of whether or not you're still sleeping with Quinn, he cares for you, and it was your choice to get involved with him. But now, your whole family is disrupted, and they had no choice about it. The more *you* suffer, the more *he* suffers, and by involving innocent bystanders, his feelings of guilt are compounded exponentially."

Mine, too. "You should have left Emily and the kids out of this. Just so you know, their father is coming for you. And he won't rest until he's gotten them back." I lunged at Balcones, grabbing for his throat.

Deftly snatching my wrists into his large hand, Balcones pulled me against his scaly body. Up close, his sulphurous breath nearly choked me. He snorted and rolled his eyes. "I have no fear of humans."

"You should fear him."

Balcones' mouth twitched into a half-hearted approximation of a smile. "Perhaps. But not today." He shoved me towards Lulu, letting go of me as his arm extended.

My friend caught me, then glared at Balcones. "So basically, what you're saying, is that Marti and I start at one end of the maze, and Quinn's MIT starts at the other, and we race to see who gets to the center first. Is that correct?"

"Essentially," Balcones replied, with a smirk that made me want to slap him.

"What happens if we win?" I asked.

"I don't want to spoil the surprise by telling you."

Lulu's lips pursed. "What happens if we lose?"

"I would strongly recommend against that. Did I mention that Phoebetor is also playing?"

"Who's that?" I asked.

"The God of Nightmares. You met him a few minutes ago. Well, I've got to go spring the trap on an MIT team. Enjoy the game0021
"

Balcones stepped through an invisible door and was gone. I ran over and tried to locate the portal, but my hands found only empty space.

Sunday, August 14, 11:45 AM
The In Between

"Argh! Why did you follow me here?" Virginia snapped, as she, Nick, Malik, and Bruce landed in a heap on the floor in Balcones' between room, the same one where Quinn had been held earlier.

"What did you expect?" Nick shot back. "You know where my kids are."

"Virginia, you are such an idiot – you let Quinn escape. I told you never, ever let yourself be alone with him. And what did you do? I can't believe I trusted you."

All four of them turned to see a paunchy man standing at the far end of the narrow room, shaking his head.

"Balcones!" she said. "I can explain."

"That's Balcones?" Nick asked, incredulous, as he looked at Malik.

"What do you mean by that?" Balcones was indignant.

Nick stood up, as did the others. He crossed his arms and leaned back slightly. "I just didn't expect a demon to look like a middle-aged fat guy, that's all. I was expecting something more…demonic."

Balcones' cheeks went bright red and his eyes flashed.

"You shouldn't have said that," Malik whispered.

The skin on the Balcones' face seemed to implode, leaving behind the scaly bronze skin and reptilian eyes of his normal demon face.

When he spoke, his voice was harsher and more sibilant. "Is thisss better?"

Quinn shifted from dog form into human form and prevented Virginia from running out the other portal.

Nick shrugged. "Meh. I thought you might have horns and a tail." Both his immortality and his fury at the thing that wrought such havoc on his family overcame the very reasonable fear he should have had towards Balcones.

Malik nudged Nick. "It would be in all of our best interests for you to stop provoking him."

Balcones stalked closer. Nick stood his ground as the demon pushed into his personal space. "Hmmm. Human, entangled with those tiresome fae. Missing some children." He grinned, close enough for his sour breath to slide down Nick's cheek. "You must be the husband of Marti Keller's sister."

Nick bristled, but Malik placed a cautionary hand on his shoulder. Balcones then moved past Nick and approached Virginia. "I will deal with you later. Get out."

Quinn made no attempt to stop her this time, and she hurried through the portal behind her. Balcones moved so that he was toe-to-toe with Quinn.

"Well, I have to say that I'm somewhat disappointed. I'd hoped to get your entire MIT, or what's left of it, anyway, to play my game. But who knows, a fae, a djinn, and a human? Could be entertaining."

"And what game is that, Balcones?" Quinn asked.

"Ah. The team lead speaks. All these years, I have been watching you, waiting for this moment. I could kill you," he bared his fangs, "right here, right now...but then it would be over too quickly. Very unsatisfying. And all the trouble I went to creating this maze would just be wasted."

"Maze?" Nick asked.

Balcones smacked his lips and glanced up at the ceiling. "Are you unfamiliar with the concept?"

"No. I just think it's weird."

"Weird. Now that is something I can promise you. It will definitely be weird."

"And if we refuse?" Quinn asked.

"You won't. There's a prize at the center. Take a look." He gestured to the wall, toward the window view of the forest. It faded, and then showed a small clearing in a dense wood. Inside the clearing, a middle-aged woman held a small baby, and two boys played tag, using a pedestal that supported a large gazing ball as base.

There was a sharp intake of breath from Nick.

"Now, and I know she looks disgusting right now, but that lovely creature holding the baby is my wife. Personally, I wouldn't trust her around human children. Also, when the glass ball is touched, it activates the guardians, and they will kill whatever is in the clearing. Demons excepted, of course. Maybe the boys will be careful. But if you're sure you don't want to play…"

"Open the door. Now," replied Nick.

Balcones smiled. "Excellent. I will warn you that there are some monsters wandering about – you probably want to get to the middle before they do, because they would nothing more than to touch the ball and activate the guardians. Food, weapons, and useful items can be found in the maze, although it may take some looking." He started to turn away from them, then turned back around to grin at Malik. "Just an FYI – this maze may look very similar to an ancient forest on the earth plane, but the physical rules are a little different. So most of your genie powers won't work here."

Malik moved in close to Quinn. "Is retrieving Nick's offspring enough justification to participate in this endeavor, or should we focus our efforts on escape?" he asked in a whisper.

"I don't think we have much choice," Quinn whispered back. "Maybe we can do both, though."

Balcones looked sharply at the two of them. "Oh, Quinn?" he asked picking at something caught in one of his claws. "Just curious. Have you spoken to Marti lately? She seems very nice. A shame about your breakup." He looked out the window into the maze for a moment, then looked back at Quinn and smiled.

The blood rushed from his face to the pit of Quinn's stomach and collected there in a frigid pool. If rescuing Nick's kids wasn't important enough to MAMIC, rescuing Marti –if she was in the maze as Balcones had just implied – was definitely important enough to him. Of course, it could be a trick, demons were known for that. How did Balcones know that they had broken up? Was it just a guess, designed to mess with his head? Or had he actually spoken with Marti? There was only one way to find out. As much as he wanted to put his hands around Balcones' throat and squeeze him, he wouldn't take the bait. He refused to give Balcones a win, however small, before the game even started.

Nick's eyes narrowed. "Are you going to open the door, or just stand there and keep running your mouth?"

"As you wish." Balcones gestured to the wall.

Tendrils of chill mist curled into the room as the wall dissolved. Something in the maze was screaming; the screams came at regular intervals, and sometimes there was more than one voice.

"Bloody foxes," grumbled Quinn.

Balcones grinned.

The three stepped through the doorway into the cool forest and looked around. They stood on a dirt path that led into a dense forest of gnarled old trees. The woods stretched interminably on either side of the path. Unseen creatures made haunting calls that echoed through the trees before they were swallowed by the mist.

"The game begins…now," said Balcones.

The doorway disappeared, with no hint of it ever having existed, replaced by a bank of fog so thick it was impossible to tell whether there was ground beneath it or trees behind it.

"The sooner we get started, the sooner we finish," Nick said, moving forward.

Malik shrugged and followed. "Into the woods."

"No show tunes," Quinn said. "Seriously. No. Show. Tunes."

The animal sounds fell silent as the three entered the shadows of the ancient forest.

Although being kidnapped by Balcones was the last thing I had expected, I was so thankful I'd had the foresight to take Cassie in the house after I'd dropped off Hunter's plant. My parents might be concerned about me, but my baby would be safe and sound. It was one less thing I had to worry about. Although I don't think anything would have kept me awake, once I got still. My second wind had petered out some time ago, and after the brief adrenalin rush from our kidnapping, I was more tired than I remember ever being. I leaned against the invisible wall that kept us out of the woods and slept.

The thudding of my head into the ground and getting a mouthful of leaf litter woke me up. I spat rotting leaves out of my mouth, tasting the grit and mold.

Lulu stretched her hand out to help me up. "I guess it's time, honey."

"Yep." I touched the prayer box with the blue crystal tear that hung around my neck for luck.

Something in the trees made a whooping cry that reminded me of the howler monkeys at the zoo. As we got further into the gloom, there was a chittering noise that could have been made by either a small bird or a large insect. I hoped it was a bird.

Chapter 22
Here be Monsters

I was acutely aware of the noise our feet made shuffling through the fallen leaves on the path. If there were any monsters nearby, they'd know exactly where we were. I tried lifting my feet higher, or walking toe-heel instead of heel-toe. Neither of those made a huge amount of difference. It wasn't too far into the woods that we came to a turn off. We could go straight ahead or make a right turn.

Deep in the mist-shrouded trees, something screamed. Short, hoarse yelps, like someone being chased through the woods by an ax murderer. My heart beat faster. "What was that?"

"If I heard it at my house, I would think it's a fox. Here, I don't know, honey."

I tried to re-focus on our task, and turned back to the path. "Keep going, or turn?" I asked.

"We're supposed to go to the center of the maze," Lulu said. "Maybe one of us should wait here, and the other should go on a little way and see if it's a dead end."

I shook my head. "No, I think it would be a bad idea to split up." I looked around for a stick. "Why don't we make a mark?" I drew a deep line in the dirt, near the edge of the path parallel to the direction we were travelling. "And if we come back this way and find the mark, we'll know we've gone in a circle."

"Makes sense."

We took the turning. Soon we came to a path that branched to the left and about ten feet afterward, a path that branched to the right.

"Right, left or straight?" Lulu asked.

"We're supposed to be looking for food and weapons as well, so we may as well take the first turn and see where it leads. I wonder, though, if there's a shortcut. Maybe something hidden out in the forest?" I headed for one of the natural paths between the trees. And bounced off the solid air at the edge of the path. I used my hands, mime-style, to feel for a break in the invisible wall. It went further up than I could reach, and all the way down into the dirt. I followed it a short distance in either direction, but it remained solid.

I sighed and went to mark the path. There was already a mark there. I ran to the other path. Also a mark.

"Dammit," I said.

"Well, I guess we couldn't expect a demon to play fair. Let's take the left turn anyway."

The path spiraled into a dead end. However, there was a statue at the cul-de-sac that held a silver dagger. I took it and we backtracked. We were just coming to the point where the spiral joined the straightaway when we heard noises. We stopped, hidden by the huge trunk of an ancient tree, and peered around the corner. Standing at the crossroad were a werewolf, a cyclops, and a scorpion the size of a horse. They seemed to be talking to each other, but it only sounded like growls and grunts to me. The werewolf gestured down the path, in our direction. I held my breath. The cyclops waved his club toward the straight-ahead path. If my heart pounded any harder, they were going to hear it. The scorpion glanced down the trail in our direction, then they hurried on down the straight path. We waited until there was silence, then we waited some more.

"I think we should go back to the first path," I whispered to Lulu. "I think we're least likely to run into those monsters that way."

She nodded, and we crept cautiously down the path, turned right, then turned right again when we rejoined our original track.

"I'm pretty sure Balcones was lying about the food," I said.

"Would you eat any food you found in this place?" Lulu answered.

"Good point. I'm still starving, though."

"Me, too."

We'd been tramping around all day, and I couldn't tell if we were any closer to the center of the maze than when we started. The mist in this place never quite lifted, so thirst wasn't so much of a problem, but hunger was. Unless I wanted to grab one of the black squirrels that haunted the trees, or one of the crows that seemed to be constantly laughing at us, and eat it raw, there was nothing to be done about it. I was desperate, but not that desperate. Not yet, anyway. We'd found no food, but we were the proud owners of a silver dagger, six arrows in a quiver, four Ninja throwing stars, and a crowbar. Good thing Lulu had been wearing her backpack. Night was quickly descending on this murky wood, and I wasn't sure where or if we would sleep. Twice during the day, we'd seen the same assortment of monsters we'd seen earlier. I wondered if we'd ever run into Quinn and his MIT. Had they already gotten to the center and claimed the prize, or were they just as lost and miserable as we were?

"Lulu? What was that noise?"

"Sounded like a wolf howling to me."

"That's what I thought."

I wished I'd paid more attention at camp, when they'd taught us how to light fires without matches. Although the perpetually damp wood in this forest probably wouldn't burn anyway.

Just ahead of us, there was the dull noise of a wet twig breaking, and we froze. I could see a figure stumbling towards us in the gloom.

What on earth is he doing here?

Sunday, August 14, 12:15 PM

The Maze

"I think we should turn left, then take the right turn just ahead," Malik said.

Quinn nodded. "From here, it looks like if we turn left and keep going, we're back to the outer edges. We need to get to the center of the maze, so I don't think tramping round and round the perimeter is going to do us any good."

"Fine. I've managed to find nothing but dead ends, anyway," Nick added.

As they approached the path that split off to their right, Quinn stopped them.

"Wait," he said. "Do you hear that?" He pointed down the track. "Look! Do you see them?"

"See what? Nick asked.

"They're hard to see in the fog, you can see them hiding behind the tree. They must be lying in wait for us. One I can't see much of, but she might be a sphynx. The other one, though, she's clearly Black Annis."

Nick pointed down the connecting trail. "I think we should go that way instead of walking into an ambush. And who or what is a Black Annis?"

"She's a blue-faced hag who loves to eat humans, especially children, who wander across her path," Quinn said.

Malik glanced down the row. "I see them. Let's go before they abandon their plan to waylay us and opt for a more direct approach, shall we?"

"What if we cut through the woods and circled around behind them?" Nick asked.

Quinn crossed his arms. "And then what? You think you can take them out with the bow we found? Never mind about the arrows."

"Yeah, you're right. Waiting for them to trap us is a much better plan."

"Enough!" Malik interrupted their spat. "It might be advantageous to get into the cover of the trees; however, we currently lack sufficient resources to effectively attack our opponents."

Nick rushed toward the dark trees, and collided with a clear barrier. He stepped back and rubbed his nose. Malik and Quinn tested for the invisible wall on the opposite side of the trail, and easily found it.

"I guess that means we stay on the trail," Nick said.

The hurried down the track, deeper into the maze.

"They don't seem to be actively pursuing us," Malik said, as they watched Black Annis and the sphynx turn the corner, headed away from them.

"Maybe they're NPCs," Nick suggested.

"What?" Quinn asked.

"Non-Player Characters. In computer games, they wander around and create havoc, but they don't' really have any intelligence."

Quinn shook his head. "There's a lot of those in real life, too."

"Balcones said that the monsters would try to get to the center of the maze, did he not?" Malik said.

"That doesn't necessarily mean that they have any self-awareness, or awareness of us," Nick replied.

They trudged on.

After a while, they came to a branch that turned almost immediately after it split from the main path, so they couldn't see down it more than ten feet or so. Quinn stepped into it and listened. "I don't hear anything. Shall we try it?"

The other two responded by coming into the branch with him. The maze twisted into a tight spiral, with nothing but blind corners at each turn. They crept through it on high alert, none of them wanting to challenge the sphynx or Black Annis, should they appear. At the end of it, there was a very small grotto. Clear water bubbled up at the feet of a demonic statue. On the wall behind it, hung a ball peen hammer.

"I recommend against touching the water," Malik said.

Quinn nodded. "Agreed."

Nick sighed. "I'm taking the hammer, though."

"Night's coming. Do we want to continue stumbling around in the dark, or do we want to draw lots for first watch and try to sleep some?" Quinn asked.

"I vote we rest," Nick said.

"I second that," Malik added.

Too bad there was no way to get off the path. If the monsters came, they'd be sitting ducks.

"I'll take the first watch," Quinn said. He was bone weary, but suspected he'd have trouble sleeping, at least at first.

Nick and Malik made themselves comfortable as best they could. In his mind, Quinn went over their inventory of found items: he carried a bow (but no arrows), Malik had a battle axe, and Nick just got a ball peen hammer. *Was this a weapons cache, or a jumble sale?* Thinking he'd be warmer with fur, he shifted into his dog form and patrolled the area. After a while, he thought he heard a strange noise, and trotted off to investigate.

Sunday, August 14, 8:15 PM
Houston, Texas

Virginia was afraid.

Balcones had said he'd deal with her later. It was much later, and he hadn't shown up. Not that she'd hung around waiting for him, but she knew if he really wanted to find her, he would. She jumped at every noise, and her nerves were shot. The demon was not inclined toward leniency, and she feared what might be in store for her.

"Think!" she commanded herself. "What can I do that will get Balcones off my back? What does he want most?" She got up and paced her living room.

She wracked her brain. *Money?...Power?...To humiliate Quinn.* He'd rambled on about his revenge plot many more times than Virginia had bothered listening to. What could she do to get back in Balcones' good graces? One thing a man can't stand is to see a woman he wants being taken care of by another man. As her ruined tulpa had faded, its memories had floated into her consciousness in little random snippets. She recalled one scene where it seemed to be the middle of the night, and Marti was standing in a man's yard, talking with him. Lulu was also there. Figures. Balcones had them now. They wouldn't be bothering her tulpas anymore. Virginia couldn't hear what anyone was saying, but it appeared to be a friendly exchange. And that was really all she needed. She decided the best thing to do was go to Marti's neighborhood and see if she could find the house from the tulpa's vision.

Virginia wished she'd worn flats for the multi-block hike in Marti's neighborhood – her feet were killing her. But at last she'd found the house. The garage door was open and the man inside, shirtless, was sorting through a box of papers. He looked young, perhaps mid-thirties. He was definitely the man the tulpa had seen. For a moment, Virginia watched him, sweat glistening on his hard body, and she was acutely aware that she wasn't as young as she used to be. Still, her legs looked good in short skirts and high heels, and that's what she was wearing. Should be good enough to at least get him to talk to her.

She walked up the driveway, hips swaying just enough to straddle the line between sex appeal and solicitation. She watched him watching her and smiled inwardly. *Take that, 'ladies of a certain age.'* Virginia stopped at the edge of the garage entrance.

"Excuse me?" she cleared her throat. "I'm sorry to bother you, but I'm looking for a friend's house and I just can't seem to find it. Could you possibly help me?" She twisted a lock of hair around her index finger.

The man set the box down on a worktable and came closer. Virginia's eye was drawn to his chest and arm, which sported a tattoo of a raven in flight.

"Nice ink," she commented.

"Thanks."

"I've been looking for this address," she said as she reached into her tiny designer handbag. What she pulled out was not a slip of paper, but a makeup compact. She tossed it gently into the garage. "Oops!"

She stepped in as if to retrieve it, and caught the man's hand in hers on the way. She stepped on the compact, and they both disappeared.

The man stumbled when they rematerialized, but quickly caught his balance. "Where…are we?" he asked, looking around.

She looked around to see Balcones sitting in a chair in front of the window, flicking through a bowl of mixed nuts with his claws. As soon as he saw her, he covered his face with his palm and shook his head.

"Virginia?" he asked as he removed his hand. "Why are you here? And why did you bring…a guest?" His voice carried the false calm of someone who has had to explain something too many times to too many different people, and was a hair's breadth from exploding.

The man, however, was staring at Balcones, mouth agape.

"I thought you could use him, Balcones," she nodded toward Hadrian. "He's a friend of Marti's."

"Use him for what?" Balcones asked, with forced pleasantry.

"Isn't it obvious? Put him in the maze with Marti, to make Quinn jealous."

Balcones rubbed the bridge of his nose with both index fingers, as if he had a headache. Then he sighed loudly. "Virginia, you've outdone yourself. With stupidity. Your idea isn't going to work because," he looked at Hadrian and scowled. "Because it just isn't. Now he knows about you, and he knows about me. I can't just let him go, now, can I? He has to go into the maze. But the game's been running for hours. I have deliberately made the teams unequal – if I put him in with Marti, that changes the odds, now doesn't it? I seriously wish you would have asked before you decided to help."

"I just thought he'd be useful." Virginia pouted.

"I'm still trying to decide if *you* are more useful to me alive or dead. Currently, the pendulum is swinging toward dead."

"What are you?" Hadrian asked. The tension between Balcones and Virginia shattered like a teacup dropped on tile.

"I have come to expect such poor manners from humans. You are in my house, and you have the nerve to ask me such a blatantly rude question?" Balcones asked. "Let me tell you what I am." He got up from his chair and strolled closer to Virginia and Hadrian. With each step he took, the light in the room dimmed. Virginia edged away from him, but Hadrian tried to stand his ground, but found himself involuntarily backing up. By the time Balcones was within a foot of him, all the illumination had faded, except for that given off by the demon's fiery eyes.

Hadrian could barely breathe as Balcones stood with his face inches away, sour breath fouling the agent's air. He wanted to get farther away, but his knees were so shaky he didn't think he could walk.

"I," Balcones said, "Am a demon. I am your worst nightmare."

"You haven't seen my nightmares," Hadirian whispered, the sound of his breath husky and dark with fear.

A grin cracked Balcones' scaly face. "Well, then. This might prove interesting after all."

Chapter 23
The Spider's Kiss

Malik tried to force his mind to empty and be still so he could rest. The indignity of having to lie in the dirt like a mongrel dog gnawed at him. It was more than that, though. He was used to being powerful, able even to bend time itself. But not here. No, in this dank place, he was as weak as a common man. A tired, filthy, hungry man. Eventually, his consciousness blurred into dream fragments, and then darkness.

The first thing Malik noticed was the smell. Layers of unwashed grime, sour sweat, and urine all competed for his attention. He opened his eyes and tried to move away from whatever foul thing emitted that stench. To his horror, he realized that it was him. Instead of the designer workout clothes he'd been wearing when he entered the maze, he found himself dressed in tattered, dirty rags. Gaudy market stalls of a bazaar surrounded him, but he was utterly alone.

"No!" he shouted, leaping to his feet.

His hand hit something hard. His breath stuck in his throat when he realized that it was a kashkul, a begging bowl carved from a coconut. His hands shook as he held them out to examine them. His fingernails were jagged and encrusted with dirt. His arms were thin and bony. And he stank. Stank of filth and despair and bottomless misery.

His chest heaved with short, gasping breaths. "How?" he said half-aloud. "How did I become this?"

He flinched when he felt a hand on his shoulder.

"Dude," Nick said groggily. "Wake up. What's wrong with you?"

"Do not look at me!" Malik said, his cheeks burning with shame. He blinked a few times and the desert glare of his dream gave way to the cool gloom of the forest maze.

"Not a problem. Of all the things I can stare at in the dark, you're not top of the list." Nick turned over, his back to Malik.

"You cannot sleep, either?"

"Not real sleep, no. But I'd have a better chance if you'd stop talking."

Malik bristled, but decided that it was late, and they were both very far from home. He turned his attention to his clothing. It didn't feel right, and the odor that had awakened him from his half-slumber still hung in the air. It must be his imagination. He turned his back to Nick, and stared into the dark, wondering when Quinn would come to wake him for sentry duty.

Hadrian stumbled down the dark path, prodded by Balcones.

"We're almost there," the demon growled.

"Almost where?"

Balcones let out an exasperation-tinged sigh. "To join your little friends." He stopped. "I do not wish to be seen. Just follow the track. You cannot miss them."

"Miss who?" Hadrian asked, but Balcones was already disappearing into the shadows of the ancient trees.

Deciding he had nothing to lose at this point, Hadrian headed down the path as Balcones had directed. It wasn't long before he saw two shapes in the dim light of the maze, but he could not make out their features.

"Hullo!" a female voice called. "Hunter? What on earth are you doing here?"

"Be careful, Marti," a different female voice said. "That may not really be him. How would he even get here?"

Marti and her family, Belinda, and Lulu were the only people who called him by his undercover name of 'Hunter.' Belinda was in the hospital, so he reasoned that the second female must be Lulu.

"It's me," he said. "I don't understand how I got here. I don't even know where here is." He was about ten feet away from Marti, so he stopped walking.

"Lulu is right. How do we know you really are Hunter?" Marti asked.

"Well…" Hunter started, but couldn't actually think of anything. They didn't have any biometric devices that could positively identify him.

Lulu leaned over and whispered in Marti's ear.

"Okay. What wine did you bring to my house the other night?"

"Chardonnay."

"He could be guessing," Lulu pointed out. "That's a real common kind of wine."

"Fair enough. What did we have for dinner?"

"Zucchini scampi, because you're allergic to shellfish."

Marti turned and spoke softly to Lulu for a moment, then they both took a few steps toward him.

"We're trapped in an interdimensional maze, if that helps any. What's the last thing you remember?" she asked.

"I remember everything. That's not the problem. I don't understand it."

"Then tell us what happened," Lulu said.

"I was in my garage, doing some work, and this blonde woman came up and asked for directions."

"Blonde?" Lulu asked. "Let me guess – middle-aged, short skirt, and high heels?"

"Yeah. How did you know?"

"Long story. Her name is Virginia," she said. "What happened next, hon?"

"She threw a makeup compact into my garage, and the next thing I knew, I was in some strange room with, for lack of a better description, the Devil."

"That's got to be Balcones," Marti said. "I'm sorry you got tricked into this."

"Balcones? Yes, that's what Virginia called him."

"He's just a garden variety demon, honey, nothing special, not as demons go, anyway," Lulu said.

"None of this can be real. There's no such thing as demons or teleportation devices, at least not yet. This has to be either a dream or some elaborate hoax." That's the only thing that could explain Balcones. Hadrian shuddered.

"I'm sorry to be the one to break it to you, but it is completely, one hundred percent real. I had a tough time with it, too, when I met Quinn," Marti said.

Hadrian scanned the path, hoping to find some evidence of a projector. "And Quinn would be?"

"He's a kelpie. But I thought he was a dog. Mostly, though, he's like a man," Marti said. "He hunts demons for a living. Balcones has some issues with that."

"I see." He had no idea what she was talking about, and thought it best to humor her. Delusional people were highly unpredictable. But then again, hadn't he just seen with his own eyes his murder suspect turn into a lion and back again? Was there some hallucinogenic contaminant in the neighborhood's water? He would request testing for it once he got back to his office.

"Just so you know," Marti said. "There are some monsters in the maze. Balcones said they would be trying to eat us, but when we did see them, they went the other way. Lulu and I had already decided to take turns sleeping – I'm on guard duty first."

"Can we try and get some rest now? Maybe if I'm asleep, I won't notice how hungry I am," Lulu said.

"Of course."

"Make yourself comfortable," she said. "There's no chocolate on your pillow at this joint, I'm afraid. Heck, there's not even a pillow."

The two of them did their best to settle in and get some rest. Lulu leaned up against the barrier between the maze and the forest. Hadrian stretched out, cradling his head in his hands. He stared up at the weird shapes formed by the tree branches, black against the deep grey sky. A yawn stretched across his face, and his eyelids felt heavy. The mournful hoot of an owl caused them to flicker open, but his blinks got longer and longer, until his eyes just stayed closed. His body stiffened momentarily to stop the falling sensation he always got when going to sleep, but it wasn't enough to rouse him.

Hadrian thought he smelled wood smoke. Rough jute rope dug into his wrists and ankles. His joints ached from being forcibly extended by the rack – if felt like he'd been there for days. He heard murmuring, but his line of sight was blocked by his own arms, stretched over his head. Metal scraped on metal and a light flared. A hooded figure approached Hadrian. He carried an iron bar, heated in the fire until one end glowed red. Hadrian tried to scream, but no sound escaped his lips.

Other hooded men appeared behind the first.

"Confess!" they intoned.

Hadrian panted in fear. *I have done nothing!* But no words would come.

"As you wish," said the man with the incandescent bar. The metal hissed as he stroked it along Hadrian's belly.

There was nowhere to go. He writhed against the taut ropes, struggling to get away from the red-hot agony that his midsection had become. Hadrian tried to yell, "Stop! Let me go!" but no sound would come from his throat, no matter how hard he pushed the air through his vocal cords.

"You are accused of being a witch. Consorting with the devil. Sending curses on your neighbors. Confess, and the priest will absolve you."

"No!" he tried to shout, but still he made no sound. He felt tears rolling down his cheeks, though, as his flesh blackened and blistered.

"Another turn," the man with the bar said.

Gears clattered and meshed together. The ropes creaked as they pulled even tighter against Hadrian's wrists and ankles. If he'd wanted to scream before, he was desperate to now. A loud pop accompanied the dislocation of his shoulder. A second followed closely behind. His other shoulder had pulled free of the joint.

At this point, he would have signed any confession. But he couldn't speak and he certainly couldn't sign anything -his hands were swollen and aching from the tight ropes cutting into them at the wrists.

"If you will not confess, you will be pressed. Do you confess?"

A primal scream of fear and rage welled up from his center, but stalled in his throat and came out as an impotent squeak.

"Very well. If that is your choice." He nodded to the other hooded men. "Leave him."

Hadrian whimpered. The small, pathetic sound was the best he could do. The pain from being suspended by his ruined shoulders was unbearable.

After suffering alone in the dark for some time, three men came in and started to remove the ropes from his wrists and ankles. Pain jagged through him as circulation returned to his hands. The men helped him off the table

Hadrian collapsed on the floor, too broken to stand. He tasted blood and realized his two front teeth were loose. He was dragged up stone stairs and thrown roughly into a cart, striking his head against the wood. Hooves clattered on cobblestones for a while, then stopped. The men pulled him out of the cart and carried him to a wooden platform., where they laid him on his back.

A priest stood before him, an over-sized bible in his hand. "Any last words, warlock, before we send you back to Satan, your master?"

Hadrian knew it would be pointless to try to speak, so he just shook his head.

A large piece of wood was placed on top of him. Footsteps, then something heavy was put on top of the wood. Then another, and another.

Hadrian struggled to breathe.

All around him, shadowy figures chanted, "Die, witch, die!"

Something seemed to be jabbing him in the shoulder. He couldn't see what it was. He didn't care – he just wanted the end to come. One person, a woman, did not chant like the others.

"Honey," the voice said. "Honey?"

Hadrian sat up with a gasp and a strangled sob.

"Are you okay?" Marti asked, resting her hand on his shoulder.

He wanted to hug her, hug Lulu, and maybe do a happy dance, at being woken up from his nightmare. He thought better of it – besides, his clothes were wet with his sweat and the dankness of the forest. His lower legs ached, and his pants stuck uncomfortably to his skin.

"I'm fine," he said. "It was just a dream."

"Looked like a doozy of a dream, if you ask me," Lulu said, shaking her head.

"It's over now." He shook his head, as if to chase the ghosts of the nightmare away. "I don't think I'll be going back to sleep any time soon – I'll stand watch while you two rest."

Marti frowned slightly and squeezed his shoulder. "Sometimes it helps to talk about bad dreams."

"I'm fine. I don't want to talk about it. Thanks, though."

"Well, if you change your mind, I'll just be over here. In the dirt. Leaning against the invisible wall."

He almost laughed. "I'll keep that in mind."

Nick was not asleep. At least, he didn't think so. He let his body relax and his eyes close, but his mind churned furiously. *How was Emily doing? Had she died while he was trapped in this crazy maze? Where were his kids? Were they alright?* He didn't trust Balcones' word that they were happily playing at the center of the labyrinth, and all he had to do to take them home was to find them. No, there would certainly be more to it, if they were even still alive.

He could hear Malik a few feet away, tossing and turning in the dirt, and he felt a flash of anger. *Just be quiet already!* But he knew that it wasn't really Malik keeping him awake. His whole world had come crashing down around his ears. His wife was clinging to life by her fingernails, or at least she was, last time he had been able to check on her. His kids were missing, and odds were they were dead. The only job he really wanted was denied him. He was trapped in a place that just couldn't possibly exist, but here it was. And to top it all off, there was no way to end this. He couldn't die. There would be no joyful family waiting to meet him in wherever it was that people went when they died. He was trapped here forever. Or maybe he was dead, after all. And he was in Hell.

"Nick?"

He raised his head. "Emily?"

"Of course! Who did you expect? McKenzi and the boys are at home with my mom. I've come to bring you back."

This couldn't be real. It was everything he wanted, handed to him on a silver platter. This could only be a trick.

"Em? I was sitting here thinking about us, trying to remember stuff. What was the name of that place we went to on our first date?"

She cocked her head. He had her.

"It was the Orange Penguin, of course. Perhaps your memory is a little fuzzy from the concussion you got when that dust head freaked out in the restaurant and started throwing stuff around."

Could it really be Emily? Impossible. And yet…how else could she have known?

"Come on, Nick. We have to go. They'll be back soon."

Nick sat up. "Who is 'they'?"

Emily looked down one of the maze paths. Fear pinched her face with its bloodless fingers. "Hurry! They're coming!"

Nick stood up. Instinct told him to run to her, leave this place. Logic told him it was a trap. And yet, how would an imposter know about their disastrous first date? He started toward the woman, his stride lengthening with every step.

She screamed. Nick started to run. But it was almost as if he was stuck in deep, sucking clay. It was a tremendous amount of work to move at all, and when he did, it was in slow motion, a quarter or less of his normal ability. Emily moved normally. So did the thing that was approaching her. Nick could not identify it. An iron helmet crowned its head and a misshapen jaw jutted beneath it. Clear slime trailed in strings from its jagged teeth. The creature wore a long cloak, and Nick caught glimpses of metal underneath, as if it was wearing armor. The thing reached for Emily, but instead of arms and hands, it had thick tentacles with clawed suckers.

"No!" Nick yelled, his voice, deepened and distorted by the slow motion. His legs pumped harder, but he moved no faster.

Emily screamed again as a tentacle twined around her arm. She pulled back, using her free hand to pry at the tentacle latched onto her arm. Another tentacle grabbed her free hand.

"Stop it! Let go!" she shouted.

Nick could not break free of the slow motion barrier. He grunted from the exertion, but he still felt like a mastodon in the La Brea tar pits watching its mate being set upon by dire wolves.

"Emily!" he screamed, his voice warping to a freakish depth.

A third tentacle snaked its way around her throat and tightened, strangling her. Her face reddened and her eyes bulged. She started making choking, gagging sounds in her futile struggle for air.

"No! Noooooo!" Nick shouted again, and tried even harder to run. He would never make it in time. As a police officer, he knew that it takes at least two minutes to strangle someone to death, but at the rate he was going, it might take him two hours to get to her.

Nick suddenly became aware that he was lying down, panting. He leapt to his feet, seeing no one but Malik.

"Where is she?" Nick yelled, his voice husky with fear.

"Who?"

"Emily! My wife. She was right there!" He pointed down the maze path.

"There has been no one here but us. I do not even know where Quinn has gone. He is supposed to be on watch duty."

Nick did not take Malik's word for it, and ran down the trail. He took the only possible route and turned right – straight into a dead end. There were no tracks or evidence that anyone had ever been there. His heart was still pounding, pumping adrenalin through his body. He slammed the flat of his hand into the invisible barrier with an exasperated growl.

Lulu did not want to sleep. She sagged against the barrier, hoping that if she went into a meditative state, her body could rest but her mind would stay alert. This place was custom-made for nightmares. She and Marti had only seen the monsters in the maze three times, but the entire day she'd felt a heaviness, as if something malevolent was stalking them unseen. Lulu supposed it could have been Balcones – he was surely observing them for his own entertainment. But this seemed closer, practically breathing down their necks.

And she felt she was flying blind. She was so used to Thutmose, her spirit guide, always being around her, but she could not sense him in this place. Even with Marti and Hunter there, she felt abandoned and alone. She wondered where Belinda was, and if she was alright.

Lulu hugged herself against the chill. Marti shifted a little, and her back touched Lulu's arm. The warmth was comforting. *Maybe I'm not so alone, after all.* But she didn't feel much better. There was still the sense of foreboding, that something sinister was lurking just out of sight, waiting for the right moment to strike.

Lulu took a deep breath, feeling the air flow into her lungs, expanding her belly. She held it for a moment, then released it. She took another deep breath, then another. On the fourth breath, she felt a rib snap. She clutched at her side and felt the jagged edge of bone under her papery skin. When she looked around, she was surprised to see that neither Marti nor Hunter was there. Had they snuck off around the corner to be together? And why not? They were both young.

Lulu tried to stand, but as soon as she put any weight on her leg, the lower bones shattered. It was true - she had fallen and she couldn't get up. The cheesy TV commercials about the elderly lady who fell and was saved by her medical alert necklace had always made her shake her head. But now that she was the helpless one on the floor, they seemed particularly poignant.

"Marti!" she called. "Hunter?"

There was no response. But worse still, when she clenched her jaw in frustration, her teeth crumbled and broke. She gasped and a whimper escaped from her throat. As she raised her hands to examine the destruction in her mouth, she noticed that her arms were wasted and thin, covered in age spots and crepey skin. Blue veins, with smaller red spidery children, bulged over her bony hands.

"No!" she shouted. "Marti! Marti, where are you?"

A wolf howled in the distance.

Okay, get a hold of yourself. You did not age thirty years in ten minutes. This has to be a dream. Wake up. Wake up!

Lulu gradually became aware that her tailbone was numb, and one of her feet was asleep. She opened her eyes, and found the Marti was still next to her, but she'd fallen over and was lying on the ground, clutching at something under her blouse. Although her facial muscles twitched a little, her breathing was deep and even – she was asleep. Hunter paced around in the deep twilight, seemingly examining the barrier between the path and the trees. Perhaps he was looking for a break in the wall.

She sighed, grateful that the horrors of old age had only been a dream. This time. She remembered her mother, though. How her mind had gone long before her body, and she's spent nearly two years in fear and confusion, recognizing no one, but afraid of the 'strangers' who surrounded her, waiting for her to shuffle off her deteriorating mortal coil. Lulu shuddered. There would be no more sleep for her tonight.

Chapter 24
Perchance to Dream

The trees off to Bruce's left shook as if something heavy was climbing through their canopies - he'd been tracking it for some time now. The dog looked up and sniffed. The branches stopped moving. There was a rasping, chitinous clicking, then eight beady green eyes glimmered in the deep shadows above him.

Bruce shifted into Quinn. "Phobetor?"

An enormous spider scrambled down the tree and stood in front of Quinn. He resumed his human form and crossed his arms, pouting. "What? Are you here to spoil my fun, too?"

"Of course not. I only want to find my friends and get out of this bloody maze. We've been tramping round it all day, and not had so much as a whiff of them." Quinn shook his head, then stopped. "What do you mean 'too?' Who else is trying to ruin your fun?"

Phobetor chuckled. "You've seen your friends several times. That's part of the jape – you see them, they see you, but neither group knows it." Then he frowned. "You know, when Balcones came to me, he said it was all a lark. Just because I am the god of nightmares doesn't mean I don't like a good laugh now and again. But now he's gone and invited some of my sisters, the Keres. And it's always the same, death and destruction, everywhere they go. Dead people don't dream, you know."

"Death and destruction? I thought Thanatos was the god of death."

Phobetor rolled his eyes. "Well of course he is. But he rules over the kind of death where you die in your sleep. Or have a massive coronary and go like that." He snapped his fingers. "The

Keres are all about murder and mayhem, and the bloodier the better."

Quinn scowled. "When are they arriving?"

Phobetor shrugged. "Any time now. For all I know, they're already here."

"Maybe we should turn the tables, and all escape before the Keres show up."

"Do you think if I knew a way out of here I'd still be hanging around, waiting for my crazy sisters to show up and spray blood and guts everywhere?"

"There has to be a way out."

"Sure there is. One of Balcones' rat holes that he uses to come and go."

Quinn cocked his head. *Tsch.* "I'm sure if we ask him nicely, he'll serve us a slap up tea and send everyone home."

"There's no need to get snarky. We're all in the same papyrela now – we might as well row together."

"There's a difference, though. You are immortal. Marti and Lulu are not. Balcones is only using them to get to me, so the worse he can make it for them, the happier he'll be." Quinn bit his lip. "What did you mean earlier that we'd seen each other, but didn't know it? Doesn't seem like Balcones' style to make them invisible when I could be watching them suffer."

"Oh, they're not invisible. Not at all. Besides the three of you, what have you seen in the maze?"

Quinn thought for a moment. "Living things? Black Annis and a sphynx."

"No. You've seen your friends. The older one appears to you as Black Annis, the younger as a sphynx. But they will run from you, because you look like monsters to them as well."

"Of course. I should have figured that out myself. So obvious, if you take a moment to think about it." One side of his mouth wrinkled into a demi-frown. Then his eyes widened. "I have an idea. Can you get me into Marti's – the younger one's – dreams?"

I leaned up against the invisible barrier that separated us from the sinister trees. Black and bare, were they all dead, or was it just winter in this awful place? I was so tired I could barely move, but of course, my brain wouldn't settle and let me sleep so I'd have some relief from the aching hunger that gnawed at my middle.

I knew Cassie was being well taken care of by my mother. *Does my baby miss me as much as I miss her? Mom must be worried sick – what must she be thinking, me up and disappearing into thin air?* While she'd shocked me by confessing to seeing ghosts, I wasn't sure she'd believe *this* story. I certainly wouldn't, if I hadn't lived it myself. Where was Quinn? Had he escaped Balcones, or was he stuck here, too? And then, of course, there's Hunter. What was Virginia thinking, dragging him into this? Lulu said she never thinks about anybody but herself, and I'm inclined to believe her. Also, had anyone bothered feeding my dog?

I watched Hunter pacing around for a little while before closing my eyes, hoping the "fake it 'til you make it" theory worked here. *What had gotten him so shaken up?* After seeing how well sleeping had gone for him, I was a little nervous about trying it. But I was too tired not to rest. As I squirmed around, trying to get comfortable, my hand fell on the prayer box pendant that was hidden under my shirt. Odin's tear. I still felt guilty over what happened to Halle, the Valkyrie. I wish there had been some other way, but if she hadn't given her life, then Nick would be dead. I'd certainly feel even worse about that, because it was all my fault he got involved in the first place. "Never forget," Odin said. Don't worry, Allfather, there's no chance of that.

After a while, I started to get that floaty feeling, where it seemed that my mind was separating form my body – it slept while my thoughts swirled around, slower and slower, until finally I just *was*. And then, I would fall asleep. Always happened. But as I floated there, staring at the infinite field of stars in my mind's eye, I felt something brush against my arm. Something with stiff, coarse hair. It made my skin crawl, and I snapped my head around to look at it.

There was nothing there. I thought I heard a faint rasping or clicking, but it could have been branches rubbing together. Then I noticed a door. Nothing else – no walls or floors – just a door floating in space. Light spilled out of the cracks around the frame. Was this some trick by Balcones? Didn't seem likely – I was already in his stupid maze – what else could he want? Besides, bright white light and demons don't often travel in the same circles.

It wasn't like I had anything better to do, so I opened it.

And I almost wished I hadn't. Behind the door was the place on the astral plane where Quinn and I had met for our nonphysical romantic encounters. They were sublimely beautiful and profoundly amazing, and couldn't happen again. Not if I wanted to protect my child and the rest of my family. I started to back out of the doorway when he called my name.

"Quinn, is that you?"

"I'm here. I've been trying to find you all day."

"Well, here I am. Are you okay?"

"For the moment. I don't have much time to talk, but I do have a plan. The only way I can think of to get out of here is to lure Balcones into the maze. Then we have to grab him and force him back through the portal. The best way to do that is if we all get to the center of the maze and wait. I'm sure he's set a trap there, so do nothing. Just wait for him to get mad enough to come to us."

"That sounds great. Except that we trudged around all day, looking for the center of the maze. We only found some monsters."

"Monsters? What did you see?"

"Well, there were three of them. A werewolf, a cyclops, and a huge scorpion."

Quinn laughed. "That's the trick. The monsters – they're me, Nick, and Malik. We've seen you, too. You look like Black Annis and a sphinx."

Marti shook her head. "I probably should have guessed that. But I would hate to have been wrong."

"I know." Quinn started to fade. "I have to get back. I think we have to work together to find the center. When you wake up, remember to find the monsters."

And then he faded into nothingness. Only the beautiful astral construction remained. A stream with a waterfall. Smell of plumerias and rain. Tropical flowers. Fantastic red, yellow, and blue birds. A canopied four poster bed. Intense green foliage. I sighed, backed up, and slammed the door.

When I woke up, Lulu and Hunter were sitting nearby, talking quietly. I yawned and stretched – a little stiff and sore, but more refreshed than I'd expected. My stomach growled loudly as I sat up. Lulu and Hunter both looked over. Dark circles underscored Lulu's eyes. Hunter's skin looked rough and grey, with dark stubble littering his jaw.

"It appears to be morning," I said, looking around. The mist was lighter than it had been before I went to sleep, anyway.

"You slept well, honey," Lulu said, a touch of jealousy in her voice.

Hunter glanced at Lulu, then back at me. "No bad dreams?"

That's an odd question. I rubbed the back of my neck, futilely trying to loosen the crick that made it hard to turn my head. "No, I don't think so. I don't really remember what I dreamed. Something about monsters in the maze, but I can't remember much about it. Didn't seem scary, though."

"Lucky you," Lulu said just loudly enough for me to hear her.

"You had bad dreams?" I asked her.

"Both of us," Hunter answered.

I nodded. What was I supposed to say? It wasn't like it was my fault. I tried to claw back the edge of the dream that had evaporated long before I woke up, but it was gone, leaving only ghostly fragments. *Monsters. Not scary. Maybe they were Muppets?* Nothing left to say about it. Best to change the subject. "What's the plan for today?"

"Plan?" Lulu echoed. "The plan is to get out of here. It's the execution we need to work on."

"If we're trying to get to the center of the maze, just following the wall won't work. That technique is only effective if you're trying to find an exit on an outer wall. Lulu said you tried drawing a line, but suddenly every intersection had lines."

"I didn't check *every* intersection, but yeah, the next couple of them had lines."

"Do you think it's possible that Nick and whomever he's with also used Trémaux's algorithm?"

"I might be able to tell you, if I knew what that was," I said.

"It's method for solving mazes that relies on drawing lines to mark the passages you've already visited. "

I looked at Lulu. "I suppose it's possible. Although we never saw them, not all day."

"You know what we need?" Lulu asked. "A bloodhound. And something for him to get the scent."

I laughed. "That'd be great, but…who has a bloodhound? Cú's got a great nose, but he's nowhere near here."

"Call him," Lulu replied.

"Why? There's no way he can hear me."

"Honey, you remember how he was able to attack Virginia's tulpa when nothing else could touch it? What if that means he can travel between dimensions? Because that's exactly where we are, isn't it? Trapped between dimensions?"

"Virginia's what?" Hunter asked.

"Long story short," Lulu said. "A tulpa is a thought-form, a mind energy creation. Virginia made one to prowl around the neighborhood to look for Marti."

I could tell from the expression on his face that didn't clarify things. But there wasn't time to explain right now. Maybe later. I closed my eyes. "Cú! Here boy! Come here, pup!" I said.

Nothing happened.

I tried again, a little louder, "Cú! Come!" I slapped the ground with my palms.

Still nothing. I felt my shoulders slump a little. "He's not coming." I stood up and dusted off my pants.

"I was so sure…" Lulu trailed off.

"Alright. Not trying to be rude, but can we please get back to the maze?" Hunter said.

I heard him before I saw him – the trilling yap of an excited puppy. He bounded out of the woods and jumped up to lick my face, his whole body wagging with excitement. "Cú!"

Hunter's mouth opened and closed a few times, but he didn't say anything.

"I knew it!" Lulu fairly cackled when she saw my puppy.

I picked the dog up, trying to calm him. That made it worse. I settled for trying to keep his tongue out of my mouth. "Okay, he's here. Now what?"

Quinn rolled his shoulders, hoping to alleviate at least some of the tight itchiness of his skin. He was going to need to spend some time in kelpie form soon, and for all of the dampness in the air, there wasn't so much as a puddle, much less a lake, to be found on the trail. As a kelpie, he breathed air, but without water to support his bulk, he'd slowly suffocate under his own weight on land.

"And you're sure it was Marti?" Nick asked, poking at the dirt with a soggy twig.

"Of course it was!" Phobetor snapped. "I don't make mistakes."

"And yet here you are, trapped like a rat in a maze," Malik replied, one eyebrow expertly arched.

A wash of pink momentarily colored the nightmare god's eternally pallid cheeks. "I-"

"Enough!" Quinn broke in. "We've enough problems as it is. The last thing we need is to tear each other apart. I have every reason to believe," he glanced at Nick, "reasons I won't go into, that it was actually Marti I spoke with. I think that we have to team up to get to the center, which is why Balcones has us looking like monsters to each other. Once we've found the heart of the maze, we'll need to lure Balcones in. I don't see any other way out but to grab him and force him back through a portal. I told Marti to look for the monsters – they were us. "

Phobetor crossed his arms. "I doubt she'll remember. You should have let me scare her."

Nick glared at him.

"People may or may not remember their pleasant dreams, but no one forgets their nightmares. I'm just saying."

Nick snarled, "Who gives you the right-"

"I am a god! I just used what's already in your head, and believe me, there was plenty to work with. Don't blame me for that."

"Seriously? All you gods are the same – self-important, entitled-" Malik broke in.

"Bloody hell!" Quinn shouted. "Get yourselves under control. You can have a comparative religion debate after we've got out of here. But right now we've got to find Marti and Lulu, rescue Nick's babies, and capture Balcones, if we can. All without springing whatever traps that blighter has set for us. And did I mention the bloody Keres are just about breathing down the back of our necks? If we're not out of here before they show up, we likely won't make it."

"Speak for yourself," Nick said, his voice dour.

"What's that supposed to mean, coming from a mortal?" Phobetor sneered.

Quinn shook his head. *I'd forgotten about that.* "It's complicated, but essentially, he was given the life force of a Valkyrie."

"I can't die," Nick added, shaking his head slightly.

"A Valkyrie, eh? They aren't all that different from the Keres," Phobetor said.

"The only similarity is that they both attend battles, seeking the dead and dying. That and they're immortal. There's almost no way to kill," Malik's eyes fell on Nick, and he trailed off. "...a Valkyrie." His eyes snapped to Quinn's. "Do you think Balcones knows this?"

Quinn turned nearly as ghastly pale as Phobetor. "I...don't *think* so."

"What difference does it make?" Nick asked, irritably.

"You've never seen a demon feed, have you?" Malik asked.

"No."

"Demons," Quinn said, "suck the life force out of their prey, pooling it with their own, and leaving nothing but a pile of dust behind. They're not immortal...but if they consumed the life force of an immortal..."

"Balcones would be unstoppable," Malik finished.

Three birdlike shadows slid out of the trees and raced across the ground. The raucous cawing of crows followed. The Keres had arrived.

I was cold, tired, and hungry. And, to be honest, extremely demoralized. It was hard to put one foot in front of the other, to try one more pathway, hoping for a different result than a dead end or a big loop. I was sick to death of being here and being away from Cassie. I was usually pretty good with puzzles, but this maze was kicking my butt. I'd utterly failed. If Hunter thought he could solve it, I was happy to let him have a try. Still, I resented being in a position where I needed rescuing. *Stupid Balcones.*

Cú had settled down to the point where he was flopped on his back, tongue lolling into the dirt. I suspect he'd been hoping for a belly rub, but fell asleep before that happened. I wasn't sure what we were going to do with him, especially in light of the fact that I'd considered changing his name to 'Mr. Underfoot.'

Crows cackled in the near distance, and I shuddered. There was something wrong about their cries. I didn't know what. Anger? Dissonance? Lulu must have sensed it, too, because she looked up and scanned the trees.

"What?" Hunter asked, seeing Lulu looking around. "It's just crows. Isn't it?"

Lulu shrugged. "Maybe. We should get moving, hon. We'll never find the way out just sitting here."

I stood up. Cú didn't stir – he was so deeply asleep he was snoring, so I scooped him up in my arms. He snuggled sleepily against my chest and went back to his nap.

"Why don't we try your method?" I asked Hunter. "Since ours clearly worked so well yesterday."

He nodded, and we started down the path.

It wasn't long before we got to a T intersection. "Left or right?" Hunter asked. He looked around for something to mark the trail with. I handed him the silver dagger from my backpack.

"Left," Lulu answered.

Hunter drew a line with an arrow, indicating our choice. We continued down the path, marking our turns. Some of them had lines when we arrived, and some of them didn't. That made me feel hopeful that perhaps Hunter was right – Quinn's group had made the marks, and it wasn't some infernal trick of the maze.

We'd travelled for perhaps half an hour, and Cú was getting heavy in my arms. I was ready to put him down before I dropped him. As we rounded a corner, I nearly crashed into Hunter, who had stopped dead in front of me.

"Monsters," he whispered.

I looked. It was the same three we'd seen the day before. "They don't seem to have seen us. Let's just retreat quietly."

"No. We'll have to fight them."

"What?" Lulu and I whispered together. "That's crazy," I added. For some reason, the ridiculous image of the monsters sitting down at a picnic with us flashed across my brain. I shook it off. That was going way too far.

I could hear the flapping of wings. *Caw! Caw! Caw!*

"No," Lulu said. "I…think…maybe he's right. We must kill them before they kill us."

"With what? Are you nuts?"

Hunter re-gripped the hilt of the dagger.

I gave an exasperated sigh and yanked one of the arrows out of my backpack. "Fine. Here's my weapon. Which one should I take on? The werewolf? It's at least six inches taller than me an outweighs me by what? A hundred pounds? Maybe the giant scorpion? His pincers are only what? Twice the length of this arrow? Three times? I'm sure that'll work out well. Should I leave the cyclops for you, or for Lulu?"

Hunter scowled at me. "They're monsters. They can't be talked to or reasoned with. What choice do we have?"

"Sometimes discretion is the better part of valor, hon," Lulu said. The glazed look from moments earlier had left her eyes.

A vein in Hunter's forehead throbbed.

The werewolf raised his arm and howled. *They'd seen us.*

Lulu grabbed Hunter's hand and started to drag him down the path, "Run, you fool!" she shouted. She didn't have to tell me twice.

"Marti!" Quinn shouted, raising his hand to wave. The sphynx and Black Annis turned and fled. Oddly enough, they'd been joined by a third creature – a spindly grey biped with over-large eyes – who was either debilitated or reluctant to move. Black Annis had to drag him, and the sphynx carried something black. It was about the size of a large house cat, and very wiggly.

"It doesn't look like she remembered her sweet dream," Phobetor said, smug grin on his face. "I hate to say 'I told you so.' Actually, no, I don't."

"Now what?" Nick snapped. "Chasing after them will just make it worse. Any more brilliant ideas?"

Quinn didn't like the glint in Malik's eyes when the djinn said, "That may be our only choice."

"I think we can outflank them," Quinn replied. "Malik, you and Nick keep going down this path. Phobetor and I will go back and take the trail that circles around. Hopefully, we'll catch them in the middle."

"Agreed," Malik replied.

Quinn turned and sprinted in the opposite direction, a pale and unhappy Phobetor trailing in his wake. "Keep up!" he shouted over his shoulder.

The path turned, then turned again. If they were lucky, Marti and company would have kept heading in the direction they took when they fled. It was possible that they would take the left turn instead of going straight, but it seemed unlikely to him – they were running in fear – and he was sure they'd take the path of least resistance. Of course, he wasn't sure what he'd do when he found them. Marti clearly didn't remember the dream.

A faint shadow, bird shaped, coursed along the dirt path, keeping pace with him. *Fantastic.* The last thing he needed was one of the war-mongering Keres sisters meddling in his plans. He glanced up as he ran, and caught a glimpse of a dark, winged shape wreathed in the perpetual mist of this place.

This cursed place! I spend so much of my life on helping these weak, pathetic humans.

There they were, just up ahead. He held up a hand. Phobetor stopped, panting. The trio ahead saw him and stopped. They tried to bolt in the other direction, but found themselves facing Nick and Malik.

"Now we've got them!" Quinn shouted, his voice throaty with battle lust. He moved forward slowly. Malik and Nick closed in from the other side.

Phobetor grabbed Quinn's arm and shook him.

Horrified, he stopped. Those weren't enemies. They were Marti, Lulu, and another human. *Did Nick and Malik have the same craving for combat and blood?*

Quinn's cohorts continued to press the group in the middle, pushing them unwillingly towards Phobetor and himself. The newest addition, the grey humanoid, carried a silver dagger, which he held in front of his midsection, daring anyone to approach.

Caw! Caw! Caw! One crow was answered by two others. Strident cries for bloodsport.

Again, Quinn reminded himself that these were friends, not foes. But he struggled to control the rage that was rising in his chest.

As the group got closer, he saw that the wriggling black thing held by the sphynx was a puppy. *Cú. How did he get here?* Had the new arrival brought him, or had he found his own way to Marti?

Nick charged the group.

"No!" Quinn screamed.

Nick kept coming.

Time dilated. Seconds took minutes to unfold. Cú leapt out of the sphynx's arms toward the trees. She turned and snatched at him, just catching the end of his tail as he soared through the invisible barrier. Black Annis grabbed Marti's arm with one hand, and the skin of the grey alien's back. They also started to pass through the barrier.

"Grab them!" Malik yelled.

Nick was closest, and he caught the knife hand of the grey creature, who'd been thrown off balance from being dragged by Lulu. Malik tried to capture the grey's other hand while he fought wildly.

"Don't use the knife. Don't give them blood. You'll only make it worse!" Phobetor shouted.

He and Quinn lurched into the melee.

"Go! Go!" Quinn ordered. "Through the wall! Now!"

Nick and Malik shifted from tugging to pushing, and the four of them tumbled in an angry heap into the forest on the other side of the barrier. The grey creature rolled as he hit the ground and leapt to its feet.

Nick tackled him and the two of them rolled from side to side, each trying to gain the advantage. Malik and Black Annis - no, not Black Annis; Lulu - circled each other warily. Quinn looked at the sphynx. Marti. She held a squirming Cú in her arms. He knew it was Marti. But all he saw was an enemy. He fought to tamp down the aggression that threatened to overwhelm him, and he panted with the strain, as if it were a physical battle. *Is that a tear on her cheek? What am I doing? I can't hurt Marti.*

Caw! Caw! Caw!

The awful screeching of the Keres tipped the balance, and he took one loping stride and leapt at Marti. She went sprawling and he scrabbled for her throat. Cú yelped as he skidded and rolled into the underbrush.

Marti struggled, but his weight pinned her to the rough ground. As his hands found her throat, his fingers got caught up in a chain around her neck. Angrily, he tugged at it. He felt the pendant that was attached to it – a locket or some such thing – give way. What felt like an electric shock shuddered through his body, and he was blinded by a flash of blue light.

Dammit! I'd hoped that getting through the barrier would at least buy us some time. But no, they had to grab onto Hunter and get pulled through with us. Now, here I stand, trying to face down a werewolf. Again. At least the last time, there had been a sliding glass door between us. And Quinn had my back. Now there was nothing but a little mist.

Cú wriggled furiously in my arms. Did he think he could take that thing on? *Don't be in such a hurry to be an hors d'oeuvre. You're staying right here with me.*

I glanced away from the werewolf's distorted canine face and saw that Hunter was rolling on the ground with the cyclops and Lulu was engaged with the scorpion. We were almost certainly going to die here in these dank woods. Memories I hadn't had a chance to make of all the things I'd miss seeing as Cassie grew up flashed through my head, and I felt a tear trickle out of my eye.

Crows squawked, and the werewolf lunged at me. I dropped Cú and heard him yelp as the monster crashed into me. I tried to get away, but the wolfman was too big. I looked into its deep red eyes as it grabbed me by the throat. Its breath smelled surprisingly of fish. It was almost as if I was observing the whole thing from just over my left shoulder – ridiculous, because I was on my back on the ground, for one thing. And yet, I calmly noted the stink of his breath and wondered if the thin, patchy hair on his snout was normal, or due to mange. Did werewolves even get mange? Random thoughts bubbled up, then drifted away as more appeared, crowding out the final seconds of my life.

I winced as the chain from my prayer box dug into my neck. The werewolf had gotten his fingers caught in it and jerked it hard. I heard it click, then I felt something small and icy fall onto my sternum.

Brilliant blue light flashed. I closed my eyes against the glare. The grief-hoarse voice of Odin whispered in my ear, "Never forget."

And I remembered.

I was catapulted into the astral love nest I'd shared with Quinn. But I wasn't really there – it was a memory. Quinn was there, telling me that the monsters in the maze were not really monsters at all, but him, Nick, and Malik. We had to work together. But how could this be? One of those three was in the middle of asphyxiating me. Was this memory real, or just hypoxia –final hallucinations as my oxygen-starved brain shut down? Still, it wasn't unpleasant, and I knew from experience that there were worse ways to die.

I had to close my eyes against the concentrated blue light that exploded out of the icy crystal on my chest. It engulfed everything like a chilly tide and blinded me.

The rough hands around my neck stopped squeezing, and I gasped for air. Something scrambled through the leaf litter, and I heard Cú's shrill whine. His paws shed dirt on my face as he clambered over me, barking and licking. His weight suddenly left me. I opened one eye just a sliver, and saw the blue light had gone. I waited another second or so, and opened my eyes.

I blinked, trying to adjust to dimness. Instead of a werewolf leaning over me, there was Quinn. He was trying to hold Cú back so he didn't trample my face. But the pup was just as happy to share the slobbery love with him. Quinn's face, however was ashen and anguished.

"I'm so sorry," he said. "I didn't want to hurt you. It was the Keres. They're driving everyone mad with fear and rage."

He stood, then helped me up. When his eyes fell on my throat, he closed them for a long moment and swallowed hard.

I looked away, on the pretext of searching for Odin's tear and returning it to the prayer box. I wanted to tell him everything was fine and it wasn't his fault. But I couldn't. He'd wanted to kill me. Even if he had been goaded into it by these Keres, whatever they were, surely he still had some volition, some control of his actions.

When I didn't answer, his eyes searched mine and he reached out to touch my face. I involuntarily pulled away.

His shoulders slumped a little and he said again, "I'm so sorry."

"I know," I replied. It killed me to pull away from him, but I what choice did I have? I should have listened to Lulu from the beginning – he was dangerous. Even though I wanted him more than ever, now.

Nick ran over to us. He reached out and put his hand on my shoulder. "Are you okay?"

No, not really. "I'm fine." Nick frowned slightly. Perhaps he knew I was lying. I held his eyes a moment longer, then looked for Lulu. She, Malik, Hunter, and some guy I didn't know were headed our way, looking only slightly the worse for wear. As they got closer, my mouth dropped open. *What? No way.* That's the weird guy from the street corner, who helped Balcones kidnap Lulu and me.

"Well, we're in the woods now," Lulu said. Her eyes lingered on the stranger.

"Did that flash mean the barrier dissolved, or is that something else?" Nick asked. He went over to the place we'd all entered and reached out toward the path. Nothing got in his way. He stepped out of the trees and onto the dirt. But when he tried to come back, he was blocked. Malik reached his hand out and pulled him through the barrier.

"Your question is answered," Malik said.

"Seems to be a one-way flow," Hunter commented. "As long as someone is on this side, we should be alright."

The man I didn't know grunted. "The rule doesn't seem to apply to my sisters," he said sourly. A large black feather fluttered down in front of us. "They get a pass on everything."

I looked up at the trees, but they were high up, and there was a lot of fog between us, so I didn't get a very good look at them.

"Let's just hold up a minute here. Who are you? Why did you help Balcones bring us here?"

"He did what?" Quinn and Nick asked in unison.

The man shifted he weight backwards and let out a deep sigh. "Phobetor. My name is Phobetor. Perhaps you've heard of me?" He ignored Nick and Quinn.

Who does this guy think he is? "No, I haven't. Why are you helping Balcones?"

His shoulders drooped. "Education clearly isn't what it used to be. *I* am the god of nightmares." He reached out towards me, but instead of a hand it was a clawed spider foot.

"Aaaah," I said jumping back. In the blink of an eye, his hand was normal again. It happened so quickly that I wasn't sure anyone else saw it. I wasn't even one hundred percent sure I'd seen it.

"Yes," he said. "I did help Balcones capture you and your friend, but it's not what you think. I'm just as much a victim as you are."

Lulu snorted.

"It's true," he continued. "Balcones approached me, 'Let's go out for a glass of mead – I have a business proposition I'd like to discuss,' he said. Just because I'm a god doesn't mean I can't try new things, now does it?"

I didn't answer, just shrugged.

"So I went with him. Thought it might be a lark, a bit of fun, you know?"

"Kidnapping is a bit of fun?" Lulu asked, her hands on her hips.

"Did I mention I am the God of *Nightmares*?" he shot back.

Nick jumped in. "You keep saying you're a god, so why can't you get us out of here?"

Malik snickered. Phobetor's face darkened and his eyes glinted with anger.

"And what's with the harpies?" Nick continued. "They don't—"

"Shhhh!" Phobetor's eyes widened. "Do not insult the Keres – they hate the harpies! You'll bring them down on our heads right now."

He looked up into the trees. Everyone else did, too. There didn't seem to be any movement above us.

"Enough! Regardless of what the Keres decide to do," Quinn said, "we need to find our way to the center of the maze. I think that's our best option."

"What if we have the dog lead us through one of the outer walls? He seems to be able to go through just fine," Hunter said.

"I'm not going to just walk out of here without my kids," Nick growled.

"And we do not know what is on the other side of the wall. If we cross through the barrier randomly, there is no means of predicting where we would end up. It could be worse than this, much worse," Malik said.

I watched Lulu sit down, back against one of the twisted trees. She closed her eyes and put her hands on one of her knees. *Wish I had some ibuprofen for you, my friend.*

Quinn rubbed his forehead, as if he could massage ideas out of his prefrontal cortex. "Phoebetor, you've been exploring the maze – do you have any insight on how to get to the center?"

"Yes. There is a small stream that flows through the heart of the maze. If we can find the stream and follow it, we can locate the center."

Quinn turned to Cú, who was sprawled out by my leg. He said something to my pup in a language that I was nowhere close to understanding. It was like a song, but instead of musical notes, it was composed of nature sounds. Cú seemed to know exactly what Quinn wanted, because he jumped up and started yapping before he trotted off into the trees. Quinn hurried after him.

"Don't let him get lost!" I called after him. As if our whole sad group was anything but lost.

Phobetor and Malik hurried to catch up to Quinn. Nick and I helped Lulu up, while Hunter awkwardly supervised. Once Lulu was on her feet, Hunter ran ahead to keep the others in sight. Nick, Lulu and I followed after him. In a stunning display of grace and skill, I tripped over a root and would have done a faceplant into the leaf litter if Nick hadn't caught me. I blamed my lack of coordination on low blood sugar.

"Thanks," I said.

He just nodded. His eyes were hard and his jaw clenched. He looked about as grim as I'd ever seen anyone look, and it scared me. I didn't think he would try to hurt me, but then again, I didn't think Quinn would try to kill me, and that had only just happened. It may well be the Keres, but outside influence or no, I still would have been dead and Cassie would still have been an orphan.

There was a shuddering in the branches above us. Unquiet wings beat the air, and the three of us looked up to see what fresh hell was headed our way.

She, and I only called her that because her torn, bloodstained dress caught the breeze from her wings and intermittently exposed her large and withered breasts, descended slowly from the canopy, fog swirling at the tips of her black wings.

Fangs, like a saber-toothed cat, protruded from wide mouth, and her eyes were all white, like an ancient Greek sculpture.

Nick stepped in front of me as this thing reached out for us with hands that were more like eagles' claws than human appendages.

Lulu bent and scooped up a handful of dirt and rotting leaves. "Get out of here!" *Tsssst! Tsssst!* She threw the dirt at the face of the Kere, who backed off some, but didn't leave.

I wasn't entirely sure if she grinned or just bared her teeth. I expect both of those expressions looked pretty much the same on her.

Lulu pulled a mini-Maglite flashlight out of her pocket and raised it toward the intruder. The creature put up her arms to shield her eyes, then hissed and returned to the branches.

"We need to hurry," I said, picking up my pace.

The Keres squabbled in the limbs above, out of our sight.

"She's right," Nick added, then took Lulu by the wrist. We'd just broken into a jog when Hunter ran towards us.

"They've found the stream. This way!"

Lulu was limping, and since Hunter was here to guide us, we slowed our pace from a trot to a fast walk. It didn't take long to reach the others.

Quinn looked up when we arrived, but turned his head and said nothing. He may as well have shoved me away from him. I bit my lip, hard, to cause one pain to distract myself from another pain. It was better this way, at least safer, anyway, even if I hated it.

Black roots tangled across each other, twining together and plunging into the murky water. The current was fast, and white foam collected in some of the denser clumps of roots. It was impossible to tell how deep the water was, and the channel was too wide to jump across. The thought of trying to wade that stream filled me with a sense of foreboding. It was easy to imagine getting a foot stuck in the knotted roots and drowning, or some huge predator lurking in the gloom, ready to snap its toothy jaws shut on the first appendage that got near it.

No one else seemed eager to go too near the edge of the water, either.

"Should we try to cross it?" Lulu asked.

Quinn shook his head. "No. The water's moving too fast. Besides, these things are often enchanted – we'd best not touch the water unless we absolutely have to. Let's just follow it for now."

We stumbled along the root-covered bank, talking very little. Hard to tell if it was exhaustion, hunger, or the miasmic vapor of the water next to us that weighed down our tongues. I don't know how long we walked – an hour and a half, perhaps two. I couldn't go any further. The blisters that had started on my pinky toes yesterday had swelled and ruptured. Now blood was seeping through the sides of my tennies. Each step hurt more than the last. We came to a fallen tree – the perfect height for a makeshift bench.

"Can we take a break? I really need to sit down for a minute," I said, sitting down.

"The more breaks we take, the longer it will be before we get to the center," Nick said, irritated.

"I really need to sit," I said, holding one red-stained shoe up off the ground. He winced, then sighed with resignation.

"I, too, would like a break," Malik joined in.

"Fine. Five minutes," Quinn replied. He took a step towards us and opened his mouth like he was going to say something, but he turned and walked into the trees. Phobetor went with him.

"I wish I had my purse – I have a little first aid kit in there," Lulu said.

"I wish I had some ibuprofen," I said running my hands through my hair. I was starting to think sitting down had been a mistake – my feet throbbed against my shoes. Even so, I didn't want to take them off – I didn't relish the thought of peeling my sock off of my raw skin.

Hunter stared after Quinn and Phobetor for a moment. He took off his shirt (which was a pleasant change of scenery) and used his pocket knife to make some holes where the long sleeves joined the shoulder. Then he ripped the sleeves off.

"I don't have any plasters, either, but I think taking your shoes off would be a good start. That raw skin will just get worse inside your damp shoes." He fished around in his pants pocket. "I do have these." He pulled out a pocket pack of tissues.

He knelt in front of me and took off one of my bloody shoes. I winced as he touched the sock. He pulled it off far faster than I expected, but I couldn't help but cringe when the dank cold air hit my wound. His hands were gentle as he packed the swollen and bloody toes in tissue, then wrapped my foot in his torn-off sleeve. *Shame about the girlfriend. And one who I knew from way back, to boot.* He started on the other foot. I started to cry. I couldn't help it. I missed Cassie so much, and I'd all but lost hope that we'd ever get out of this miserable place.

Quinn and Phobetor returned from the trees, carrying a big stick. Phobetor brought it over to me.

"It's not much of a walking stick, but it's the best we could find on short notice," he said.

"Thanks."

Quinn and Nick stood together, a little way from the rest of us, obviously eager to get back on the trail. If Quinn was jealous of Hunter's attention to me, he didn't show it. Was it self-control or just that he'd never really cared anyway? When Hunter finished with my foot, I thanked him and stood up. It wasn't the most comfortable pair of shoes I'd ever had, but the pain was now bearable. I must have looked like a medieval beggar - filthy, with my feet wrapped in rags and my shoes tied together and slung over one shoulder. It didn't matter that Quinn was off limits and Hunter had a girlfriend – no one was going to look at me in this state and think romance. *Just as well.* I felt bad that Cú had to walk, but there was no way I could carry him now.

We carried on for about another two miles, or maybe it just felt that way.

"Look!" Lulu said. "Is that the central wall? Why does it have a wall? None of the rest of the maze did."

"It is definitely a wall," Malik said. "Unknown if it is the central boundary."

Quinn held up a hand to stop us. "We have no idea what is inside, if that really is the center. There's been no sign of the Keres since early this morning, and it's a safe bet that they're up to something. Marti, since you're incapacitated, and we might be met with force at the center of the maze, why don't you stay behind so you can pull us back out through the wall if need be."

I nodded. I wasn't going to be much use to anyone, anyway, given the state I was in.

"I'll go in first to do recon," Nick said.

"Agreed," Quinn replied.

We approached the wall as quietly as a group of ragged travelers could. That is to say, not very. We stopped and Nick put his ear to the damp grey limestone to listen – and almost went halfway through.

"I'll spot you," Hunter said, "Pull you back through when you're done."

"Sure." Nick cautiously put his hands and face against the stone and eased himself through the wall. Hunter pushed his own face into the center. I thought I heard a crash, and searched the trees for the Keres. Nothing.

In less than five minutes, Hunter pulled Nick back into our space.

He shook his head, dejected. "The only thing in there was a stupid glass ball on a pedestal."

I knew how disappointed he must be to not have found his kids. I was disappointed, too.

The ground started to shake beneath us. Bare tree branches rattled and clashed against each other, and twigs rained down.

Quinn looked up. "Nick? What did you do?"

Chapter 25
Guardians

I didn't do anything," Nick snapped.

He glared as Quinn held his gaze. "There was a crash. We all heard it."

Nick's eyes blazed in silence for a few more seconds. "Fine. I kicked the pedestal. It fell. The glass broke. Satisfied?"

The shaking grew worse, and the ground started to make a deep, growling rumble that chilled me to my very core. Fissures snaked through the wall in front of us. I sat down so I wouldn't fall over.

As suddenly as it started, the temblor stopped.

Hunter glanced around. "Is that good?"

Malik and Lulu answered at once: "No."

Quinn's hands were shaking as he snarled at Nick, "You weren't supposed to touch anything. No one was —"

The stone wall exploded.

Nick tackled Lulu before she was hit in the face by a cantaloupe-sized chunk of rock. Cú and I scrambled behind a tree. Stone fragments ricocheted off trees and splashed into the stream.

"This is outrageous!" Phobetor complained from behind a nearby oak. "Balcones never said anything about —"

"Shut up!" Malik hissed.

Where is Quinn? I peered around the tree, but couldn't see him anywhere.

White limestone dust hung like smog in the air. Three enormous creatures stepped out of the rubble, head and shoulders above the surrounding trees. Their lumpy skin was greenish-grey, and while mostly human-shaped, they reminded me of walking rock slides.

"Trolls," muttered Malik. "I hate trolls."

I didn't think there were a lot of bridges these things would fit under.

The troll in the center, who was slightly taller than the other two, swung his knotty club and roared. It was loud enough to hurt my ears, and it sounded like boulders tumbling and sliding against each other.

My pulse pounded in my throat as adrenalin surged through my body. Flight was looking a lot better than fight. The trolls were stiff and slow-moving – if we ran now, they'd never catch us.

"Come on!" I yelled, standing up with Cú tucked like a loaf under my arm. "Let's go!" I glanced around at the others. *Where is Quinn?*

We started to run pell-mell through the trees. I looked over my shoulder to reassure myself of the growing gap between us and them, but I stopped to stare instead. One by one, the trolls changed from slow-moving giants to wolves that covered the ground in huge loping bounds that we had no hope of outrunning.

One of them yelped. A large reptilian head on a long neck erupted from the water and snatched the pony-sized canid mid-stride as it galloped along the stream bank. They both disappeared into the murk, and the water frothed white with the underwater struggle. Then it went still. A few tufts of canine hair floated to the surface and were carried down the stream.

Well, at least I knew where Quinn was.

The troll-wolves now seemed confused. They didn't dare to go near the bank, but they stood on their hind legs and craned their necks at the water, presumably looking for signs of their lost companion. The pair went back on all fours before they raised their heads and long, shrill howls shuddered out of them.

But what scared me were the answering calls.

They sounded far away, but I'd seen how fast those monster wolves could run.

Nick frowned. "They're calling for reinforcements."

Hunter eyed the trees, their tops shrouded in thick mist. "You think they can climb?"

Malik looked at him as if he had just asked if the moon was made of green cheese. "They are mountain trolls. They can shapeshift into anything they wish."

"Aren't the Keres up there somewhere, anyway?" I asked.

Lulu looked pensive. "What about the stream? The trolls won't go near it – could we swim to the center?"

Nick ran his hand through his hair. "I'm not sure there's even a point to that now."

"Did you fail to notice there's a monster in the water?" Hunter asked.

"That, um," *he isn't really going to believe me, is he?* "is Quinn."

"I'm sorry?"

"That is the natural form of Quinn," Malik said. "Were you not aware he was a kelpie?"

Hunter opened his mouth, then shut it again.

"Hey!" Nick shouted. "Plan now, argue later. We're about to be overrun."

The wolf-trolls had started edging closer.

"Get to the water," Lulu said.

That backed them off, although Hunter shifted uncomfortably and kept looking into the stream. I could see something large and dark beneath the surface, and I hoped it was Quinn.

"There may be portals at the center," Malik said. "We may find less danger in entering an unknown portal than we face here."

"He's probably right," Lulu said.

I caught sight of movement in my peripheral vision and whipped my head towards it. The black, slick-skinned head that rose out of the water had a mouth large enough to bite me in half. Its eyes were black from edge to edge. If that wasn't Quinn, we were in real trouble. It reminded me of a Komodo dragon, and I wondered if kelpies also had a toxic bite. I didn't want to find out.

We eased past the trolls, who snarled at us, then picked up speed as we headed towards the remains of the central portion of the maze.

The round center of the maze was surrounded by a wall, with the break where the maze path entered the interior. Only about half of that was still standing, the side furthest from us. The wall closest to us had been smashed by the mountain trolls, and was nothing but scattered rubble.

In the center, near the stream, lay the broken pedestal and shattered gazing sphere. Hunter seemed drawn towards it, and he picked up a piece of glass. He looked like he'd been zapped by a heavy static charge. I thought he might have cut himself, but I saw no blood.

"What now?" Phobetor said, over-loudly.

Hunter threw the glass down. "We have to get out of here!"

Caw! Caw! Caw!

The Keres fluttered down from their hiding place, blocking the maze path. The two trolls had come up to the broken wall quickly and silently as wolves, then shifted back into their giant stony selves. At least a dozen wolves lurked at the edges of the trees. Whether they were actual wolves or trolls, I couldn't tell. Still, they would not approach the stream, where death, in the form of Quinn, lurked.

Balcones stepped through a portal and appeared directly in front of us, shaking his head. "It's so hard to find good help. If you want something done right, you have to do it yourself."

He turned to Phobetor. "You. You were supposed to keep them awake and off balance, and here I find you strolling around with them like you're all best of friends." He shook his head. "Must be true what they say – 'Never send a god to do a demon's job.'"

Phobetor's eyes glowed green, but he fumed in silence. The Keres shrieked and screeched to each other, and I felt anger wash over me like acid rain. This was all Quinn's fault. If it wasn't for him, I'd be home with Cassie right now. My jaw clenched as I turned towards the stream, and I felt my hands curling into fists.

Phobetor's body twisted and warped, and he took the form of a huge spider. He scuttled up into the trees and vanished into the mist.

"Coward," I spat.

I turned to Lulu. Her eyes were huge with fear, and I felt even angrier. One of the trolls raised its arms in the air and roared. The wargs in the forest began to wail, deep, throaty howls of rage.

Bring it. If we're going to die in this wretched place, let's get on with it. Maybe we can take some with us.

"Where is that cursed kelpie?" Balcones asked, looking around. I want him to have a front row seat as his friends are torn to shreds."

His eyes fell on Cú, who sat at my feet. "Pathetic," Balcones sneered. "This is the best MAMIC has to offer? Their standards have fallen over the years." He took a step forward and reached out his hand towards my puppy.

Two things happened simultaneously, so I'm a little fuzzy on some of the details. Out of my peripheral vision, I saw something grey fall out of the trees and land on the Keres. They began to shriek and yell as they were caught in a net of rope-sized spider web and pulled up into the canopy.

In front of me, Cú suddenly grew to the size of a bull. Balcones took a step back. So did I. Cú's ears flattened against his head, and a deep snarl rumbled through his body. It made the hair on the back of my neck stand up, and I knew he was on my team. I was behind him and a little to the side, so I couldn't be sure, but it looked like his eyes were glowing red.

Balcones muttered something that I assumed was cursing, but it was not in any language I knew. I had a sudden appreciation of Quinn's gift to Cassie and me - a silly little puppy that could turn in an instant into a fearsome protector. Perhaps I'd underestimated how much Quinn cared about us.

One of the wargs stalked into the heart of the maze. His yellow eyes were bright against his charcoal fur. "Balcones," he said in a deep, raspy voice. "You lied to us."

"I most certainly did not," the demon sputtered.

I looked at Malik, who shrugged. Lulu stayed close to Nick and Hunter. Clearly, none of them wanted to get close to the huge growling beast that Cú had suddenly become, even if he was keeping Balcones at bay.

The warg bared his teeth. "You told us that there would be great carnage, and enough fallen humans for us gorge upon. I see only five, and one of them has hardly any meat on its bones." The wolf eyed Malik. "That is barely enough for my mate and I, much less the entire pack."

Yellow eyes, too many to count, glowed between the gnarled trees. I shuddered. So many sharp teeth beneath those eyes. They could easily overwhelm us, Quinn and Cú notwithstanding. If Balcones was going to have a falling out with the wargs, the last place I wanted to be was in the middle of it, especially if we might still be on the menu. The atmosphere felt spring-loaded, as if any movement would set off the trap.

Movement to my left as Nick charged toward Balcones. "Where are they? Where are my kids?" he roared. "We got to the center of the maze. Give. Them. Back."

Balcones chuckled, and the angry warg lunged at Nick. Its teeth raked Nick's arm as Cú threw himself at the beast, sending it sprawling. It got ungracefully back on its feet and snarled, but it backed away, tail tucked between its legs. I could hardly blame it – Cú was almost three times its size.

As the green Valkyrie fire crackled down Nick's arm, healing the gashes left by the warg, Balcones' eyes started to glow and his mouth opened in an awful grin. He strode toward Nick.

"No!" Malik shouted. "Nick, run!"

Nick just stood there. Did he think he had a shot at Balcones?

Cú wheeled around from where he had vanquished the warg, but he wouldn't reach Balcones before Balcones reached Nick.

Water spewed from the stream as Quinn's monstrous kelpie head shot out and grabbed the back of Nick's shirt, pulling him into the water.

Balcones howled with anger. "Get him!"

The mountain trolls both roared and the earth shook as the one with the club smashed it against the ground. They lumbered toward us.

The wargs, however, melted like ghosts into the forest.

"Get in the water! Go! Go!" yelled Lulu.

We turned and pelted towards the stream. "Cú! Come!" I shouted over my shoulder.

"I cannot swim!" Malik shouted.

Hunter grabbed him by the arm as he jumped into the water, dragging the djinn with him. Lulu and I were close behind. Cú loped up, easily catching us. We didn't have time to stop and dive, we just leaped off the bank into the dark water. I had no idea how deep it was, and I sucked in a deep breath as my feet left the ground.

Instead of splashing over my head into the murk, I landed very comfortably on something large and slick. The first thing I thought was 'dolphin,' but that would have been ridiculous.

It was Quinn.

In kelpie form, his body was about as long as a Chevy Suburban, but not as wide. Nick dangled from Quinn's teeth, swearing furiously, as Quinn carefully swung him over to his own back. It seemed that the kelpie expected us all to ride him down the stream, like some bizarre amusement park boat. While we were trying to scramble into position, Cú leaped off the bank to join us. *He's going to knock all of us into the water, and maybe even sink Quinn.* But as he jumped, he shrank from gargantuan shaggy dog to little smooth puppy. Hunter caught him and handed him to me. Lulu was still draped across Quinn's back between Hunter and I when he started to move, but we were all mostly in place.

Balcones ran along the bank, but even weighed down, Quinn cut through the water like a motorboat, his powerful flippers propelling us along fast enough to churn the water up onto the banks in a froth.

We had to hold on tight as Quinn ducked under the still-standing section of wall that had passed over the stream. Balcones cursed and shouted behind us. The trolls roared with him. But every beat of Quinn's leathery paddles put that much more distance between us and them.

We had escaped. Sort of. We were still in Balcones' maze, and not sure where we were headed, other than downstream. But it was better than nothing. My only regret was that we didn't have Nick's kids with us.

I shivered. We were traveling fast, but I didn't think we were going fast enough to make me feel so cold. I didn't want to completely change my balance, but something wasn't right. My skin felt tight and painfully cold, especially around my throat and chest. I raised one hand to my sternum. The water on my skin and my wet clothes had frozen. I held the prayer box away from my throat and noticed that icicles hung from it. *That's odd.*

While I didn't I relax and enjoy this river cruise from hell, at least Balcones and the mountain trolls weren't breathing down the backs of our necks. The root-twined banks and bare trees could have well been a video loop, but subtly at first, the banks began to rise around us, as if the stream had somehow cut its way through a low hill. The bones of the hill were a dull grey rock that failed to glisten even where the water lapped up against it. Still, I couldn't help but hope that this change in scenery meant something. Different had to be good, right?

"Sharks!" Malik screamed.

No way. I turned to look. Sure enough, two sets of black dorsal fins and tails, single file, rushed towards us. They were huge, maybe even larger than Quinn. And they were gaining.

Hunter had also turned to look. "We have to get out of the water!"

Quinn thrashed his thick tail and added some speed, but not enough. They were still catching up.

"Sandbar. Up ahead!" Hunter yelled.

As the stream curved a little, there was a pile of sand flattened against the bank. The two problems with the sandbar were that one, the bank stream overhung it – it would be difficult at best to scramble up it; and two, if we didn't get up the bank, we'd be trapped on a narrow sandbar between two huge sharks and a rocky wall at least twice my height. Those brutes could easily beach and grab us. I watched in morbid fascination as the sharks steadily closed on us.

Quinn barely slowed when he hit the sandbar. We were all launched onto it, and he shifted into his human form before we'd regained our balance. The lead shark opened its mouth as it got closer. Its teeth were probably each the size of my hand. We had almost made it out. I held Cú tighter and looked around at my companions – Malik standing apart, resolute; Hunter trying to pull his foot out of the sucking mud at the edge of the sandbar; Nick and Quinn moving towards me. The shark started to rise out of the water, rearing back for the kill. One last glance at Lulu. Tears streamed down her cheeks.

And then I knew what to do.

I yanked the prayer box hard, breaking the chain, then I threw it into the water in front of the shark. At the touch of Odin's Tear, ice crackled and groaned as it snaked up and around the sharks, trapping them fast as the stream solidified. They struggled, though, and they were huge.

"Everybody off the bank!" I shouted. "I don't know how long the ice will hold."

Nick and Hunter lifted Lulu, then Malik, and me up so we could struggle over the edge of the step bank.

Quinn shifted back to his kelpie shape, and awkward on dry land, and used his head, crane-like to lift Nick and Phobetor up to join the rest of us. The ice holding the sharks began to crack. Shards of it started to calve off. Only Hunter and Quinn remained on the sandbar.

Quinn lifted Hunter up, and as soon as his feet touched the ground, I shouted, "Grab Quinn's neck! Grab his neck!"

A huge slab of ice crashed from the head of the second shark and it was able to wriggle, churning the ice into slush.

Uncertainly, Hunter put his arms around Quinn's neck. I grabbed Hunter from behind and pulled back. Quinn shifted into Bruce, and the three of us toppled over into the moldering leaf litter. Before I'd even gotten into position to stand up, Quinn was already in human shape and on his feet.

"Those aren't sharks – they're trolls." He reached out to help me up, and I felt the familiar electricity of his touch. There was so much I needed to tell him. But it would have to wait. He said something to Cú that I didn't understand, and the pup got bigger – perhaps Great Dane size, and started sniffing the air. He turned slightly right and headed away from the stream. We trotted after him. I kept looking over my shoulder, knowing the trolls would be after us as soon as they freed themselves from the ice.

We kept on jogging through the woods after Cú. Sometimes we stopped while the dog paused to re-calibrate his course. But these breaks were never for long. Between my bloody feet and Lulu's sore knee, she and I struggled to keep up. We had just started up again when there was a crash.

"Ow!" followed by some swear words from Lulu.

"What's wrong?" I asked.

"I think I've broken my ankle," she replied through gritted teeth.

I knelt beside her. It looked bad – it was swelling rapidly and was already starting to discolor. "Can you rotate it?"

A sharp intake of breath. "No."

I looked at Nick. "Go find me some sticks, at least half an inch in diameter."

A shadow slid over us.

"We're out of time. They're coming!" Malik yelled.

Quinn shifted into his horse form and Nick and Hunter heaved Lulu onto his back.

"Go, Cú!" I said, hoping that he understood me as well as he understood Quinn.

The dog loped off and we ran after him. I nearly fell over as I turned my head in time to see two hawks transform into wolves as they swooped towards the ground. "Faster!" I shouted.

Cú was headed straight for a particularly gnarled tree. *What are you doing? Move!* He was aimed dead-center and would crash headlong into it in the next stride.

Instead, he disappeared.

Quinn and Lulu followed close behind him, then Malik. Hunter was next and Nick and I brought up the rear. The wolf-trolls galloped faster.

I tried to go faster as well, but I ended up stumbling and getting my shirt caught on a branch. Frantically, I pulled on the stick, trying to snap it, but it was too thick. I could hear the footfalls of the wolves, and I froze, paralyzed by fear and mesmerized by their ferocious beauty. Something yanked me upward, and I heard fabric tear.

Quinn had snatched me off the ground and was sprinting the ten yards or so to the tree. The panting of the troll-wolves was all I could hear. One of them leaped for us as we got to the tree. Quinn turned and threw himself at the trunk. I cried out as a hot mouth closed on my foot and fangs scraped off the rag bandage.

But a taste of my blood and one of Hunter's shirtsleeves were all the troll-wolf got.

Quinn and I landed in a heap on the other side of the tree. But we were in a completely different place – the tree was a portal. Malik stood up and chanted something. Was he sealing it against the tolls?

Quinn's face was inches from mine. I kissed him. When I pulled away, I said, "I owe you an apology. The Keres. I didn't understand how strong they were–"

He kissed me.

"Uh-hum." Nick cleared his throat. Twice.

Quinn pulled away, then he got up and helped me to my feet. I took a few disoriented steps.

"What the hell?" Hunter asked, looking around.

There was nothing but pale blue light – no ceiling, walls, or floor. It was hard to tell which way we were going, or if we were going anywhere at all.

"This is a shortcut," said Malik. "You might think of it as a wormhole."

Lulu held onto Nick to keep her balance. "Where does it go?" she asked.

"Good question," Quinn answered. "Let's find out." His voice sounded flat and dimensionless, as if it came from an anechoic chamber. It made me not want to talk.

He shifted into a horse again so that he could carry Lulu. We followed Cú, who seemed to know exactly where he was going. After a while, he barked and wagged his tail.

"We're back at your house, Marti," Malik said. "That's the where. I'm not sure about the 'when,' though."

"What is that supposed to mean?" Nick asked. Hunter nodded, as if he had the same question.

"Time is relative to the dimension you are occupying," Malik said. "It doesn't usually line up with the time flow in other dimensions. It may be that you visit Faery and while you are there, it seems like you were there seven days, but when you get back, you find seven years have passed. Or perhaps you return three days before you left."

Nick frowned.

"Time is not as linear as most people believe it to be," Malik added.

"Let's just take a peek and see when we are," I said. I wanted to see Cassie so badly I could taste it.

We stepped out of the blue light into my back yard. I peered through the kitchen window and could see that Mom and Dad were watching TV in my living room. That's where Lulu and I had left them when Balcones grabbed us. I could see the clock on the microwave, and we'd only been gone half an hour or so.

Nick and Hunter helped Lulu off of Quinn, and he shifted into human form. Cú was back to pup size.

"We've got to get Lulu to the doctor," I said.

"I'll take her," Nick said. "I'm going to the hospital to see Emily, anyway."

"I'll come by a little later." I felt a surge of guilt. I was getting to go home to my baby, and he wasn't. Just the thought of never seeing the twins or McKenzi brought tears to my eyes.

"We'll find your kids," Quinn said.

"Yeah. I'm sure that's your top priority," Nick replied.

Malik started to say something, but Quinn raised his hand. "Now that Balcones knows you've got a non-human healing ability, he may or may not guess what it really is. He will be after you, though, to find out, and he's got the perfect bait." He took a deep breath and let it out. "It's very rare for a human to be on an MIT, but under the circumstances, I think it might be best for everybody if you joined my team. Temporarily, of course, until your children are recovered. I know you want Balcones captured or dead at least as much as I do."

Nick nodded. "Temporarily. But only because you know more about all this demon/supernatural stuff than I do. As soon as my kids are home, I'm done."

Lulu was trying to stifle a groan, but wasn't quite successful.

"Here," Hunter said. "Let me help you." He supported her as she hobbled over to the back porch. "Nick, you should probably go get your car."

Nick grunted and left.

"I don't understand anything that just happened," Hunter said. I wasn't sure if he was talking to me or to Quinn and Malik.

"Would you like to forget it?" Malik asked.

Hunter thought for a moment, then shook his head. "No. I don't think I would. I just want to figure it out."

"Malik? Why don't you go with Hunter and answer his questions?" Quinn said.

The djinn looked askance to the sky, not hiding his displeasure at the assignment, but he said, "Very well then. Shall we go?"

Quinn turned to me and brushed a wisp of hair from my cheek. "You're still a target. So is Nick, now. I understand if you don't want me around, but I can't just leave you unprotected. We need to –"

I kissed him, not a deep, longing kiss, just enough to make him stop. "We'll talk later. Right now, I need to see my family."

He stood forlornly in the back yard.

"Well, don't just stand there. Come inside."

Bonus Material

Foundling

Afractious gust of autumn wind ran chilly fingers down Etienne's back, but his stone skin was immune to such things – hot, cold, wet, dry, it was all the same to him. He perched on a flying buttress and looked out over the darkened city of Paris. Lightning from a distant storm flickered through the thunderheads, momentarily changing them from grey to orange.

He was almost too old for his mother to tuck in at night, but he loved the stories she told him. His favorite was the one about how the bravest of the gargoyles had came down from the mountains and started living in the tops of stone cathedrals the humans had begun to build. One stone carver accidentally discovered that demons and gargoyles were mortal enemies, and he began carving gargoyles on everything, hoping the demons couldn't tell the statues from the real thing. Maybe she'd tell him that one again tonight. He stretched his wings and yawned.

Footsteps approached. *At last. What had taken Maman so long?* But before he could turn to greet his mother, a hemp sack was thrown over his head and he was yanked off balance. He squeaked and struggled, but to no avail. Gruff voices argued around him as he was jostled and bumped along.

"No! You'll damage him. What kind of wedding present for a king would that be, eh?"

"Yeah? Well he won't stop fighting now, will he? If I drop him from here, it will do a lot more damage than a punch 'round the earhole ever would."

"If you're such a weakling you can't handle a child, I'll take him off you. They won't pay for damaged merchandise."

The jostling stopped. He heard the flap of wings, and then there was a sudden lift. He was flying now. Flying away from his home and family. How had this happened? His mother had told him stories in about evil gargoyles. A few were rogues, and some of them even had dealings with demons. He'd thought they were just tales, but now here he was, stuffed into a sack and being stolen away. Would he ever again stand with his father on the top of the bell tower, looking out over *la belle ville Paris*? Or hear his mother's beautiful voice? Rancid black despair welled up from the bottom of his being and swallowed him whole, and he wept.

"You're too low!" the first voice shouted.

Too late. Etienne's head collided with hard stone, and he knew no more.

"That one looks a little small. I'm not sure it's suitable."

Etienne awoke and opened his eyelids just a crack. He sat in a large armchair. The burlap sack had been removed, but his arms and wings were bound. An iron collar with a chain tethered him to a thick metal ring set in the floor. Two figures argued in front of him.

"But you have to train them young. The adults are impossible to break." A greasy smirk spread across scaly lips. "Believe me, I've tried."

Were these demons? Etienne tried to swallow his fear, but he was so thirsty it hurt his throat.

"Look! It's awake," the first voice said. "Stand up. Let's get a good look at you."

Etienne was terrified, but he imagined what his father would do. He stood up and tossed his head disdainfully.

"It's got some fire. You've got to give it that," the second voice chimed in.

The first grunted. "It isn't like I've a lot of time before the wedding. Fine. It will do."

He took a small pouch from his robe and counted out a number of gold coins, which the second demon snatched greedily.

The first frowned. "You will make sure it is stowed properly – I don't want it damaged on the trip to Scotland."

"As you wish," the second replied with a slight bow.

He opened the heavy lock that connected the chain to the ring and tugged on the chain. "Come!" he grunted.

Etienne remained where he was. The demon yanked hard on the chain and the gargoyle landed face-first on the stone floor.

"Idiot!" screamed the first demon. "I told you not to damage it. N-O-T, understand?"

"I'm sorry," the second demon groveled. "But you have to be firm with them. It only takes a few times-"

"Get out. I'll deal with it myself. And if this cub is damaged, I'll have your hide hanging on my wall."

The second demon backed out the door, apologizing as it went.

"Up you go." The demon pulled Etienne off the floor. "King Alexander of Scotland had very well better appreciate all the trouble I have gone through to get his wedding gift. He will most certainly owe me a favor."

The padded crate that held Etienne did have air holes that he could peek through, and while his night vision was excellent, there was too much cargo for him to see a lot. The straw that was sewn into cloth pouches and attached to the sides of the crate was musty enough to make his eyes water. Surely that's what caused the constant dribbles of liquid from his eyes. Stale bread and strips of dried meat had been left in the box for him to eat, but he wasn't hungry enough to even nibble the powerfully salty food. Etienne didn't often hear footsteps, but when he did, it was always with the vain hope that his parents had come for him. But they never did. Only sour-smelling sailors ever came into the hold.

He missed his maman and papa so deeply that the ache in his heart kept him awake at night. Etienne's hands had been bound when he was shoved into the crate, but his rough teeth had made short work of the hemp ropes. Once his hands were free, it was a simple matter to shed the binding from his wings. He used his time to plan and practice his escape. If only someone would open the crate.

The rocking of the boat as it rode the swells had never been gentle, but it suddenly became stomach-churningly violent. The ship soared on huge crests, dropped hard into deep troughs, then rolled and pitched like a wounded animal.

Wood creaked and groaned in protest against the assault. Etienne was slammed from one side of his box to the other. The ship rose to a sickening height, tilting and tossing the gargoyle against the wall. He floated, gravity-free, for a moment as the boat fell into the valley between the monster waves. There was a groan, then an ominous pop. The ship began break apart as it sank into the greedy sea. Mooring snapped with the shattering hull, and casks and crates were free of their dark prison. Some raced toward the angry sky above, some tumbled slowly to the cold seafloor.

Etienne's crate floated briefly, but the heavy sea swamped the openings, and it fell through the broken hold. The box shifted and one of his hands got stuck in an air hole, keeping him from the rapidly shrinking air bubble at the top of the box.

Something crashed into the crate, hard enough to splinter the wood on one side. Another crash. A hole appeared.

He was free of the crate, but not free of his predicament. Etienne struggled, trying to flap his wings against the roiling water. But wings are designed to work best in air, and he found the strain against the seawater painful.

Terror gripped him by the throat as he saw what had smashed the crate. The creature's head was bigger than he was. It had large black eyes and recurved teeth filled its open mouth.

Etienne fainted.

When he opened his eyes again, he was in a cozy cottage, wrapped in a blanket in front of a well-laid fire. A boy a little bigger than him sat on the floor nearby. Beyond him, a man slouched in a rickety wooden chair and knitted a woolen hat, and a woman sat at a spinning wheel, making yarn.

"*Bonsoir, Monsieur et Madame. Je m'appelle Etienne. Où suis-je?*" Etienne asked.

The couple looked at each other. The man frowned and shook his head. "Sorry, lad I dinnae ken what you're sayin'."

Still, they offered Etienne a thick wedge of brown bread and some hot porridge. He ate every crumb of the bread and a second helping of porridge before he curled up beside the fire and fell into a dreamless sleep.

Etienne snapped awake. Something was wrapped around his arms and legs, trapping him. Panicked, he snatched off the restraint and tossed it away. *Where am I? This isn't my home!*

The woman who had fed him last night looked surprised as she watched the woolen blanket hurtle toward her and crumple onto the floor at her feet. "Are ye hot then?" she asked.

Etienne had no idea what she said. He stared at her, trying (and not quite succeeding) to blink back the flood behind his eyelids.

Rain pelted down on the roof.

Slowly, the woman eased out of the chair with her knees on the blanket. Her eyes glistened with sympathetic droplets, and she held out her arms. And even though he was almost too old for such things, he went to her and threw his arms around her neck. Silent tears trickled down her neck and onto her shoulder.

It will be okay. My parents are surely looking for me. It's just a matter of time until they arrive.

Etienne soared above the surface of the river, a dozen or so feet above the water. From this height, he could spot the flashing scales of migrating salmon. Two black horses galloped along the riverbank, following him. His eye caught a glint of silver in the water, so he slowed and hovered over the schooling fish. They were headed to their spawning grounds as fast as they could go, but they were no match for Etienne's speed.

The two black horses raced ahead of him, then waded into the river with surprisingly little splashing. His shape-shifting foster family fascinated him. They called him 'Ocean,' partly because they couldn't pronounce his name, and partly because they found him in the ocean. He had been called Ocean for more years now than he had been called 'Etienne,' but he held onto that name, because in his mind, he could still hear his mother's silky voice calling him that. Etienne kept that memory locked tightly in his heart.

The two horses were deep enough to swim now, so they let go their equine shapes and morphed into their natural kelpie selves. Gregor, who had rescued him, and his son, Colbán, had long ago devised this gargoyle-assisted fishing technique. They caught salmon that were so abundant this time of year, some for themselves, and some for Colbán's elderly neighbor. She was human, and alone, and would probably have starved to death years ago, if not from the gifts of fish and bread that Iosobal, Colbán's wife, secretly left her.

As the grotesque kelpie heads rose from the water, mouths filled with fish, Etienne grasped them with his clawed hands and feet, flying the load downriver to where his foster mother, Máel Muire, and Iosobal waited with the couple's five sons. There, the women and the two eldest boys would clean, salt, and smoke them to keep the larder filled when food was scarce in winter, and even the plentiful brown trout all but disappeared. They did it for hours, this fish processing assembly line. Finally, the shadows lengthened and it was time to rest.

Etienne had just dropped off the latest round of salmon, and was searching for Gregor and Colbán to tell them Iosobal was ready to call it a night. He envied Colbán sometimes. His foster brother had a beautiful wife and five young sons. Etienne dearly loved his adoptive family, but Scotland was not his home. Most of his memories of Cathedral Notre Dame had dimmed, but he clearly remembered standing on the bell tower with his father, and his mother's angelic voice singing to him. Perhaps, when the fishing season was over, he would try to find his way home.

All these years, and his parents had never come for him. Did they not know where to look? Did they think he was dead? Or did they just not care? He felt sure he that if his own child had been stolen from him, he would never stop looking. Had they given up? Etienne was old enough now to fly back across the Channel and return to his people. Truth was, he had been for some years now. But sometimes suspicion is easier to bear than confirmation. And yet, that distant bell tower called to him - a clear, bright beacon in the misty past. Sooner or later, he must seek it out, but what awaited him there? A joyful reunion? An angry confrontation? What if no one had missed him, or cared that he'd returned?

He was so wrapped up in his own thoughts that he utterly failed to notice a small boat with a handful of men in it – most likely poachers at this time of day. He was headed dead at them, and at this speed, he would knock them over like skittles. He arched his back until it hurt, furiously flapping his huge wings, trying to pull up and avoid the fishermen.

He almost succeeded.

His feet struck one man in the jaw, and he flopped over the side and in the water. Etienne gaped in horror. He did not swim. Neither, apparently, did the fisherman. His companions yelled and brandished their fishing spears at Etienne as their colleague sank rapidly below the surface.

Something dark was rising. Colbán's great head broke the surface, the submerged fisherman held gently in his teeth. The men clearly did not understand that Colbán was returning their friend. They stabbed at him and raked his smooth flesh with their spears.

"No!" Etienne yelled. "Fools! Stop it!" But they paid him no mind.

Colbán tried to toss the semi-conscious human into the boat, but missed. As he started to dive, one wicked spear caught him directly in the eye, going entirely through his head.

Blood.

Etienne had never seen so much of it. It gushed from Colbán 's ruined eye, from his nose, out his mouth.

Gregor surfaced near his son, and the attack turned to him. He was out of their reach, however, as he tried to help his mortally wounded child.

Rage took hold of Etienne.

He dropped like an avenging stone from the sky and smashed a hole in the boat. Then another. Men screamed as spears bounced harmlessly off his stone skin. Bones crunched and snapped as his rock-hard fists pummeled them into the water. Into the domain of the kelpie. Not one of them, not even the wreckage of their boat, was ever seen by mortal eyes again.

Etienne turned to help Gregor. He wrapped his arms around Colbán's neck and helped Gregor drag his son's failing body on to the shore. Hoofbeats pounded in the distance. Seven black horses galloped toward them, going flat out.

Iosobal skidded to a stop and shifted into human form. She ran to her fallen husband and dropped to the ground next to him. Máel Muire was only a few steps behind her.

Iosobal stroked her husband's long neck and face, "Colbán?"

Máel Muire tried to cradle her son's head in her lap, but in his kelpie form, it was far too big. Blood stained her dress.

Colbán let out a deep breath, then seemed to collapse in upon himself. Where Etienne's foster brother had been was now a kelpie-shaped pile of peat moss covered over with a gelatinous green substance.

The two women began an unearthly keening wail. Gregor tried to comfort his wife, but she would not suffer his touch.

From deep in the forests that surrounded the river, night's children – the great grey wolves – began to howl along, as if they recognized the abject misery of Colbán's family. Five skittish colts had become five crying boys. Etienne circled his wings around them and they all wept together.

Iosobal was the first to speak. "From this day forward, I lay my curse on all humankind. To come into my sight will be their doom. I will feast on their hearts and leave their bones to the wolves."

This is all my fault. If I hadn't been so careless, none of this would have happened. I may as well have killed Colbán with my own hands. Etienne could not bear to speak to his foster family, even though his grief was just as deep as theirs. Would they blame him as much as he blamed himself?

He looked at the tear-stained faces of Colbán's sons. "As your father's brother, it is my duty to help you grow up strong. I will always, always be there for you. But before I can do that, there is something I must do first. I must make a short journey. Laurie?" he addressed the eldest boy. "Please tell your mother that I will return before Hogmanay. The year will not turn without your Uncle Ocean! But there is a long overdue task I must complete. *Comprends-tu?*"

Laurie nodded. Etienne squeezed them just a little harder with his wings, then he released them. With a last look at his grieving foster family, he flapped he great wings and rose into the air.

Which way from here is Paris?

Thank you for investigating with Marti and joining the MIT on another demon hunt. Have you read the entire series?

Belinda's Books

Other Books by Artemis Greenleaf

If you enjoyed this book, I would really appreciate a review or a share on social media. It helps people find the book.

Thank you!
♥

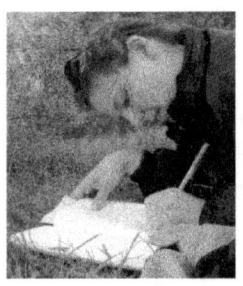

Artemis Greenleaf has always been fascinated by the mysterious, and she devoured fairy tales, folk tales and ghost stories since before she could read. In 1995, she had a near-death experience which turned her perception of the world upside down. She lived to tell the tale (and often does, in one form or another). Artemis lives in the suburban wilds of Houston, Texas with her husband, two children and assorted pets. She writes novels, short stories, and non-fiction, and her work has also appeared in magazines. For more information, please visit artemisgreenleaf.com.

You can sign up for Artemis' newsletter with giveaways, news, and new releases here:
http://eepurl.com/b4sQBj

Connect with Artemis online:
Website: http://artemisgreenleaf.com
Facebook:
https://www.facebook.com/ArtemisGreenleaf
Twitter: http://twitter.com/AGreenleaf
Pinterest:
http://www.pinterest.com/artemisgreenlea/

www.ingramcontent.com/pod-product-compliance
Lightning Source LLC
Chambersburg PA
CBHW060357180626
46817CB00007B/2465